A Promise

in

Provence

Book Two

Kyle Hunter

Monceau Publishing

Cover design by Erika Alyana Sañga Duran.

ISBN: 978-1-7322682-9-6

Books by Kyle Hunter that will take you places

Circle Back Around

One December

Provence Series

Prodigals in Provence 1

A Promise in Provence 2

Love in Provence (Boxset of Books 1 & 2)

The Second Chance Series

Marissa Rewritten (a novella) 1

Julia Redesigned 2

Chapter One

Lauren Abbott pressed both palms against the cool stainless-steel surface of the dishwasher, savoring the sharp chill against her steamy hands, then snapped it shut and pushed the 'on' button. She lifted the left cuff of her chef jacket and glanced at her watch. Ten fifteen.

A few deep breaths were futile in providing extra strength to finish out a seemingly endless shift. She'd still have to scrub down the metal counters and disinfect them. The appeal of working as a chef in a successful suburban D.C. restaurant had expired months ago. Of course, back then, it hadn't exactly been a choice.

"It's gonna be bad out there," said Bryan, who'd started in the kitchen only a week before. His face tensed as he cast a glance through the kitchen window toward the swirling flakes of snow. "We shoudda left hours ago."

Lauren followed his gaze and silently agreed. How much more white glitter would fall before she made it back into her own bed?

A faint aroma of grilled salmon still laced the air. The kitchen was calmer now as the evening wound down. The familiar voice of Chef Daniel, the owner of the Fins and Feathers Restaurant, rumbled from the dining room. He was shouting again, his complaints unintelligible, apart from the way he emphasized particular words, like *always, customer,* and *waiting.* He was often red-faced, from his bushy black eyebrows down to his white collar, as if in the midst of a colossal catastrophe even when there was none. Even when the customers had left over an hour ago amidst reports of seven inches of snow. By this time, the doors would be locked and the restaurant empty, except for the busboys who blew out candles and pulled the soiled linen cloths off the tables and into a pile.

Christmas Eve, and Chef Daniel's holiday special, flame-broiled surf and turf at prix fixe, had gone over like gangbusters, snowfall or not. No employee had taken a break all evening. Instead, each one did the work of three. Lauren leaned back against a counter as exhaustion rippled through her, down her back and pooled in her legs. A glance outside confirmed a steady swirl, like a cloak of dust in the blackness of the night.

Chef Daniel barged back into the kitchen with a loud bang through the swinging metal doors. Lauren flinched. He appeared more subdued now, though he still growled a few decibels lower about something that had happened at table eight. Lauren straightened and put her rag back into motion. Three other white-clad cooks scurried around the kitchen mopping up and putting food into the large double-door walk-in refrigerator. They tried to stay out of his target range until he returned to the dining room with an impatient stride.

A tap at the window caught Lauren's attention. She glanced up and saw the outline of a man peering in through the steam on the panes and the backdrop of swirling snowflakes. She squinted, then a wave of recognition. Mark, bundled in a parka, a wooly cap encasing his head. What was he doing here on Christmas Eve in the snow?

Lauren shot him a perplexed look with a tilt of her head, but her hands kept moving, changing the circular motion to back and forth strokes. Mark mimed a steering wheel turning as his troubled brown eyes beseeched her. He wanted to drive her home.

She shook her head and mouthed, "Thanks, though," adding a friendly smile. She couldn't. It was too soon. And she had no idea what time she'd be finished for the night. She caught his eyes through the frosty glass and shrugged with her palms up. She pointed to her watch, hoping he'd understand.

His shoulders drooped but he nodded then mouthed back the words, "Be careful." He waved and trudged away.

Her eyes burned for a moment, though no tears followed. Instead, a lump spread in her throat and began to throb. She swallowed. Mark had come out on a snowy night to accompany her home. That was Mark. Part of her wanted to let him, to allow him to navigate the icy roads while she rested against the car seat, entrusting her safety to him.

But she knew she couldn't. They would only start talking again about their relationship and it would all lead nowhere. Again. She wasn't ready because, well, what could she tell him? She didn't know herself, so how could she explain anything to him? Right now, she just needed a break from it all. From this restaurant. And from him.

She swiped the rag over the newly disinfected stainless-steel prep table again and blinked. Why did seeing Mark always do that to her? Fill her with guilt and regret so heavy it felt like she'd swallowed lead?

Finally, she was able to work the buttons down the left side of her white smock, pull the toque off her head, and slip into her down coat. Only one thing would do now, to slide between the sheets of her bed and leave the difficult questions of her life for a few hours. That was her preferred way to spend that particular Christmas Eve.

CR   CR   CR

Mark McCandless sighed, his breath rising from an unsearchable cavern inside his body and filling the night air with a puff of vapor. He wasn't surprised that Lauren had refused to leave with him. He would have waited for her to get off work. He didn't want her out in this tempest. He himself had fish-tailed more than once on the route from his house to the Fins and Feathers. A fill-in job, she had claimed, until she figured out what she wanted to do with the next chapter of her life.

Her next chapter opened up a hollow space inside him. It was the one thing that drove him to his knees.

Large, sticky flakes of snow swirled faster now, clinging to his knit hat and his face. It would have been futile for him to insist that Lauren come with him just because he was worried. She could be stubborn and would have been infuriated at his interference. She had to do this herself. And whatever passage she was traveling, whatever discovery she felt she had to make alone, he'd have to let her find it. He didn't have a choice.

The Lauren he'd dated for the last two years would have greeted him with a soft smile, worried that he'd come out in the snow. Once he'd safely accompanied her home, she'd have insisted on warming him up with some spiced hot cider.

In the last six months or more he'd seen small fissures open up between them. Little by little a distance appeared in her gaze. He'd helplessly watched her pull away in steady increments until finally she said the dreaded words. She needed space.

Space, well, he could give her that if she wanted it. He only hoped the space didn't stretch wider and wider until he could no longer even see her silhouette.

The cars in the parking lot were already coated with at least two inches of snow. Icy flakes pelted against his bare face. He blinked against those that hurtled into his eyes. His wool cap was already coated with crusty flakes, as was his collar, and a few rogue flakes slipped underneath, stinging his neck with wet cold.

He squinted into the darkness. It took him a moment to identify Lauren's blue Kia SUV, wrapped like a cake in fluffy, white frosting. Hopefully, its tires and weight would get her home safely. He'd send a prayer. It was all he could do.

Despite his dark thoughts, Mark smiled. She'd looked so cute in her chef garb, her shoulder-length brown hair mostly tucked up into the puffy, white cap, though numerous strands had escaped on either side. A frown followed. Best not to let his thoughts go there.

He gripped an ice scraper in one hand. The stiff brush on one end was perfect for a night like this. A year earlier Lauren had broken hers scraping ice off the windshield after a particularly nasty ice storm. As far as he knew, she hadn't replaced it, and this was the first snowfall of the year. She wouldn't realize until she arrived dog-tired at a snow-covered car that she'd never bought a new snow scraper.

He brushed the snow off of the windshield first, long strokes piling a stack of wet flakes toward the street. Then he circled the car and took care of the back and side windows, finally finishing off with the mirrors. There would be more snow accumulated before she drove home, but this would help. He set the scraper on the windshield above the wipers and turned to locate his own car.

Over the last year, each time she returned from a tour in France, she seemed to miss him less, allowed less time to catch up and reconnect. He missed her terribly when she and her friend Bree left for two weeks at a time to lead tourist trips to France with their travel business, Le Bon Voyage. But when she returned with a slowly fading light in her eyes, the one that used to say how much she missed him, it was more painful than her absence had been.

Driving slowly through the net of hurtling snowflakes, he gritted his teeth and told himself she'd be okay. She'd get home, resilient, capable woman that she was. Woman who no longer needed him. Or wanted him.

She'd be okay, that was true. But without Lauren, would he?

છ   છ   છ

On the way home Lauren spun wheels at stoplights, fishtailed at turns, and held her breath for much of the journey. Finally, she maneuvered her car into what she guessed was her parking space in front of her apartment, though she wasn't absolutely sure. There weren't even tracks in the snow to indicate a road beneath.

She killed the motor and sat for a moment in her car, relishing the cocoon of stillness only a snowfall could offer. When she was little, she used to bundle up and go outside just to listen to the silence and see what kind of monster tracks she could create stomping around in freshly fallen snow. Her older sister, Michelle, never understood why she was so drawn to the silent wonderland. Lauren would stay outside as long as she could until the chill seeped into her parka. Or until her mother came out in her old red ski jacket to join her, tossing a snowball at her and making tracks of her own before urging her inside.

Lauren pushed the frozen car door and stepped out to begin the trek toward her apartment building. Icy flakes filled her shoes and dampened her socks. Mark had kindly left her a scraper, bless him. Otherwise, she'd still be in the Fins and Feathers parking lot, finding creative ways to clean off her buried and frozen car.

She shivered and tried to pick up the pace across the caked sidewalk toward the building, but nearly slipped several times. At last, she slid into the warm hallway and rubbed her hands briskly to reboot her circulation. She mounted the stairs, feeling like she was seventy instead of thirty-two. Next to her apartment door was the crouched form of a child.

"Hey, Shelby. What are you doing there?" She smiled down at her neighbor's ten-year-old daughter who peered up at her from under a pink and yellow knit hat. "It's so late. Did you forget your key?"

"Yeah. I was at my friend's house until ten then got a ride. My mom said she'd beat me home, but she didn't. I guess she's running errands or something." Shelby pulled herself up and yanked off the cap from her round face, causing her wavy blond hair to spring up in all directions.

A likely explanation. Shelby's mom was late more often than not. But it was Christmas Eve. And it was eleven-thirty. The poor kid had been waiting an hour or more.

"Come on inside, don't wait in the hall." Lauren unlocked the door and ushered the girl into the darkened living room. She hit the switch and a sudden splash of light filled the room. "Maybe if you had a nice necklace with your key on it you wouldn't ever lose it." She pulled off her down jacket and helped Shelby with hers. "Want something to snack on until your mom gets home?"

"Sure."

While Lauren rummaged in the cupboards searching for those fig cookies she always had on hand, Shelby wandered around the kitchen observing and commenting. "Your canisters match your towels. It's cute. I like this one with the flowers." She touched the top of the largest of three canisters. "Everything's so clean, it looks like you never cook in here. You're a professional cook, though, aren't you?"

Lauren's head was partially inside the cupboard. "I saw them in here just yesterday." She pulled back from the cupboard and turned back to Shelby. "I'm a chef, not the main one. Sometimes I like cooking for myself and my friends when I'm not working at a restaurant. But I'm not motivated now, since I do it all day."

"I understand. I would feel the same." Shelby nodded, her head bobbing emphatically. She turned and continued exploring the bright corners of Lauren's kitchen, the refinished vintage dish cupboard, a side table laden with a massive food processor that didn't fit anywhere else in the kitchen, botanical framed drawings on the wall.

Shelby had always struck Lauren like a half-child half-adult, one moment using the tone and vocabulary of an adult, the next moment, erupting in childlike glee over something simple. Lauren smiled, as warmth stirred inside her for the girl. Shelby reminded her so much of herself at that age. And for some of the same reasons.

"My mom is always late. This morning I reminded her that tomorrow was Christmas, and she should be home on time, but I guess that didn't work."

Where were those crackers? There, wedged in the back of the cupboard. Well, maybe some almond butter on the crackers would do the trick. Lauren opened the fridge and pulled out a jar of almond butter. "Maybe your mom is finishing up her Christmas shopping for *your* gifts. Ever think of that?"

"Yeah, maybe." Shelby had turned to watch Lauren. She rocked back and forth on her shoes, hands in her pockets.

Lauren ventured weakly, "It'll make you more independent to be on your own every now and then, don't you think?" She'd try the positive approach, since Shelby's mother wasn't likely to change. In fairness, the woman was probably doing the best she could with a job and a child to raise alone. And she *had* left Shelby a key.

Shelby shot Lauren a look as if to clearly say that she wasn't buying it. "I'm only ten. I have time to be independent."

Lauren laughed. "You're right. Here, sit at the table. This is almond butter on the crackers."

"You don't have any cookies?"

"No, I'm out of the fig ones, and the others have too much sugar. On top of that, and if I had them, I'd eat them all." That wasn't the reason she didn't make cookies. Of course, she'd never *buy* them, but she hadn't a teaspoon of Christmas spirit that year. She'd forgone the usual lavish holiday decorations, lights, Christmas cookie exchanges, and continuous Christmas music.

"But you're skinny. You can have some cookies and you'll probably stay skinny. This cracker isn't as good as a cookie. It's dry. Tastes like—I dunno, sawdust or something. A cake of sawdust. The almond isn't bad, though."

Lauren sighed and slid down in the chair, with her own almond cracker on a napkin in front of her. She should have gotten a few things from the grocery store that week. The next day was Christmas and nothing would be open. Wish she'd thought of that.

"Sorry, it's all I've got. Hey, how about an apple? Almond butter is real good on apples." Shelby shook her head.

Lauren slathered more almond butter on a cracker, suddenly ravenous. "What are you guys doing for Christmas?" She glanced up in time to see Shelby delicately rescue an oily blob of almond butter about to drip off of her cracker.

The child made a face and said in a dramatic voice, "Aunt *Alice.* We'll be having Christmas dinner with *her.* She's okay, but she talks *all* the time—I mean, a lot—about people I don't know, especially ones dying of cancer or sick with some other disease. I don't know why she likes to talk about that. It's depressing." She rolled her eyes and shuddered. It was funny coming from a ten-year-old. "Are you going somewhere?"

"First, I'm going to relax." Lauren leaned back in her chair. "I just worked a twelve-hour shift and I'm almost asleep as we speak. Tomorrow I'll be meeting some friends." She hoped she was, anyway. Diane hadn't confirmed yet and it was nearly midnight. Her best friend, Bree, had left the day before for Arizona with her boyfriend to visit his mother for the holidays.

And Mark—she flinched as something twisted inside—she'd normally be spending the holiday with him, maybe with his parents too. Not being there with him or with his loving, stable parents—people who accepted her and loved her like their own—was a palpable loss she'd rather not dwell on.

She took a breath and tried to brighten. This year was simply off by a few degrees and would get better. So, she'd just stay alone with the complete disorientation that had colored her life for over a year.

"So, what happened to the guy who used to come over all the time?" Shelby must have been reading her mind. "You guys break up?" Lauren stared back at the girl and something on her face must have sent a warning. "Oh, never mind. I'm nosy. My mom always says that."

Lauren frowned and sighed. "No, it's okay. He has other things to do this year." Yeah, like wonder why she won't celebrate Christmas with him. She hated hurting him, especially after dating for so long. She just couldn't keep going without being sure. It was the humane thing, to let him go and to find herself. By herself.

"Where do your parents live?" Shelby was on a roll with questions capable of jamming a blade into all of Lauren's wounds.

"They're dead." She thought she saw Shelby flinch. "Long time ago." That helped to soften the truth for the hearer, even if it didn't for Lauren herself.

Lauren heard a knock on the door. Relief coursed through her. She might get to sleep before midnight after all. "That's probably your mom." She slid the chair back and went to the door, hoping it wasn't Mark.

Lauren opened the door and Shelby's mother stood there, an annoyed look on her face, as if Lauren had stolen her daughter instead of giving her refuge. Her tired face was ruddy with cold, mapped with tiny lines that belied the youthful puff of golden hair. "Hi, Eileen. Yes, she's here."

Shelby's mother stepped into the apartment as Shelby emerged from the kitchen to greet her. "I'm sorry, Baby. I had to drive real slow to get here without slipping and having an accident. I was worried when I didn't see you at home. You musta lost your key again." She turned to Lauren. "Thanks for letting her stay a bit."

"Oh, she was no trouble at all."

"Merry Christmas, Lauren," said Shelby and her mother nodded in agreement with a pinched smile.

After the door shut behind them Lauren stood silent for several seconds. The stillness of the apartment was almost too loud. How would she stand it for the next three days until the restaurant opened again? The restaurant was the refuge she hated, but a refuge nonetheless. She'd find some friends still in town or browse for housewares or décor. That always lifted her spirits.

Restless, Lauren walked to the window then back to the dining table. Her small apartment was bathed in creamy yellow and turquoise, her favorite colors. She'd coordinated everything in a way that was both beautiful and cozy. Normally, it was a comfort to be there. Her nest. She went abruptly to the window and back again, needing to break the ice block of sad inertia. But first, sleep. Things would look clearer, more hopeful, in the morning.

She cast a glance toward the foyer where the phone sat on the small table. The fading memory of his face had been flitting in and out of her thoughts for the last few days. She'd listened to his message a number of times and it always brought a smile and a tiny shiver.

Lauren stared at the phone then slowly walked toward it. She pushed the small arrow where the messages were played. She listened again to the voice she hadn't heard in person for months.

"Bonjour, Laur-hen." The musical accent always made her smile. "Merry Chreesmas to you, my dearest. I hope you are at a party but steel thinking of me. Will you come to France when the wea-der ees better? I invite you, when you want. Whenever you want. *Joyeux Noël. Heureuses fêtes, ma Chèrie.*"

Jean-Pierre. He'd left the message three days earlier, but she'd been too busy at the restaurant to call him back. They spoke a couple of times a month, sometimes in French, other times in English. She knew he wanted to practice his English with her and had shown improvement since she met him seven months earlier during her last trip to France, her final trip with Bree.

Another puzzle in her existence, Jean-Pierre. Was *he* the reason she felt as if a continent lay between her and Mark? Had Jean-Pierre somehow caused her to feel so little for the man she, at one time, thought she'd marry?

For sure, it was a puzzle. And she didn't have a clue to its answer. So, here she was, no more Bon Voyage, no Mark, and no France. Only the shadowy persistence of a charming Frenchman.

Chapter Two

Lauren pulled the full-length curtains wide and closed her eyes, letting the sun warm her face. After a winter that had trudged on in a glum parade of gray days, the cold had finally broken, and the world seemed reborn. On the street below several people strolled, cleaned cars, walked dogs. The sound of their voices and laughter rose up to her second-story balcony.

With the rise of temperatures, her spirits lifted as well. Things were about to turn for the better, she could feel it. Feathery pink cherry blossoms burst out on the trees as if shouting to the world that winter was finally over. She liked to think so, in any case. A smile came at the thought of fat, jolly flowers singing in joyful defiance against the cold that had gripped the city for months.

Despite the change of season, not much else had changed in *her* world. She still had to report to the Fins and Feathers Restaurant for her shift in about an hour. Through the winter months she'd hoped for more clarity as she cocooned in her apartment whenever she wasn't pulling a long shift. Yet, her life still resembled a badly smudged mirror. During her morning prayer and coffee time she often asked for her next steps, but wondered if the silence itself must, in some way, be a part of her growth process. Didn't the preachers say that waiting brought about its own rewards? She must have heard that recently but was beginning to hunger for the fruits of her patience before it developed a cynical edge.

Her cell phone rang into her thoughts. She looked at the name displayed on the screen and sighed. Her sister, Michelle. *Be nice.* Why was it so hard? Being nice wasn't as difficult as avoiding a verbal gaffe. Michelle was making efforts and so should she. "Hi, Michelle." She forced cheer into her voice, feeling guilty for the desire to make it a quick call.

"Hey, Lauren. What are you up to on this lovely Saturday? At least it's lovely here. Hope it is there, too."

Lauren slid down to lean back on the couch. She had to run to the post office before it closed at noon, but it would probably have to wait until Monday. "It's a perfect spring day. About seventy degrees. Too bad I have to go to work in an hour. Restaurants gear up over the weekend."

"Oh, yeah. I forgot." Michelle's voice was quiet. Silence followed.

"What are you and Justin doing today?" Lauren voice was bright, forced.

"Oh, the usual. Working around the house, doing laundry. He wants me to see this big mower he's thinking of buying. I know we can't afford it but it's nice to see him excited about something. Maybe we'll pay in installments."

Lauren nodded, searching for something to say that wouldn't be taken as criticism of her brother-in-law's spending habits. "Is the new medication helping him?" Instantly, Lauren regretted her words. She should have asked more questions about the lawn mower or something more upbeat. Anything else. Too late now.

She heard a long sigh from her sister. "It's early to tell, but I think so. He seems more optimistic about the job search, at least. He had an interview on Wednesday."

"Oh, that's good. I'm sure that'll cheer him up. Let me know what happens."

"I will."

The banal chatter was probably better than no communication at all. They might talk about something real but had both probably forgotten how. Lauren knew it was her fault, this inability to break through the barriers that she and her sister had erected over the years.

A few months earlier Michelle had started calling, which she hadn't done in a decade. She'd never said why she'd begun the random Saturday phone calls. Lauren guessed it was the realization that, despite everything, they were still family. The only one each of them had. The tragedy that had torn them apart years ago was a finished chapter. No sense in letting the pain course like fresh blood, anchoring them in the past. No benefit in thinking it could never be repaired.

And yet, the effort to move forward in the relationship felt like concrete blocks around Lauren's feet. It wasn't easy to pretend they were best friends or close sisters when they'd turned away from one another in their darkest hour, each one hurting in her own corner.

Had Michelle hurt, or merely run away? The question arose at odd moments through the mist of lapsed time.

"Do you miss going to France now that you quit the company?"

Michelle's question startled Lauren. Her sister was making efforts at going deeper but Lauren wasn't ready to go that far with her. "Um, I think I made the right decision. But yes, I still miss France. And Bree is doing great, she really is. She doesn't need me now. She's handling it like a pro."

"That's great. No guilt, then."

Lauren felt a twinge. "No, Bree and I have an understanding. She's fine. It all turned out better for her." That fact alone might have erased Lauren's guilt, but she still felt she could have handled things differently. She wouldn't admit that to Michelle.

"I bet she was shocked when you pulled out."

Lauren frowned. Where was Michelle going with this, after all these months? Lauren had left her and Bree's company the previous summer. "I think she'd known for a few months that I wasn't happy anymore. It might not have been a total surprise. And it was for the best, I think. I'm not in my niche yet, but I'm sure I'll find it soon."

"Restaurant work isn't your niche?"

"No, probably not. Not unless I have my own one day. It's not creative enough for me and I spend my time responding to other peoples' emergencies. I don't like that."

"And what about Mark?"

Lauren paused. This was starting to feel like an interview. She chafed against responding, opening up the whole subject of Mark again. "We're still friends but taking a break from—uh, being a couple."

"That's a long break. What's it been, nine months? Maybe you should just move on."

Maybe you should mind your own business. Irritation rippled through Lauren's composure. She forced a chuckle. "Are you writing an article on my private life or something?"

Michelle let out an awkward laugh. "No, I just don't want to see you stuck in a situation that doesn't make you happy."

"Don't worry about me." Lauren's words came too quickly. "Just live your life the way you always have." She wanted to bite her tongue. Or her lips, or maybe her whole face just then.

Michelle was quiet. "Not sure what you meant by that, but I need to go now. Justin is headed toward the truck so we can go check out the mower."

"Okay, I just meant enjoy your weekend. Hope the mower works out okay."

"Thanks. Bye, Lauren."

Lauren hung up and groaned as she fell back against the couch. So often she managed to say the wrong thing to her sister. Michelle approached tentatively, maybe clumsily, but Lauren would push her backward with some stupid statement. She didn't do that with anyone else.

When had the drift begun? Before Mom got sick, or at least before she'd gotten bad. Seemed she'd always been sick. But in the early days it wasn't as obvious, because she still made cookies with them, walked them to school, played hide and seek around the house until their giggles gave them away. She'd find them behind an armchair and gather them up with a hug. That was before.

Somehow Mom's illness had driven a wedge through the sisters as each one coped in her own tortured way. But Mom had been gone seventeen years. Wasn't it time to finally let it all go?

Could she let go of the abandonment she'd felt, alone to take care of her mother's crazy mood swings while Michelle, two years older, had been out with everybody on the block, partying the night away? Could she pretend it had been okay, even though Michelle was the older sister and should have shouldered more of the burden?

Lauren sighed. She ought to let it go. As a Christian she ought to. Seventeen years was enough.

The parking lot of the Fins and Feathers was mostly empty, except for the familiar cars of its employees. The restaurant wouldn't open for dinner until five, but everyone reported for duty from mid-afternoon to prep the menu and set up the kitchen. Lauren buttoned her chef coat and arranged her toque on her head, tucking her ponytail up into the roomy pouch that hung lower in back.

Chef Daniel strode into the kitchen just then, looking more subdued than usual. Over the clanking of pans and the hurried kitchen traffic he flicked his hand dismissively in the air and called, "I need five minutes, everyone, before we get prepped for tonight."

When the team had gathered around him, faces blank with expectation, he cleared his throat. "This week we had an inspection, as some of you are aware. Though we try to keep everything maintained to the highest level, some of the broilers are old and some of our other equipment needs to be replaced as well. I knew that it was a matter of time and the inspectors confirmed that they needed to be replaced very soon. Replacing the equipment shouldn't take that long, but since I was planning on renovating the dining room at the end of the year, I have decided to do it all at the same time. So, in two weeks the restaurant will close and stay closed for a minimum of two months."

A collective groan rose up in the room as Chef Daniel continued. "I will certainly need you all here when we reopen, but I understand that you'll need to be employed in the meantime. I leave that to you to decide what to do, but I hope you'll all be able to come back."

Lauren stood frozen in her spot, her thoughts in freefall. Despite her shock at the news, she couldn't block a wave of relief from rippling through her. At the same time her mind let out a silent whine. *This was all you had, and now it's gone too.*

Chef Daniel turned to Lauren and met her eyes. "I hope you'll be able to come back, Lauren. I'll make you my sous-chef. You're always cool under pressure. Nothing like me!" He gave her a rare smug grin which she was unable to return. Everyone considered her calm and serene, her colleagues, her friends. She didn't know if that was her normal nature or some mechanism she'd taught herself over the years. Safer that way.

During the ensuing hours of her shift, her mind bounced around to different options for the next chapter of her life. Seems she'd already done that thoroughly when she left Le Bon Voyage the previous year.

She could always find work in another restaurant, but the thought left a sour trail in her stomach. It was good to have something to fall back on, but not quite this soon. She'd prefer, well, never.

So, here she was again, in a baffled state of limbo. Was she just being too difficult, too choosy as she tried to find her niche, a job where she'd be happy? The wave of emptiness, the mental scratching for options—these were all too familiar. She was again out of place.

Only now she had *no* place.

ℂℂ ℂℂ ℂℂ

The hockey puck landed with a *thwonk* into the goal. Mark lifted both hands and added a victorious hoot. His best friend, Logan Simpson, skated over and gave him a high five. "Well-played, my friend. I believe I have officially lost."

"Officially, yes." Mark grinned and slapped him on the shoulder. "I wonder if I'm getting too old for this anyway."

They skated toward the perimeter of the rink and sought the bench where they'd left their belongings. Still heated by exertion, Mark pulled off his fleece jacket and took a long swig of cold water from a thermos. After his heartbeat began to slow down, he leaned over to untie his skates. "How's Dina feeling these days?"

Logan pulled off his skates one by one and tied a small rope around the blades to connect them. "She's entering that ideal phase of pregnancy, if there is one. She's at seven months, so she's not sick anymore but isn't feeling like an elephant just yet."

Mark laughed. "I haven't been through it but can imagine the last month being uncomfortable in every way. Bet you're excited. First kid."

"Yeah, but it's only just now getting real, you know? It's always been just us, and now I try to imagine this other little person as a part of our family. I like it."

Echoes in the cavernous space increased tempo as more skaters entered the rink. After the confinement of skates, Mark's Nikes felt heavenly, and he wiggled his toes around inside them. Being with Logan did him good too, considering all the frustration he'd been feeling lately about Lauren as they approached a year of "space". He needed to let her go, but just couldn't summon the strength. She was never very far from his thoughts.

As if reading his mind, Logan asked, "Any changes from Lauren? Is she still being hard-to-get?"

Logan's question struck like a well-aimed, though unintentional blow. Mark shut his eyes for an instant.

"Oh, I'm sorry, man. I didn't mean to stomp on the wound. Foot in mouth, Logan." Logan held up one hand, as if in surrender and above his bearded face, blue eyes squinted an apology.

"It's okay. I'm trying to get used to it. I was just thinking I might have to move on. I'm just so convinced that we're supposed to be together, that this is what God wants."

Logan's gaze was compassionate. "Maybe you're misreading him? Is that possible?"

Mark blew out a breath of frustration. "Yeah, I guess. It feels— never mind. I do have to let go."

"Do you think there's another guy in the picture?"

"Not that I know of. She just said she needed space to figure things out." Beyond her cryptic claim and through his months of racking his brain, he couldn't add any missing pieces. "As far as I can tell, her feelings simply changed. Not abruptly, but over a few months. I guess it happens with some couples, and now it's happened to us."

When Logan was silent Mark added, "Sometimes I wonder if I'm too dull for her. I've never been out of the country, except Canada, and she's been to Europe more times than I can count. She even lived there for a while during college. Maybe she wants someone more exotic."

"You, dull? You've gotta be kidding. I wouldn't be best friends with somebody dull, Bro. Maybe you don't jump out of airplanes, travel the world, or chase after terrorists, but I'm pretty sure that's not what she's looking for." He grinned and raised his dark eyebrows as if hoping to elicit agreement.

Mark gave him a grudging smile. He *had* actually jumped out of an airplane once but saying so would be beside the point. "Thanks for trying."

"No, really. You're a great CPA, an ace hockey player able to beat even *me*. On top of all that, you're a talented actor, wood-worker . . ."

"Okay, okay. Listing my hobbies doesn't reassure me that I'm what Lauren is looking for." Logan spoke as a best friend. But not as a woman.

Logan locked serious eyes on Mark's. "You *know* those things don't really matter. What matters is that you're a man of integrity, stability, and faith *and* you have a heart of gold. I'm serious. If

Lauren doesn't want that, lots of women *will*. Don't doubt yourself. It's her loss."

"For what it's worth, she did say it wasn't me, but her. She's been confused about her life ever since she left her company. She's not sure what's next for her and needs to figure that out before she'll know what to do about *us*." Mark shrugged with a nonchalance he didn't feel.

"What did she do again in France?"

"She and her friend Bree led small group tours to Provence. She was the culinary and wine expert in particular, but really, they both took care of all the details."

Eager to end that vein of the conversation and Logan's well-meaning encouragement, Mark stood up and gave him a tight smile. "Ready to get something to eat? I'm starved."

As they walked toward the parking lot Logan said, "Lauren always struck me as so steady and calm. The idea that she'd just lose her feelings for you doesn't fit, in my mind."

"She's steady and calm on the outside." Mark wouldn't say too much. Lauren's past was her own business. He knew of turbulence beneath the surface of Lauren's calm demeanor. "It's her way of dealing with hard things, I guess. Anyway, we're not going to talk about her all day. I'll let you know if anything changes."

"And I'll pray, Bro. And ask Dina if any of her single friends might be open to meeting a great guy who's a devil on the ice rink."

ଔ   ଔ   ଔ

When her shift finally ended Lauren drove toward home the long way, by a few new subdivisions that faced tranquil cow pastures on a curvy two-lane road. It was pitch dark by that time so she couldn't see very much of it. Just knowing it was there soothed her, as did the aroma of grasses and animals. The evening breeze that flowed into her open window was laced with the chill of early spring. She released her tight shoulders and let it wash through her muddied thoughts.

Her job would end the following week. Then what? Maybe in the few short days that remained she'd have a spark of insight about her next step. Another restaurant, a catering shop, a cafeteria in a school or somewhere else—several ideas came into her head and most of them flatlined on the motivation scale. All her life she'd had a sense of what she should do next, even if it was revealed only at the last minute. Maybe this time would be no exception, but for now, she didn't have a clue.

A trip might give her clarity and a change of air. She could spend a few days in Baltimore with Michelle, trying to rebuild a family feeling. She could visit her college best friend in California. She hesitated burdening Bree with her decisions. Not only had Bree heard it all before, but she had her hands full with the company *and* her wedding in just a few weeks.

Lauren finally got home after eleven. She was tired but not sleepy. The television didn't draw her, nor did the book she'd started last week, still laying on the table where she'd left it, a bookmark hanging out like the tongue of a tired dog.

What did draw her was the telephone. He'd called again yesterday and left a message. She'd tried to put off calling him back too soon. Didn't want to look eager, and still wasn't sure what to do about him. If she called him back, of course he'd try to persuade her to come, like he had done in his not-so-subtle way over the last several months.

Her finger hovered over the button. She pushed it. Jean-Pierre's musical voice filled the room as he greeted her, said he missed her, told her about his week.

He ended his message in a similar way as those before. "*Ma Chérie*, I hope you think of coming to France to visit. It is very beautiful now here. It is just starting to be warm and the plants are blooming. I hope you will come. I don't see you since last summer. It is very long for me."

Lauren smiled. He could have given up months ago, but he still tried to draw her across the ocean. A thought that tickled her mind and had bounced around in her head for at least a week . . . now she didn't have a reason to give him for not going.

A trip to see Jean-Pierre might bring clarity about Mark. Maybe even about herself. This was likely the best time to go see him, before looking for a job and getting into a new routine. After all these months, she could finally see if this simmering lure that had begun last year had any substance.

To see France again would also do her good, give her closure after her hasty withdrawal from the business. Those were good reasons, weren't they? Was it irresponsible to go to France now, when she was standing there with no job, no prospects? Was that the mature thing to do? She always did the mature thing, made the wise choice. Steady Lauren. Cool under pressure.

Lauren sighed and wandered toward the bathroom to wash her face, her mind still churning. On the other hand, what was holding her back? Not a job, not a relationship. Not family. Really, nothing. Still, she wasn't convinced that it was the time to travel to Europe. For months she'd told herself that she needed to let Jean-Pierre down gently. He likely wasn't a Christian. But something pulled her toward him, something she couldn't put her finger on. Something tingly, dangerous, intriguing. And she hadn't felt that way in so long.

She shouldn't even think about it until she'd had plenty of sleep and got through the rest of her final week at the Fins and Feathers. Then, well. Maybe.

Chapter Three

"Mom, are you home?"

The stillness in the house was palpable, like scaffolding bracing the house, holding it together. Lauren tiptoed down the shadowy hallway, her sneakers soundless on the wood floors as she approached Mom's room.

Maybe her mother was taking a nap, as she'd been in the habit of doing in the afternoons since returning from The Place. That's what she and Michelle called the psychiatric hospital where their mother had spent so much time in the last three years. The Place was a better name than the Looney Bin or the Psyche Ward. Lauren had long ago avoided classmates who'd taunted or snickered those terms regarding her mother.

But her mom was getting better. Lauren just knew it. That very morning she'd looked so calm and serene, more peaceful than Lauren had seen her, like, ever. That had lifted Lauren's teenage hopes, propelling her to ace her third period chemistry exam. It was going to be okay. Their family was going to heal. They would be normal. Finally.

The treatments had worked, four months of them while Mom had been inpatient. Since her return home two weeks earlier, her color had returned, traces of the humor Lauren had so missed and nearly forgotten about, it had been so long. The frequent hugs . . . almost like her old self. She'd even teased her daughters that morning before they'd left for school and the memory of her wide grin, so rare, stayed in Lauren's mind all through the day.

Even though Mom was recovering, she tired easily. Lauren didn't want to wake her up from her nap but would just look in on her real quick. Whenever Mom was sitting in her favorite chair watching TV or when she was napping, Lauren looked at her frequently, as if wanting to make sure she was still there, as if assuring herself her mother hadn't disappeared, gone back to The Place.

As Lauren approached the doorway, she could see her mother's feet at the end of the bed. She must have been tired, because she'd forgotten to take off her shoes. Her mother lay diagonally across the bed, which she'd never done before. Her head was turned toward the window. As Lauren circled the bed and her gaze fell on her mother's still-open eyes, a cold wave washed down her and her throat constricted.

Lauren reached down and grasped her mother's hand, now cold. Shook it, pumped it. Nothing. It fell back to the mattress, icy and limp.

"What did you do? What did you do?" A whisper, a whimper escaped Lauren's lips.

Louder then, strangled words, a wail from deep inside her, primal and raw and unearthly, like a bleeding, dying animal in the wild. "What did you do? What did you do" . . . just before she collapsed sobbing on top of her mother's still, cold body.

ཀ ཀ ཀ

Mark arrived early to the coffee shop and selected a small, square table near the window. He felt unsettled, vigilant, almost dreading seeing Lauren again. She'd taken initiative to meet with him and he had the impression she wanted to tell him something that would end up being a bombshell.

He had no illusions that she'd sit down and draw close to him, elbows folded toward the middle of the table, a soft expression in her eyes, close enough that he could smell her perfume. Even less did he dare dream that she might sit on his lap like she used to, her arms snuggled around him, and her head tucked into the cove of his neck. He didn't expect her to tell him she really loved him, had missed him terribly during their "break." An ominous grumble of foreboding settled in and he couldn't shake it.

The front door swung open, and he lifted his head in time to lock eyes with Lauren as she entered. Her hair was loose and hung in soft waves around her pale face. She was wearing a dark green tunic dress he'd always liked with black half-leggings.

Mark rose and went to her, kissing her on one cheek. "You want the usual?" he said, attempting a smile.

She gave him a strained smile in return. His dread deepened. "Yes, thanks."

He gestured toward his table then went to the counter to order a latte for her and a hot tea for himself. After placing their order, Mark returned to the café table and settled back into his chair. "How are you? It's been a little while." He knew exactly how long it had been. A month and a half with no word. Not. One.

She lowered her eyes and shook her head slightly. "Good— um—I'm so sorry, Mark, I didn't intend to let so much time go by. We're still friends, after all. Friends don't do that."

"I didn't say that to guilt you, Lauren. I just missed hearing from you and hoped to have news. I hope you've been okay. I was worried."

"Always worried about me." Her light teasing was hollow and didn't reach her eyes.

"Not always. Without news one assumes the possibility of bad things. So, I prayed."

Lauren looked away from him out the window at an overcast sky. "I don't deserve you, Mark. You're the best. You're so steady and faithful. So caring."

"Then why don't you love me anymore?" It slipped out, though softly. He couldn't help himself, and knew he was close to groveling. But the question had churned through his tormented mind so often over the last year, his thoughts about her were torn to shreds from overuse.

She turned her face back to him. "Mark—" Her hand reached out across the small table and gripped his forearm. "I don't know how I feel. I *might* still love you, or—or maybe not. I just don't know. That' s what I've been trying to tell you."

Mark's name was called by the barista. Lauren rose. "I'll get them." Maybe she wanted to break the tension, change the subject. Escape the conversation. She returned, a steaming mug in each hand, and sat down.

She looked at him, her face now purged of expression, and said, "I'm going to France for a little while. I think it will help me to sort things out. I can get closure on my final chapter with Le Bon Voyage." She bit her lip and lifted her eyes to his. "And—"

"And?"

She sighed and looked at her hands. "Last year when I was in France, I met someone."

Mark stiffened, feeling like a cannonball had fallen into a cavern in his stomach. She'd met someone. Up to now he'd been so thankful that she'd never said those words. Now his gratitude and hope melted like ice inside him.

"You never said." His voice sounded dull, quiet, but he couldn't help it. The aggressive noises from the espresso machine and the barista banging grounds into the trash banged on his nerves.

"It's nothing serious, really," she added with a slight laugh. "I met this man, Jean-Pierre, who owns a restaurant. We had a connection. So, we've stayed in touch. Just phone calls once in a while, that's all. But I think one reason I'd like to go to France is to see what it's about, if anything." Her words were coming quickly, breathlessly, as if she just wanted to get them out and leave them writhing between them on the table.

"You want to go live there near him." It was a statement, not a question. He didn't know what else to say.

Lauren shrugged. "Just for a while. He told me I could work in his restaurant if I wanted to during my visit. He lives in a town in Provence called Cavaillon. It's close to where Bree and I were last year. It's a mid-sized town near Avignon, if you know where that is. He found a place for me to stay, with an older lady he knows who has an extra room."

She'd thought everything out. Planned everything. She'd decided.

"How long will you be gone?"

"I don't really know, maybe a couple of months. Possibly longer. I just need to give myself time to make sure."

"And once you know?"

Lauren leaned forward. "It depends on what I learn. There's always a possibility that I'll come back no more certain than I am now. I keep praying for some message or something about what I should do, and what we should do about us."

"But you've already done something about us." He kept his voice calm, steady, though his insides ripped and the pain gripped harshly. "You've stepped back for almost a year now. I wanted to give you space, but Lauren, I want you back—"

Mark turned his face away from her as his fingers drummed the table, almost with a mind of their own. He'd stated what she already knew. Kept telling himself this would be the last time to say those words to her. But he felt powerless to hold back. He cleared his throat and his eyes found hers again. "I'm sorry, I don't mean to put pressure on you. But, Lauren, you know that one day—" he shrugged, "I'll give up and consider it over. You *know* that day is coming."

She nodded solemnly. "I know." Her voice was a whisper. "I don't even deserve to have you still sitting here being my friend."

He leaned toward her then and said fiercely, "Still *loving* you, Lauren. I love you. I'm waiting, not because I'm some saint, some fantastic friend. Of course, I'll always be your friend. Always. But I want what we used to have together, though we don't have to be exactly like we were. We don't have to be at that point again right away. We can start by just casually dating, if that's what you want. Just know that I still love you and I'm here, for now, because I don't know how to *not* be here."

Lauren gripped the table edge with one hand. Her face looked stricken, the skin around her mouth pale and drawn tight. No tears emerged, as if she was holding down a tidal wave by sheer will. "I don't know what else to say, Mark. I can't make something happen, and I'm doing what I can now by going to France. I hope it will help me." Her eyes pleaded with him and she repeated in a whisper, "That's all I can say."

Mark gave her a tight-lipped smile and took a long swig of lukewarm tea. He looked past her head through the plate glass window where patrons sat on the terrace, as he willed away the sting that taunted his eyes.

He blinked. "Do what you need to do. And I'll do the same, I guess." His phrase sounded clipped to his ears, final. Harsh. He added more softly, "Will we talk once in a while?"

"Of course. I'll stay in touch."

He wanted to believe her but already saw a faraway look in her green eyes, as if in her mind she were already in France. Those green eyes he loved, fringed by dark lashes, her full lips, pursed as she lapsed into private thoughts. She might not call but he certainly would. He wouldn't let her forget about him.

For a while, anyway. After that he would have to forcibly close the door on their past, and even harder, turn away to move forward.

At that moment he couldn't even think of it.

ʘ ʘ ʘ

Even though more than a month had passed since her job at the restaurant ended, Lauren felt incredibly behind on trip preparations. And her departure loomed ahead in just a few days.

She dropped her plants off—two dozen of all sizes—with a church friend named Shannon then drove across town to Bree's apartment. Bree had just returned from her honeymoon and was still gradually moving things over to the house she and her husband had recently bought. "Come over any time," Bree had told her. "I'll be here all afternoon doing some packing and going through applications for the next tour."

Lauren parked in front of the building and cut the motor. She sat still, remembering when she used to come daily to Le Bon

Voyage office, the business they'd both established four years earlier in Bree's spare bedroom. A wave of melancholy swept over her. So much had changed in just a year. Now Bree was married and Lauren was like an untethered sailboat with no destination.

It was during the third year of the Bon Voyage's existence that doubts began to gnaw before and during each trip. Eventually, Lauren concluded that she wasn't meant to stay in the company and should be doing something else, though she didn't know what. It had been difficult to break this news to Bree, but in the months that followed Bree regrouped and stepped into her new role like a champ, as the sole owner of the small enterprise. That was a huge relief to Lauren, and a joy to see Bree's life move in a definite direction with the company and with her new relationship. Now if only Lauren could figure out what *she* should do.

Bree pulled open the door at Lauren's knock. The sight of Bree, her blond hair drawn up into a pony tail with feathery wisps floating around her head, flooded Lauren with comfort. Bree drew Lauren into a tight hug that felt like therapy. Lauren squeezed back.

"I've missed you!" Bree pulled back. "Come in. I'm glad you had time to come over. I wouldn't want to miss saying goodbye." They'd spoken on the phone since Bree's return from her honeymoon in Italy, but it wasn't the same as wrapping her arms around her best friend, feeling anchored in a long-term friendship when the rest of her footing was in mid-air.

As Lauren entered the apartment she was assailed by its familiarity and the daily rhythm of three years of business there. Now the walls were bare of all but a few nails and smudges and stacks of boxes filled each corner of the living room.

She sat down on the couch as Bree carried in a tray with glasses of tea and placed it on the coffee table. "Want some tea? It's herbal."

Lauren grinned. "I just had some at Shannon's when I dropped off my plants, but sure, it's a hot day. I could use some more."

"I'm glad Shannon could help you out with your personal forest. She has enough room for them on her sun porch, I guess, and you know for sure they'd die if I kept them. We'll be in and out for the better part of this month, and still moving in, of course." Bree poured the tea and handed Lauren a cool glass.

"How is the new house coming along?"

"Slowly but surely. It's livable but not put together yet. It's such a cute little place, well, you saw it before the wedding, but once it's fixed up you can come over for dinner. Everything happened so fast this year, it's like a dream." Her serene face clouded suddenly, and she stared at Lauren. "You'll come back, won't you?"

"Of course. I mean, I'm almost certain." When Lauren had asked herself the same question, the gush of anxiety that followed forced a mental about-face. Don't go there. Just take one day at a time.

"I'll miss you while you're gone. Selfishly, I want you to come back, even if I still go to Provence once in a while. You're still my best friend."

"And you're mine." Lauren's voice softened and she reached out to squeeze Bree's arm. Her throat was suddenly tight with emotion. "I'm so thrilled with how things turned out for you, Bree."

Bree's face softened and her eyes grew moist. "That means a lot, Lauren. I just thank God every day for—for my new life, not just Travis but all of it." She shook her head and finished with a smile. "So, tell me what you'll be doing in France."

Lauren set her glass down and leaned back on the couch. Her eyes roved around the room that was so familiar but seemed strange to her now. By the time she returned from France Bree would be fully settled into the new house and this place would belong to someone else.

She sighed and turned to Bree. "Jean-Pierre has found a place for me to stay. I might have already told you that. I'll work in his restaurant as a hostess, just so I'll have some structure while I'm there. I'm not sure it's a good idea to work with him, but it's a place to start." Being in a high-pressure job side by side with Jean-Pierre would show her very quickly what kind of man he was. A perfect way to expedite her discovery process.

"At least you'll see what he's *really* like, instead of just the sweet-talking Frenchman with a sexy accent." Bree grinned at her, her blue eyes glinting with mischief.

Lauren laughed. "My thoughts exactly. I'll be honest, part of the reason for my trip is because I don't know what else to do with myself. I need to shake out some old thought patterns and see things from a new perspective. Jean-Pierre is a part of that, but not all of it. I think a change of environment will help me see what I need to do next. I sure hope so." To her own ears, Lauren sounded like she was trying to convince herself and Bree. To sound like she'd really thought it through.

Bree nodded, looking relieved. "I—I thought at first that it was strange that you were willing to leave everything here and just go there. Last year you seemed eager to leave France. And then, you've always seemed so stable and reliable and that seemed—" Lauren could tell that Bree was struggling to be diplomatic.

"You mean it seemed wild and crazy?"

Bree laughed. "Not completely, but it did seem out of character. I mean—you just met this guy and, I don't know, he's a stranger to you. I know you've kept in touch, so maybe you know him better now."

Lauren met Bree's eyes. "I know it doesn't seem worth it for me to go. But I haven't felt that—that spark for so long. I need to follow it up. Anyway, it may fizzle very quickly once I'm there."

"Have you told Mark yet?"

Lauren stared down at her hands for a moment. "Yes. We met for coffee yesterday. It was hard. I told him about Jean-Pierre."

"Oh." Bree nodded, eyes wide. "I guess that was difficult for him to hear. He didn't know about Jean-Pierre before?"

Lauren shook her head. "I didn't know how to tell him. And before I decided to go to France, there wasn't a reason to tell him."

"Do you think it's over with Mark?" Bree's voice was quiet.

Bree's question took Lauren by surprise. The finality of the words caused a pang inside, even though Lauren had asked herself the same question dozens of times. "Not necessarily. We were together for so long that he's a part of my heart. But I want to determine if that's because I'm so used to him, which isn't a good reason to stay together, or if he's my destiny. That's part of the reason for the trip. I hope to get that answer."

Bree nodded, sympathy showing on her face. She reached out and grasped both of Lauren's hands. "Me too. Maybe being in France will show you that you still love Mark. But I know it can go either way."

Lauren tightened her lips and nodded. "I wish that would happen. I really do. If I had to make a list of what I want in a guy, it would be Mark. I always thought I was so lucky that he loved me. But now I feel so—platonic, I guess. I can't go forward feeling this way. I know that in the daily relationships of life love is a choice. But it doesn't seem to be enough by itself when it comes to dating and marriage. You have passion and excitement for Travis, don't you?"

Lauren grinned when Bree blushed. "I sensed it the moment you two met, that sparks were going to fly, in a good way. So, you agree that it's important."

Bree nodded. "Yes, of course. I really want that for you too, to feel deeply for a man, yet also know in your soul that he's a good man and God's choice for you. If Mark isn't God's choice for you, even if he's a great guy, then I don't want him for you. The jury is still out on Jean-Pierre, but maybe it won't be either one of them."

"Maybe I'm back to zero in that area too." Lauren leaned back against the couch, suddenly feeling heavy, empty.

"That's not a bad place to be, Lauren." Bree's eyes engaged Lauren's. "Being at zero is okay, because there *is* a plan for your life. You just don't know what it is yet."

Lauren smiled and nodded. She used to be the one to say uplifting things to Bree, who had been a self-admitted worrier and control freak. Lauren had been the steady one in the pressure days of Le Bon Voyage, especially just before a trip. But things were completely reversed now, with Bree beaming peacefully, settled in her future.

Lauren wondered if she'd ever have the same thing one day, a loving relationship, a stable future. A happy story ending. Maybe she was undeserving, or just unfortunate. She shook the thought away. It wouldn't lead to anything good. "Of course, I'll keep in touch," she said quickly.

She'd likely need a lifeline back to home, especially when she first arrived in France. She'd call and hear all about the house, the new film company Bree and Travis had started, new projects with Le Bon Voyage. Lauren, too, would give news.

She only hoped she'd have something to say.

Chapter Four

Lauren's palms grew moist as the train approached the Cavaillon train station from Avignon. The arid and hilly countryside sped by, dotted with farms and clusters of homes topped by orange tile roofs. Despite her anxiety, the foreignness of the landscape was somehow a comfort, not only because it was Provence, which felt like her second home, but because it was far from all that stagnated in Benson, Virginia.

The ride from Avignon was short and now it seemed far *too* short. During her flight the previous night across the Atlantic to Paris Charles de Gaulle airport and the high-speed train to Avignon, one fact hovered continuously in her mind. She would see Jean-Pierre for the first time in a full year.

It wasn't only excitement that she felt, but also a heaping dose of pure nerves. She had crossed the ocean for a stranger. A stranger who might have expectations of her and their relationship. For her, it was a fact-finding mission at various levels. Jean-Pierre was one of the variables, though not insignificant. He was a man she'd met, felt something for, with whom she'd stayed in touch. Maybe she shouldn't have, but it was too late now.

The conductor announced her stop *dans quelques instants*. In just a few moments. She reached to gather her bags. Soon she would disembark . . .to her new life, maybe. To an adventure, possibly. To a mistake, probably. Perspiration broke out on her neck.

As the train slowed down, a yellow stucco building with an orange tile roof came into view. A metal footbridge hung between the two platforms. Inside the train the passengers were already spilling into the aisles, pulling small bags from the overhead rack, gathering their children. The rumble of voices in staccato French cadence increased with the movement in the train car.

Lauren cast her gaze through the large window beside her seat and scanned the platform for Jean-Pierre, thankful she had a recent photo. It had been several months since she'd even been able to conjure his image in her mind, though she would likely know him anywhere. She didn't see him through the window, but he was probably sandwiched in the crowd that waited on the platform.

By the time she hauled her suitcase from the rack and down the metal steps of the train, the crowd on the platform had thinned, but still no sign of Jean-Pierre. She stood motionless on the platform and panned her gaze up and down the concrete expanse. A feverish thought landed in her mind. What if he didn't come? What would she do? Get a hotel. Call him a few times. At worst, she could just tour around for a couple of weeks and then go home. Or she could find a restaurant job somewhere—

"Lau-rhen! You are here!"

Lauren's head jerked up and she saw him rushing across the platform like a disorganized professor, longish wavy hair tucked messily beneath sunglasses on his head. He looked like he had the two times she'd seen him the previous year, a flash of light orange from his untucked camp shirt, long khaki shorts and loafers without socks. As he approached it all came back, the clear blue eyes, the engaging white-tooth smile from a slightly weathered, tanned face. Something stirred inside. Lauren grinned back as a wave of relief coursed through her.

When he reached her, he pulled her forward by her shoulders into an embrace and kissed her soundly on each cheek. Then he swept up her suitcase in one hand and offered her his other arm. "I'm so sorry I was a leetle beet late. You must be very tired, Chérie. It's so nice to see you. You look the same as before. *Très jolie.* You have not changed."

Lauren fell into step beside him, her hand curled around his muscular forearm. "I'm pretty much the same, I'm afraid."

"Good, good!" He laughed. "I am so happy you decide to visit. We did not have time last summer to spend together. And now you are here."

She didn't know if her sudden drowsiness was due to relief or sheer exhaustion from nearly twenty-four hours of travel. "Where are we going first?"

"I will take you to see Madame Carnot, the lady who rents you a room in her home. She is a very nice lady, like a grandmother. You can rest from your trip, then if you like, I will come take you to dinner. Is this a good plan?"

Lauren nodded, anticipating her bed at Madame Carnot's house. "Yes, it's a good plan. I'm very tired now, but I'll be better by this evening."

"*Merveilleux!*"

Lauren observed her surroundings in a foggy state, feeling like she'd emerged from a dream. Was she really here? Two tall trees graced either side of the station and cast long shadows on the dark green grass. She and Jean-Pierre crossed a pedestrian square then the parking lot, finally arriving at his car, a white Citroën. They loaded her luggage in the small trunk and he pulled out into a shady avenue of Cavaillon. Her memories of last summer floated back in disjointed strands. A comfortable breeze flowed into the car through the open windows as she watched the town go by.

Jean-Pierre chatted along the way as he pointed out landmarks of the town, gesturing out the window on either side of the car. At that point she didn't know what to say to him and was content to let him chatter on.

"Over there we have our own Roman ruins at the Place du Clos." He pointed out the window toward stone arches standing in the middle of a small field close to a hillside. "Of course, that is not where they were built. They have been moved several times. It's quite interesting, though, if you like ancient history. Beyond that is a steep trail up the small mountain and paths around a very old church."

As he drove Lauren observed his profile. Dark brown hair threaded with bits of gray curled down past his ears. A pair of sunglasses sat on top, giving him a windblown yet casually stylish appearance. His strong, square jawline spoke of confidence, masculinity, and perhaps a forceful personality. His arms and legs were tanned. She could picture him under the Provence sun haggling with fishmongers and merchants at the open markets, as he'd been doing the day she met him last summer.

Soon Jean-Pierre slowed the car. Lauren looked up through heavy eyes and saw they were in a neighborhood lined with stucco houses each with an orange tile roof and surrounded by a wrought iron fence about five feet high. He stopped in front of one of them, small and white and well-kept, with neat rows of rose bushes against the house and a white gravel path leading up to it. Amidst the white stucco a bright blue wooden door welcomed them.

"Madame Carnot is waiting to meet you." Jean-Pierre was out of the car and unloading her suitcase when an elderly woman clutching a knitted shawl around her shoulders came through the blue door and onto the path.

"*Bonjour, les jeunes,*" she called to them, with a warm smile of greeting.

Pierre took Lauren's arm as she pulled herself out of the small car. He effortlessly carried her big suitcase in the other hand and began speaking French to Madame Carnot, telling her about going to the station and about Lauren's need to rest.

"Bonjour, Madame Carnot." Lauren shook hands with the older woman.

The woman continued smiling, creases multiplying in her pale face surrounded by a fluff of pure white hair. Through a tangle of wrinkles behind her glasses, her gaze was alert. "Bonjour, Lauren. Bienvenu at my home. *Chez moi.*" She gestured toward the house and they filed into the darkened hallway. Enticing smells that flowed from the kitchen reminded Lauren how long it had been since she'd eaten only a hasty croissant near the Avignon train station.

Madame Carnot led Lauren into the kitchen while Jean-Pierre hauled her suitcase up the staircase to the first-floor guest bedroom. A small loaf-shaped cake awaited on the table, with a slice of it on a small plate. As the woman poured tea, she continued chatting about how long she'd been in her home, how nice Jean-Pierre was, and how much he did to help her. Lauren listened and nodded at appropriate times as she savored the cake and warm tea. She fought a wave of dizziness and fatigue and hoped that her hostess wasn't always this talkative.

"Merci, Madame Carnot, for the cake and for letting me stay here with you." Lauren tried not to eat the cake too quickly or have too much of it. She wanted to observe her surroundings, but her vision was getting blurry. There would be time to explore later.

Jean-Pierre returned to the kitchen and said to Lauren, "I will come to fetch you at seven. Is this good?" He politely refused a slice of cake offered by Madame Carnot.

"Yes, that's perfect. I should be more rested by then." Lauren smiled and walked him to the door.

Jean-Pierre made a small bow and said, "*A toute à l'heure,*" then disappeared through the front door. Lauren turned to Madame Carnot and excused herself, unable to stay even for courtesy. Her eyes were heavy, and her thoughts were muddled as she trudged up to the first floor.

When she entered the bedroom, she stopped. A large pastel bouquet of lilies, roses, and carnations flowed out of a ceramic vase on the small, round bedside table. Madame Carnot probably would not have left them here to welcome her, unless she had a thriving garden in back of the house. The rest of the room was plain, but clean and comfortable looking.

She approached the stand where the flowers beckoned and saw a small card leaning against the vase. She opened it and read, "Lauren, welcome to France. I hope your time here is full of joy and discovery. I look forward to discovering you. Jean-Pierre."

She couldn't suppress a smile at his words, sweet and bold at the same time, clearly expressing his intentions, drawing her in. She knew her goal was the same, whether she'd admit it or not. Wasn't that why she came to Provence? To test the strong feelings that she'd experienced when she'd met him last summer?

Of course, she couldn't base her life on a feeling. Doubtless, her friends back home probably thought she had suddenly developed a split personality, so completely out of character was it for her to do what she was doing. But she was as puzzled by her lack of feeling for Mark as she was by her simmering attraction for Jean-Pierre. She was simply stumped about her whole life.

Those thoughts were exhausting to her, even when she hadn't spent the night in an uncomfortable airplane seat and traveled across the country. Her quest had begun. She was there in Cavaillon. The next chapter, though, would have to wait for a few hours' sleep. When she awoke, she would face what she'd done.

The shrieking voice of the alarm reached into the cluttered fabric of Lauren's dreams. She'd been with Mark at his house. They'd been cooking something for a weekend meal laughing together. It had felt comfortable then turned to something cold.

As she emerged from the cloudbank of sleep she didn't immediately know where she was. Her mind strayed for a moment to her dream about Mark and she felt a twinge of emptiness but pushed it away.

Opening her eyes fully, she saw the sheer, white curtain plumping gently with a breeze that tumbled over her seconds later. Her eyes roamed the room, observing more detail than she had upon arriving. An antique armoire stood in one corner awaiting the contents of her suitcase. The beige walls were bare of decoration, save an ornate crucifix facing the bed.

A wave of relief and guilt assailed her, both at once. She hadn't thought of Jesus very much in the last twenty-four hours. Maybe she'd been afraid he'd tell her not to take this journey. But the reminder that, despite her choices, he was with her and would stubbornly stay by her side was an immense comfort. "Thank you for being here," she murmured. "Do what you need to do in me. Please."

Lauren could have slept much longer, but didn't want to confuse her system. Two hours was plenty. She felt much better. The clock read five fifteen. She had enough time to get her things organized and prepare herself for dinner with Jean-Pierre.

There wasn't much in her suitcase that wasn't wrinkled, but she found a light blue sundress that had just a few creases, and the dress looked like it might be perfect for a balmy summer evening on a first date with Jean-Pierre.

The door chime rang out at five past seven. Lauren called out goodbye to Madame Carnot and opened the door. Now in a more alert state, Lauren noticed how tall Jean-Pierre was, at least six feet, unusual for a Frenchman.

"You had a good sleep? Do you feel better?" Again, he proffered his arm to her. She was enjoying this old-world chivalry.

"Thank you for the flowers. They're lovely, and a nice welcome." Suddenly, she felt shy.

He nodded, seeming embarrassed as well. "*Bien sur.*" Of course.

He opened her car door and his cologne wafted toward her. In her mind warnings were shouting all while her heart warmed to his attention. During the short drive to the restaurant, she talked more than she'd been capable of earlier. She found herself relaxing in his company, as she had the year before when she first met him.

"Tell me more about your restaurant, Jean-Pierre. Have you had a good year since I last saw you?" It was a good conversation opener even though they'd chatted about the restaurant in the previous year's phone calls. Now she'd be an active participant instead of a spectator. She hoped she was ready.

"Ah, *oui.* It has been a good year. I am very close to having a star. I mean, a Michelin star. It's an award every restaurateur in France wants to have. Of course, I served very good food even before this, but I have recently been recognized."

"What does it take to get a star?"

"No one knows one hundred percent, but it is many things. The ingredients have to be as good as possible, the meals, of course, the whole dining experience has to be consistently good. That means décor, technique, everything. The Michelin people visit the restaurant but no one knows who they are. They do not announce themselves before or after. Then the reviews show up in the papers and you know they have paid a visit."

"Then they give you a star?"

"No, not right away. They want to be sure it isn't only one time that everything was very good. They visit again months later, or wait even longer than that. So, the best thing a chef can do is keep trying to improve and be better. That's what I try to do."

Lauren nodded. Seemed like loads of pressure. "I see. But your restaurant is popular even without the star, right?"

"Oh, yes, it is. We have to turn people away sometimes, especially on weekends. We ask them to reserve, but sometimes they do not. But it is okay, because if they are turned away, they are more eager to return. It is a good problem."

Suddenly Lauren felt like she had a million questions. Was this part of an answer for her? She hadn't had such an interest when she worked under Chef Daniel. Maybe it was too soon to give up the idea of one day owning her own restaurant. Working with Jean-Pierre would be a good beginning, to discover not only the career, but the man.

"Here we are." He parked the car parallel to the curb. It looked like a crowd was already there, by the looks of the small parking area and the curbs up and down the street.

"This place is owned by a friend of mine, Serge. I am very picky about where I will dine, since I know what it takes to have a good restaurant. This one is good. I say this not just because he is my friend." Jean-Pierre let out a hearty laugh. He got out of the car and led Lauren inside to a warm, attractive dining room with stone walls and wood beams on the ceiling. They were seated at a cozy table bathed in flickering candlelight.

Soon, a burly man in a white chef coat appeared at their table. Jean-Pierre stood and shook his hand heartily. They bantered in fast French for several seconds, then he turned and gestured to Lauren. "I present you Lauren, from America. She is here visiting for a little while and will be working with me. And this is my friend, Serge."

"Ah, finally *Chez Jean-Pierre* will have some class!" Serge chuckled and extended a hand to Lauren. He bent and kissed her hand.

"*Enchantée.* I'm happy to meet you." She gave him a subdued smile and settled back in her chair while the men continued talking shop for several minutes, too fast for Lauren to follow. She'd been out of French for a full year. It would likely take a couple of weeks to get up to speed.

Once Serge returned to the kitchen, Jean-Pierre launched in his easy way into a conversation that soon had Lauren feeling like she had never left. Throughout the evening she noticed the chemistry she felt and her ease with him. The time flew by. They discussed the restaurant business, Provence, and her last year in the States.

"Last year you told me about a boyfriend that you had. You are no longer with this man?"

Lauren was surprised by his abrupt question and uncertain how to answer. But of course, he would want to know. Had she broken up with Mark for good? She didn't feel she had, but it certainly looked that way to everyone, including Mark. "We are just friends right now." It was honest, even if she hadn't fully answered Jean-Pierre's question. "I—I wasn't sure of my feelings for him so I thought it was better to just be friends."

Jean-Pierre nodded, but something on his face expressed doubt. "Maybe I can convince you that he's not the man for you." A wily smile spread across his face, and he winked at her. Then he lifted his head and gestured for the waiter. He said no more about Mark or about himself. He turned back to her. "Dessert? A digestif? Or fromage?"

"A bit of cheese would be nice. I've missed French cheese." She could almost taste the crisp baguette with a creamy brie or mild goat cheese spread on it.

He grinned and told the waiter, "*Un plateau de fromage, s'il vous plait.*"

"I wanted to ask you what you'll have me do in the restaurant. You talked about needing a hostess. I prefer that to cooking, but it depends on what you need." She should just flat out refuse to cook, but her skill set revolved around food. Maybe she should be open. It might be different than the Fins and Feathers.

Jean-Pierre stroked his chin which showed a shadow of stubble. "I have thought about this. I don't need a cook now, except sometimes when we have an absence, but you can begin as a hostess. Would this be good for you?"

She nodded and let out a breath of relief. At least she'd have an easy job that wasn't cooking. She still needed a break from the stress of working in a professional kitchen.

"I may also have you visit the markets when I need things. This would be very helpful." He looked up as the cheese plate arrived and a fresh basket of baguette rounds. The waiter proffered a new bottle of red wine, which Jean-Pierre tasted. He nodded to the waiter, who poured two glasses.

"You should take the next two or three days to explore Cavaillon, so you can remember it. Tomorrow I will have a short visit from my son. He has some problems we have to deal with."

Lauren felt a jolt. "I didn't know you had a son," she said lightly, though a grinding began in her stomach. "You never mentioned him."

Jean-Pierre gave a dismissive wave. "He is a big son, twenty-three. I was a father before the age of twenty. I was too young to be a father. He lived with his mother, who became an alcoholic, and now he struggles with this as well. He lives in Savoie, in the southeast of France, but comes here sometimes. He needs some advice about some problems he has. I try to help him as much as I can."

An unsettled feeling needled her inside. Why hadn't he told her something so important? "You didn't tell me," she repeated. "Are you close to him?"

"Not so much in the past, but we are getting closer. This is why I didn't say anything."

His answer did nothing to reassure her but she decided she'd stay open. It was their first day together, after all, certainly too soon to make waves about details he'd omitted. Even important ones. Maybe he'd been afraid of her reaction if she'd known of an adolescent failure he'd experienced. Or possibly he'd forgotten he hadn't told her.

"So, tomorrow you can rest and discover Cavaillon," he said, as if eager to change the subject. "You can visit the restaurant whenever you want to. It's called *Chez Jean-Pierre*, of course. Maybe on Thursday we will go to the marché and I will show you what I will need you to buy for me whenever you go there. In two days, we can spend time in the afternoon in a nearby village you will like. There are some lavender fields. You like to bicycle?"

Lauren nodded. "Yes, and I play tennis, too, if there are courts nearby. Of course, I'll need a partner." She lifted her eyebrows and grinned at him.

He laughed. "I can provide you a bicycle, but I cannot be a tennis partner. I have a friend, Hélène, who plays. I can send her to you."

"It's not important. Biking sounds nice. I'd love to see some lavender fields."

"And you must stay until July, when we have our melon festival. You probably know about Cavaillon melons."

"Yes, they are the best in France."

"*Absolument*. They are famous here. People come from all over France to taste the melons and come to the festival. There's a parade, people cooking all kinds of things, and at ten in the evening the Camargue horses are released to run through the town."

Lauren's eyes widened. "Really? I can't miss that. Sounds fantastic."

"One hundred horses. La Camargue is not far from here. These horses are famous too. They live in the marshes and are mostly wild."

Lauren smiled. Seemed like she would have a good summer working with Jean-Pierre, able to enjoy the surrounding beauty of the region along with its seasonal events.

Going to the marché would be a pleasure, too. She'd always loved the noisy, colorful open-air markets, and wandering amidst shaded stands flowing with fruits, vegetables, flowers, and spices. For now, she'd withhold her assessment of Jean-Pierre. Time would tell her volumes about him. And hopefully about herself.

Chapter Five

Mark knocked on his friend Logan's door and waited. Both conviction and regret frothed uneasily inside him. Conviction because he knew he needed to get back "out there" in relationships with women, as several of his friends had been urging him for months. He needed to draw a line with Lauren and assume she was no longer in the picture.

The blind date Logan had arranged was supposedly the perfect hinge to this new chapter of his life. He'd made a step in that direction by agreeing to meet the woman, though some misgivings hovered in the background, since these first encounters were too often just plain uncomfortable. He'd smother down his reluctance for this evening.

The door swung open and Logan pulled him into a man-hug, complete with two hard thumps on his back, a bit more vigorous than usual. Mark coughed.

"Come on in, Mark. Good to see you, buddy. What can I get for you?"

Mark shrugged and his gaze panned around. "What do you have? Mineral water would be good for starters."

"Sure thing. Come in first and meet Becky."

Beads of perspiration broke out on his neck. He hadn't done this in so long, and with Lauren, figured he never would have to again. But here he was. The first date.

As he entered the living room an attractive dark-haired woman rose to her feet. He noticed she was slightly plump, but stylishly dressed, with off-white pants and a tangerine-colored tunic. She turned to him and extended her hand. "Becky Barrett. Nice to meet you, Mark."

He smiled and took her hand. "Nice to meet you, Becky." So far, so awkward. Becky seemed like a take-charge kind of gal at this point. But it was too early to know.

Fortunately, Logan arrived with a bottle of chilled water and handed it to Mark. Dina also waddled in, looking ready to pop, but her face was beautiful, glowing with happiness, her eyes shining.

As they hugged Mark gave her space for her bulging middle. "How are you, Dina? Bet you are ready to bring this bundle home." He sat down in a facing armchair and took a sip of water.

"You know it, Mark. It'll be nice to have him *outside* of me. His room upstairs is all ready for him. We can't wait, but we're trying to be patient."

"How do you all know each other?" Mark asked his only sure-fire opening question.

Becky smiled and sat forward on the edge of the couch. "Dina and I used to work together, before marriage and motherhood took her away. We've stayed friends ever since."

Her eyes were dark but framed with sooty lashes with a lot of mascara and eyeshadow. She was pretty, but had a different style than Lauren, who was more earthy, less fixed up. Lauren almost never had every hair in place, and he loved that about her. Her beauty seemed fresh and genuine—

Best not to think of that. Anymore. He wanted to stay open to *this* evening, *this* new chapter. He nodded to Becky. "That's great, these friendships that last a long time. What do you do now?"

"I'm still at the credit union. I'm in lending now. It's interesting and I meet a lot of people. I like working with numbers, too. I hear you're an accountant." He heard her silently saying, *We have a lot in common, Mark. We both like numbers.*

"Yes. I work for myself now." He settled back into his chair, relaxing his shoulders. "Everyone seems to think that numbers are boring, but I'll have to agree with you that numbers can be fun. They're predictable. And they don't argue with you or make any requests." She gave him a bland smile and a hollow chuckle, as if she wasn't sure what he was talking about.

A buzzer went off in the kitchen. "That's for us. Time for dinner, everyone." Dina struggled to her feet and Logan hopped up to grasp her arm.

Mark and Becky went to the dining room and sat down at a prepared table. Dina and Logan disappeared into the kitchen but scraps of their discussion about the meal drifted back to Mark. He looked back at Becky, determined to exercise his best social skills. "Are you originally from Virginia?"

Becky flipped her shoulder-length dark hair over one shoulder and grinned. "Is *anyone* originally from suburban D. C. Virginia? No, I finished grad school in Ohio and moved down here about nine years ago to join the many other transplants. I have one sister and she moved down with me. We were both looking for warmer weather and wanted to be near a big city."

"I guess you found it." Smile. Silence.

"What about you?"

Mark shot a glance toward the kitchen. Where were they? "Uh—I was raised in the Philadelphia area. I have two brothers, but I'm the only one down here."

"I guess we were almost neighbors, Ohio, Philly. Your brothers both stayed up north?"

"One did. My younger brother, Chris, has a couple kids and lives in Bucks County. My older brother, Finn, is the exotic one." Mark was starting to relax now. "He's based in Atlanta but is a travel and wildlife photographer so he stays on the move all around the world. He just got back from South Africa."

"Oh, that's interesting. Sounds like a fun career." She smiled a nice, genuine smile and he noticed she had lovely teeth, straight and brilliant white.

"He's the more interesting one in the family."

"Oh, I'm sure you're very interesting too, despite working with numbers!" She laughed and he smiled back at her. "Do you have hobbies as well when you're not crunching numbers? Not sure where that expression came from."

"Yeah, I have wondered that too." They both laughed.

At the moment of their shared laugh Logan returned. "Glad you are getting along in here." He grinned and placed a steaming bowl of garlic green beans in the middle of the table and a bread basket on the side. He pulled his chair out and sat down.

Becky turned to Logan and said, "Mark was about to tell me about his hobbies, so don't distract him. I want to hear about that."

Mark stifled an inward groan. He disliked talking about himself, but figured it was a necessary bridge to cross when on a first date. "When I was a kid my dad told us boys that we all needed to find two hobbies. One we could do with other people, and another we could do alone. That way, we could stay entertained even if our friends weren't available. I've always been thankful for that advice."

"How smart your dad was. So, what did you pick?"

Logan handed the green beans to Becky as Dina came in with another steaming platter piled with a variety of seafood. A tangy aroma of grilled fish filled the room. "Mark is a whiz of a hockey player," said Logan. "He also does amateur theatre."

"Though I haven't done that in about a year," Mark said. "No time, once I was working for myself. I do a little woodworking when I can. That's my solitary hobby, I guess. That and reading."

Dinner progressed in a predictable but not uncomfortable way. Mark couldn't be ill at ease in the company of his best friend, regardless of the circumstances. And they were eating a wonderful feast. Later, Dina brought dessert from the kitchen. "Coffee or tea, anyone? I know it's pretty warm for it, but I'll make some if you like."

Around the table everyone declined coffee but eagerly eyed the strawberry pie with whipped cream. Mark leaned back in his chair, content with the evening but unsure of whether or not he would pursue another meeting with Becky. She was pleasant enough, attractive, though not very athletic or outdoorsy, he learned.

They likely weren't a good fit, was his guess. Of course, it was way too early to decide that, but he usually leaned on his first impressions. He'd always had a keen ability to size up a person fairly early. When he'd met Lauren, he'd known right away he wanted to date her, that they would click. There'd been no question, after only ten minutes. In fact, he'd been sure after their first date that he would one day want to marry her. That certainty had never left him.

Which was what had kept him from giving up on Lauren over the last year, despite the popular opinion that he should. Was it time to start doubting that conviction? Was it finally time to give up? Mark pressed his lips together and gave a slight shake of his head.

"Something wrong, Mark?" Dina asked.

His eyes shot up to hers and he grinned sheepishly. "No, just thinking of something else related to—uh," he waved the air dismissively, "to a project I'm doing. Sorry, I zoned for a minute."

"No problem, how about some more pie?"

"No thinking about work, Pal. This is weekend." Logan's white-tooth grin showed through his close-cropped beard. "Otherwise, we'll all be happy to help you with whatever has you preoccupied."

Mark laughed, embarrassed now. No way would he tell them what he was thinking. He said, "I have a conviction about a project . . ." he began, groping for words. "It's a project I'm not sure I should let go of yet."

"That's an interesting topic," Becky said. "When should you give up on something and when should you hang in there, since the breakthrough might be just around the corner."

Logan reached for the pie plate. "Great pie, Hon," he said to Dina, then turned back to Becky. "Very good question. I guess you have to look at what you've put into it, whatever it is, how likely it is to pan out—"

"Do your research, look at your competitors, if that applies," Dina added. "If it's something like starting a small business, of course, you have to give it plenty of time to take root. But by the same token, you have to do your market research beforehand."

"I can tell you have a business background, Dina." Mark smiled at her, appreciating her effort, and gratified that she seemed to have no idea of the topic he had in his mind.

"MBA Wharton," Logan said proudly. "My wife is no flunky. Our kid's going to be a genius."

Dina laughed. "He's a proud father already, and the kid hasn't done anything yet."

"That's parenthood for you, at least it should be like that." Becky dabbed her still-red lips with a napkin.

Dina leaned forward on her elbows and looked at Mark. "Getting back to the topic. You have to decide what the prize will be if you persist." She was clearly enjoying the discussion, maybe because she'd been out of the business world for at least a year. "And what the cost will be. If the cost isn't greater than the prize, then the time and effort you spend is more of an investment."

Mark felt something buzzing inside his brain moving down to his heart. He suddenly felt pinned in place by this idea of conviction. Was God telling him something about Lauren? He leaned forward to hear more of the conversation. Maybe there would be additional clues for him.

"I think what you've already put into something is one factor in how soon you'll give up." Becky's eyes were animated as she looked around the table. "I have a friend who started a blog about two years ago. For almost that entire time there was not much activity, though she posted faithfully every week. She was about to give up, then all of a sudden everything shifted. I think she's got some sponsors or something and was able to quit her day job. One thing that kept her from giving up sooner was all the time she'd put into her posts. She didn't want all that giving of her heart and wisdom to be lost."

"Understandable." Logan nodded. "That's creative energy you put out. Mental energy, too."

And emotional energy. Heart energy. Clearly, in the romantic realm, it took two. But the investment Dina spoke about, Mark had surely made. But was he giving up too quickly? Lauren was in France with her Frenchman. What could he do?

Dina had said to look at the competitors. That brought to mind the Frenchman. Jean-Paul, no, Jean-Pierre. What could Mark do about *him*? Go to France?

The thought came to him like a javelin, causing a sharp intake of breath. He tried to appear that he was tracking with the conversation, but his thoughts had taken a detour. Should he go to France to get on Lauren's turf and try to win her back from Jean-Pierre? Maybe he'd been too passive all along, being the nice guy, the patient one, waiting for her to come back to her senses and return to him.

Maybe he should go there and confront her with his conviction. Maybe that was his final step before he could allow himself to give up for good.

The evening wound down and Mark managed to stay interactive, even as his thoughts ricocheted around in his skull. He'd give his idea more thought, and lots of prayer . . . but he was already mentally leafing through the steps of preparing a leave of absence from his office.

He could work remotely, to a large extent. He'd plan on three weeks, give or take. Likely, Lauren would be angry at first, but maybe he'd eventually win her over.

He had to try. He couldn't give up without doing this one last thing. Once he did, it could go either way. At the worst, he'd know how to say good-bye.

℘ ℘ ℘

Lauren pulled her kerchief down on her brow and flicked a drop of perspiration from under her sunglasses. Her legs ached as she pedaled the gently mounting slope of the departmental road toward Ménerbes. On her first day in France, she'd expressed an interest in biking to Jean-Pierre over dinner but didn't realize he would organize an excursion two days later, a fifteen-kilometer bike trip to Ménerbes from Cavaillon.

Jean-Pierre cycled easily a few yards in front of her, seeming fully relaxed, though they'd been riding on hilly slopes for nearly an hour. From time to time, he pointed out a town or landmark as they passed by.

Despite the challenge to her current fitness level, it felt good to be out under the Provence summer sunshine, passing by farmhouses, hilly slopes, vineyards, and villages. Lauren felt more alive than she had in months. Jean-Pierre had offered the option of biking to a closer village, such as Robion, half the distance, but Lauren had heard so much about Ménerbes, she wanted to go.

"Wasn't that the town made famous by Peter Mayle in his book *A Year in Provence*?" she had asked him when he suggested the outing.

"*Eh, oui*, it's the same one, and everyone heard of the Luberon region after this book," Jean-Pierre had said. "But it is not so crowded now as then. Monsieur Mayle moved on to another town, Lourmarin, I think."

Aside from its literary fame, Lauren knew about Ménerbes from her previous trips to France. Reputed to be one of France's most beautiful villages, in the past it had also drawn many artists like Picasso and Nicolas de Staël, to establish or restore homes there.

Lauren could see the tile rooftops of the village up in the distance, buildings rising like a rocky crown from the vineyards, cherry groves, and fields below. Perched up on an outcrop and surrounded by medieval ramparts, it gazed out over the tranquil valley.

The winding access road to the town appeared steep and Lauren's legs were already feeling like jelly. Just when she was about to request a break, Jean-Pierre turned back and called, "Why don't we walk our bicycles the rest of the way up this hill? You must be tired, and I am also."

"I'm eternally grateful, though it surprises me that you're tired. Makes me feel better." She grinned at him and, needing no more prompting to dismount from the bike and find solid ground under her sneakers. She caught up to him and they pushed their bikes up the paved road toward the village. "Fifteen kilometers is a lot further than I realized." It was only about nine miles, but she was still panting as she spoke. "I must be out of shape."

Jean-Pierre laughed. "You won't be, after your visit here. I ride these hills when I have time off. I rarely have time off, but I force myself to get away. It takes away stress from the restaurant and keeps me in good health, too." That would explain his lean legs and torso, as well as a golden suntan that accented his clear blue eyes. Lauren drew her gaze away, embarrassed by her observations, and the tingling she felt inside at his nearness.

Finally, they arrived at the entrance to the village. Blue-shuttered stone houses that looked centuries old beckoned Lauren toward the winding streets, accented by large flower pots spilling over with petunias, impatiens, and ferns. Soon they arrived to a lively town square. Lauren looked around and everything she saw confirmed it had been worth the effort getting there.

"This is so lovely." It seemed an understatement, as she surveyed the scene from another century, solid stone buildings, a clock tower in the center of the square, shops with colorful awnings, clusters of café tables.

"Where would you like to start exploring, at La Citadelle on one end, or Le Castellet on the other?"

When Lauren gave him a quizzical shake of her head he explained, "The Citadelle is a fortress where a siege between Catholics and Protestants went on for five years in the sixteenth century. Then over there is the castle, which is from medieval times, so it is interesting too, but we can only see it from the outside. Or

64

perhaps the town square here, in the middle of the two?" Jean-Pierre pushed his sunglasses up on his head and awaited her response, a look of mischief on his face.

"Is that like choosing between history and eating? Hmm, I think I'll opt for eating now and doing the history after. What do you think?" Lauren cocked her head as she looked back at him. She'd noticed a grumble of hunger twenty minutes earlier. The gathering of café tables shadowed by colorful parasols was enough of an invitation.

Two hours later, following a satisfying lunch under the shade of trees and umbrellas, they strolled through the hilly streets of the village and browsed in some of the shops.

Later, Jean-Pierre said, "If you aren't too tired, the Abbey Saint Hilaire is just three kilometers further. I think you'll enjoy seeing it. It is from the 13th century."

Refreshed by food and rest, the next few kilometers didn't seem very far, though the ascent to the abbey proved to be another steep ride. The imposing building of pinkish stone covered with orange tile sat atop several terraced layers of green earth, the valley full of vineyards and arbors, lush green growth spilling out before them in all directions. They dismounted and stood silently on the hillside that fell away to the valley. Lauren breathed deeply as she gazed around her, drinking in the green expanse.

"*Magnifique*, eh?" Jean-Pierre stood beside her, joining her in visually savoring the pristine valley. After a few more moments of quiet contemplation of the scene, they turned and continued pushing their bikes up the final stretch of the road, which turned to gravel as they approached the abbey. A few cars were in the abbey parking lot, but the landscape was otherwise deserted.

"The abbey is bigger and in better shape than I imagined, given that it's nearly a thousand years old." Lauren scanned the building's rustic stone walls and medieval-looking towers, all covered with the curved terracotta tiles on the roof so common in the region.

Jean-Pierre gestured toward the abbey with a nod. "The nuns left in the eighteenth century but in the nineteen sixties it was bought and restored. All of these vineyards you see in the valleys there belong to the abbey. People can go inside it and look around, for a small donation." He turned to her. "Do you want to see the inside of the abbey or sit on the hillside to look at the valley from here?"

The panoramic valley stretched out, licked by the late afternoon sun. The view was even more stunning at the higher elevation. "Let's go down one level there and sit first, why don't we?" Lauren pointed to a grassy terrace touching a row of stone half-walls. "We can see the abbey after."

She moved her bike next to his and they stepped down the hill to settle on a bank of grass. "Did you say there is no Mass or personnel here at the abbey now?"

"No, just the couple restoring it and trying to share its history with people who visit."

"Do you—" Lauren wasn't sure how to ask him what she'd wondered for months. It seemed a good time and place to ask, sitting next to a building dedicated to God. "Do you have a personal faith, Jean-Pierre? Were you raised in a church or with religious beliefs?"

Jean-Pierre didn't seem surprised or offended by her question. He turned his face toward her, and it glowed in the orange light of the mellowing sun. His expression was serious, thoughtful. "I was raised like every French child, back then, at least. My parents took me to Mass during my childhood. Today most families do not attend or take their children. Then when I was a teenager, my good friend died. I was so sad I abandoned the church after this." He shrugged then gazed out across the valley. "But I have often wondered about God and sometimes feel curious about Him. I know there is something else there." He flicked his head to gesture toward the sky.

Lauren placed her hand on his forearm. "I'm so sorry about your friend. At a young age it's especially hard to lose someone. But you're right, there *is* something there, a God who loves us and wants us to know Him." She watched for his reaction. He was looking at her, sitting close enough for her to smell his cologne. She felt a stirring of attraction, but also of hope. He hadn't scoffed or refused her question.

"Life is so difficult sometimes," he said. "And we make bad choices. I made many bad choices in the past."

"But it isn't too late, even after bad choices or tragedy. I discovered the love of God after I lost my mother." Lauren's heart was pounding as she said words she hadn't pronounced in years. "I felt comfort and saw the bigger picture. I believe He has been with me ever since then."

Jean-Pierre gave her a small smile which seemed sad to her. Which bad choices was he thinking about? Perhaps having a son so young, or the fact that he hadn't raised his own son, who now had alcohol problems. "I hope so, Lauren. Religion in France is a touchy subject, you know. Most people don't want to discuss it. There's a very bad history. Very bad. And a lot of ceremony, which I don't like so much."

She nodded. "I understand. And I feel the same way about ceremony. History is full of mistakes made by people who misunderstood God and what He wanted. They made mistakes and we make mistakes. But God doesn't. He keeps reaching out, not with religion but with His love." She knew she was saying the right things, but aware that it wasn't coming from a deep enough well of experience. She also had partially shut God off somewhere along the line.

One side of his mouth quirked up and his gaze could only be described as tender. "You explain things so well, *Ma Chérie*. It's beautiful. I think I understand some things for the first time in my life."

A tentative swell of joy bubbled somewhere deep inside her. Then it collapsed when he said, "Tell me about your mother. What happened to her?"

She hadn't expected his question, his uninvited entrance into her secret sorrow, which only Bree and Mark knew about. She stared at him a moment, feeling her mouth go dry, wondering how to summarize, how to change the subject.

A sudden desire filled her, a yearning to expel the pain and tell the raw truth she'd told almost no one. As he gazed down on her, blue eyes full of gentleness that surprised her, he made her feel like she *could* tell him the truth. She swallowed. Moistened her lips. "My mother was mentally ill for most of my life. She was in and out of mental and regular hospitals for as long as I can remember. Then one day she—she took her own life."

Jean-Pierre winced and shook his head. "I'm so sorry, *Chérie*. This is awful. How old were you?"

"Fourteen."

"Were you the one who found her?"

Lauren nodded. "Yes." Her answer was barely a whisper. "She was laying on her back across her bed, almost like she was taking a nap. At first, I thought she was. But she'd taken pills." Lauren had looked on the dresser and bedside table, everywhere in the room, sure her mother would have left a note. Finally, she saw a torn piece of paper laying on the bed beside her with the words, 'I'm sorry' on it.

With the jagged truth out of her chest and hanging in the air between them, she remembered too sharply each detail burned into her memory. She heard her own voice in her ears shouting, *What did you do? What did you do?* Shock, tears, then anguish and anger followed. Even a frayed shred of relief. Her mother's torment was over. And their up and down existence might find calm for the first time in her life, even in the void and the grieving.

Jean-Pierre was silent. Then he spoke quietly. "God gave you comfort after this?"

Lauren swallowed the stale grief. "A couple of years later I found a church where I started attending. I learned about God's love, despite circumstances we go through. And yes, He helped me through it all. I found faith after that tragedy."

"I'm very glad. Maybe I will find faith also."

She smiled and met his eyes. It had been a good decision to share her story with him. "I hope you will, Jean-Pierre. It's a wonderful journey when you meet Him."

"I am very sorry for your mother. But I am happy that something good came from this for you. You seem peaceful now about everything."

He hadn't seen the despair back then, nor the hollow ache she still carried around every day. But her faith did help her suppress the grief and escape her sadness. She'd learned how to bottle up her feelings and give them to God before they got too messy. He'd stayed by her during all those years. He was still there, even if she sometimes felt far from Him.

Speaking the truth out loud felt somehow cleansing. It was part of her history, but she'd hidden it for years, not because of shame, but to avoid reopening the scars that had taken so long to stop throbbing.

Lauren pulled her thoughts from her reverie and noticed that Jean-Pierre had shifted closer to her. She welcomed it, welcomed his warmth after her confession. The humming inside became louder. Sharing her story bound her to him in a new way, forging a new sinew between them.

"Thank you, my Lauren, for telling me this sad thing. For trusting me." He was silent for a moment, continuing to gaze at her with clear blue eyes of compassion. Then he said, "I feel like I know you so much better." He hesitated as his eyes roved to her lips and back to capture her gaze. "I want to kiss you, but I'm sorry if it is the wrong moment."

She lifted her eyes to his and tilted up her face. He leaned toward her and brushed her lips with a light, tender sweep. His hand cupped her chin and pulled her face closer as he deepened his kiss, exploring her with his lips. She circled his neck with her arms while he drew her closer. She tried not to compare him to Mark. It was different, but wonderful.

She was starting to think that he, too, was wonderful. *Slow down, Lauren.* It was too soon. Only a few days.

Her thoughts were muddy, and her emotions turned toward him, reaching to him. She felt lost in his arms as the warmth of his lips invaded her senses. Finally, he pulled away and cradled her in the circle of his arms for several minutes, his chin resting on top of her head. Then he spoke against her ear. "Are you ready to go inside the abbey? Maybe God will meet us in there."

She pulled back and smiled up at him, still filled with the heady feeling of his face against hers and his arms wrapped around her. He grasped her hands and helped her to her feet. She said, "Yes, I think He will."

Chapter Six

"*Merci.*" Lauren smiled at the burly vendor and took the plastic bags, one of onions and one of leeks, from his hand. She slipped the heavy bags into her canvas market bag, rearranging the half-filled space to avoid crushing the mushrooms. After pulling the drawstring shut on her provisions for the coming few days at the restaurant, she shifted the sac on her shoulder. That ought to do it for the list she had wadded in her jeans pocket.

She pulled the crumpled list out and reviewed it a second time to confirm that she'd gotten everything Jean-Pierre wanted. In Cavaillon the market took place only Mondays and Thursday evenings, but there was always a market of farmers and fresh food vendors somewhere in the region every day of the week.

That day she'd spent the morning in Isle-sur-la-Sorgue, five miles away. She was thankful that Jean-Pierre sent her out two or three times per week to get staples as well as special items, like chanterelle mushrooms and black truffles. The truffles, with the unappetizing appearance of nubby black rocks, were prized in the area and outrageously expensive. Jean-Pierre had his favorite truffle merchant, Guillaume, whose market stand was in town only on Thursdays.

The Thursday market at Isle-sur-la-Sorgue was far less crowded than Sunday, when the famous antiques market took place. Although Lauren was finished with her errands, she didn't really want to leave the bustling market and return to Cavaillon. Not yet. In fact, she could stay there all day, absorbing the sights and sounds of this centuries-old market tradition.

Just hearing the low roar of the rushing water as it flowed through canals around the city and seeing the historic water wheels brought it all back, the last time she'd been in Provence with Bree and Le Bon Voyage. Lauren smiled at the memory, filled with a sudden rush of nostalgia. The previous year they'd spent a day in Isle-sur-la-Sorgue with their tour group. It had been an eventful day and the trigger for so much more in Bree's life. Lauren sighed deeply. So much could change in a year, and in fact, *had* for both her and Bree. Lauren's future wasn't as settled as Bree's, but day by day she was starting to relax, enjoying the present. Mornings spent biking, hiking, or visiting local markets, evenings helping at the restaurant, the warm attentions of Jean-Pierre . . . she could certainly find a worse way to spend her summer.

In the days after her bike trip with Jean-Pierre, thoughts of her mother entered her mind at odd moments, as though verbalizing the tragedy in a safe relationship had pried open the sealed box, even if just a little. In the wake of those thoughts was a stale ache, but no longer the blinding despair that, for years, had caused her to block the event from her conscious mind. Maybe she shouldn't have avoided speaking of it or thinking about it all those years. With Jean-Pierre she'd done both and had not fallen apart. This had surprised and encouraged her. And the conversation had deepened her budding feelings for Jean-Pierre.

During Lauren's second week in Cavaillon, she began working as hostess at the *Chez Jean-Pierre* restaurant, a role she completely enjoyed. Greeting patrons warmly and showing them to a table pushed so many of her hospitality buttons.

Despite the hectic rhythm of running a popular restaurant, Jean-Pierre seemed determined to court her. He often took her to sample fine restaurants in other towns, or he planned day trips, a visit to a goat or herb farm or kayaking through the Gorges de Régalon, with limestone cliffs towering on either side of the river. Frequently during their day off they biked together.

She'd also developed a habit of biking alone in the cool of the morning, exploring nearby villages and drinking in the Mediterranean beauty of the scrubby countryside. In a short time, as he'd predicted, she felt leaner and more toned all over her body. As for her relationship with Jean-Pierre, three weeks wasn't much time to conclude anything, but her attraction to him hadn't waned as they fell into a comfortable rhythm.

At times a question teased her mind—could that be a picture of a future with him? Visiting local farms together to source new products, biking, hiking, and other outdoor activities during the warmer months? Talking about food and recipes together? When these invading and premature thoughts arrived unbidden, she tried to flick them away, though they left a path of warmth that spread through the pit of her stomach.

She'd spoken with Mark twice shortly since her arrival, though less often as time went by. Of course, she wanted to stay true to her promise to remain friends, but she also was still testing her feelings for both men. For some reason she wasn't ready to officially end her involvement with Mark even if, after a full year in a platonic state, it hung by a fine filament.

Her phone rang in the small, woven bag that hung across her chest. "*Chérie,*" Jean-Pierre sounded breathless. She heard the noise of cars and staccato French phrases in the background. "I have just spoken to my brother, and he would like us to come for dinner tonight at seven. Is this good for you?"

The weekends were so busy at the restaurant, they'd gotten into the habit of taking a day off Thursday evenings and Sundays. Since they often did things together, she'd been more or less waiting to see what he'd come up with for that evening. Finally, she'd be meeting his family. Ready or not.

"Sure, I'd love to meet him." Jean-Pierre's brother and his wife lived in nearby Cheval Blanc. He spoke frequently of his brother and Lauren had the impression the two were close.

Lauren left the market area near the Notre Dame des Anges church and returned over bumpy cobbled streets toward the parking lot, but when she reached the outer canal, she sat down on a half wall to feel the mist of the foaming water. The canal was noisy here at one of its wider points, as white water frothed endlessly over rocks and under the bridge. She closed her eyes and breathed in the cool air rising off the canal. She could still hear the clamor of the market several streets away and smell the fresh-baked waffle cones from the ice cream shop just behind where she sat.

Were things moving too fast with Jean-Pierre? Not because she was going to meet his brother, but in general? They'd fallen into a rhythm since her arrival three weeks earlier, seeing each other daily either at the restaurant or on bikes or other outings. He often kissed her goodbye, at some longer than others, but didn't pressure her for more, which she appreciated. Since he wasn't yet a Christian, she wasn't sure what his expectations were.

They hadn't talked again about spiritual matters, but when she'd expressed a desire to find a church, he said he'd like to come with her. She wanted to find one for herself, but even more so for Jean-Pierre before he lost interest. She hadn't done it yet and the task weighed on her. How likely would she be to find a community of believers in Provence? Centuries earlier, Protestantism had flourished but had then been forced underground, amidst violent opposition that endured for nearly two hundred years. There were several Catholic churches in town where small groups of faithful members gathered. Yes, there must still be small congregations here and there, even if the current spiritual landscape of France was as rocky and dry as the physical terrain.

Lauren murmured a prayer for guidance, both for a church and for her relationship with Jean-Pierre. She truly hoped God was listening, not put off by her confusion and lack of consistency with him. "I know better, Lord. I'm just not sure how to pray most of the time." Her whispered prayer lifted a weight from her as she owned up to what God already knew about her ups and downs. "So, I'll just ask you to do your will and stay close to me." It was all she could say just then, but she knew it was enough.

Several hours later she stood with Jean-Pierre on the porch at the home of his brother, Luc. It was a typical Provençal home, stone with a tile roof and a fragrant collection of hyacinth and thyme blossoms on either side of the walkway. Lauren gripped the stems of the bouquet she'd bought to present to the hostess and silently chided herself for the butterflies in her stomach as she wondered how she would be received as Jean-Pierre's new American lady friend.

The door swung open, and a man filled the opening, clearly Jean-Pierre's brother, equally tall, with the same square jaw and direct blue-eyed gaze. The man gave them a boisterous greeting and stepped forward to grab Jean-Pierre and plant a kiss on each cheek. They began chattering in French, too fast for Lauren to follow.

Jean-Pierre turned to her. "Lauren, this is my brother, Luc. Luc, I present you Lauren, my friend from America. She came last year to Provence, and she has returned this year."

"*Enchanté*, Lauren. I have heard about you. Welcome to my home." He kissed Lauren's cheeks as well and ushered the two of them into a cool hallway and toward a living area. A petite dark-haired woman entered the room. "This is my wife, Fabienne."

"*Bonsoir*, Fabienne." Lauren held out her free hand, but Fabienne leaned forward to kiss her once on each cheek, as her husband had done.

"Hello, Lauren. I'm so happy to meet you, *enfin!*" Finally.

"Me too, Fabienne. These are for you." Lauren held out the bouquet and Fabienne took them with a broad smile.

"*Merci*, Lauren. You are very kind." She looked at her husband. "We will start with an apéritif, *non*?"

They settled into the living room and Fabienne served salty snacks and before-dinner liqueur. Luc and Fabienne inquired politely about Lauren's life back home and how long she'd be staying in France. She felt sure they were stumped as to why she was in France and what she was hoping to accomplish there. Snag Jean-Pierre? Find a career in a restaurant?

Neither she nor Jean-Pierre mentioned Mark. When she told Luc and Fabienne that she'd been laid off from a restaurant in Virginia, they nodded, and she had the impression that was a good enough explanation to cover all that remained unspoken. Probably, they understood perfectly, and she was the only one who was confused about her life.

The dinner conversation bounced from politics to international relations, the war in Syria to France's relationship with various other countries, the United States, Russia, the United Kingdom, in a loud and continuous thread. Although her French had caught up in great strides since her return to France, there were times when she couldn't catch everything. At one moment, she thought Jean-Pierre and his brother would begin arguing, but seconds later, they were laughing and throwing good-natured insults at each other. Fabienne participated less than the brothers, but also had her own strong opinions, all given with a mixture of certainty and humor. In other words, it was a typical French dinner party.

Lauren's way of communicating was much calmer, more conciliatory. Jean-Pierre no longer translated anything for her and, at times during the evening, seemed unaware of her presence. Her lack of participation was her own fault since she wasn't knowledgeable enough about the politics or international relations in France to contribute an informed opinion. So, she hung back, silent for most of the meal, observing the emotional outbursts, hand gestures, and laughter which she felt incapable of sharing.

If she'd been reading French newspapers over the last few weeks, would that have equipped her better to share in the conversation, instead of feeling like a mute piece of furniture in the room? She knew her personality was different than theirs. Part of it was cultural, part was her calm nature. She didn't have highs and lows like they did. She'd taught herself that skill after the tragedies in her life almost wiped her out.

But at that moment as she watched them and listened to the banter, the disagreement, the laughter, she'd never felt more on the outside, more jealous of their ability to express, feel, laugh, and cry without thinking. Without calculating. Without protecting.

"I am glad you were able to meet my brother," Jean-Pierre said when they were in the car on the way home. His voice was quiet, a sharp contrast to his earlier rowdy volume with Luc and Fabienne. "I could not tell if you enjoyed yourself. Did you enjoy yourself?"

Why did his inquiry sound like an accusation? "Yes, it was a lovely evening. I like your brother and sister-in-law. You seem close with Luc."

"Ah, it was not always this way. But as adults, yes. He is a close friend now." Jean-Pierre was silent as they continued the route toward Cavaillon. When they finally reached Madame Carnot's little stucco house and parked, he turned to her. "Lauren, are you always very quiet, or were you feeling shy tonight with my brother?"

His question took her by surprise. She'd hoped he hadn't noticed her effacement, since he'd been caught up in the evening. "I—I guess I'm pretty calm in general. I'm not like that with you when we're alone, as you know, but I am a bit reserved at first when I don't know people well. Does it bother you?"

Jean-Pierre shrugged and returned his gaze toward the windshield in front of him. "If this is your personality, no, of course not. I am not accustomed to this, but we are different, and this is okay." He turned back to her. "*Chérie*, I like you very much. I want you to be who you are, but I think you hold many things inside you, like you are afraid to let them go out. There is a precious Lauren inside, I think, who I haven't met yet. Is this true?"

Lauren stared at him, unable to respond. She hadn't ever asked herself that question, but his words touched on a question inside her, opening a wall she'd shut years ago. Her eyes stung and she blinked. Blinked again. Was part of her discomfort that evening due to an inability to be herself, an emotional barrier in addition to culture and language?

"I—uh, maybe. I haven't thought about this. I don't know. I was calm tonight because I only just met your brother, because I don't know enough about the news stories you were discussing, and the French was fast for me—" She stopped and lowered her eyes. She was defending herself more than explaining and she shouldn't have to defend herself.

Jean-Pierre shook his head and grabbed her hands. He pressed his lips to her knuckles and held her hands a moment. "I understand, *Chérie*. I do. This is new for you and you are from another country. I have to be more patient and remember this. One day, though, I would like to hear your opinions. Even your strong ones and even the mean ones." He grinned at her and his white teeth glinted in the darkened car. "Do you have mean thoughts sometimes? I want to hear them. I want to hear everything. Do not be afraid, Lauren. You can tell me."

She stared at him. His words had delved into her, touching a deep bruise she didn't fully understand. His words unleashed a stream of tenderness as well. She leaned forward and wrapped her arms tightly around his neck, in that moment, loving him. His arms encircled her back and he breathed into her hair.

It was crystal clear what he was saying and what he wanted, but she didn't know if she could give it to him, as much as she wanted to. To him, to everyone she encountered—her true self. Maybe only Mark had seen the depths of her soul. And Bree. She'd let Jean-Pierre see more of it if she knew where to find it.

Lauren pulled back from him. "I'm sorry I disappointed you, Jean-Pierre. I'll think more about your question. I can't become French, you know. I have my own temperament and culture, but I will try to express more things from my heart with you." Jean-Pierre responded with another hug and a tender, lingering kiss.

As she entered the house and turned with a final static wave at Jean-Pierre, her mind was still filled with the question. Was she hiding her true self? How could she know, after years of tucking that part neatly away?

Along with that, she'd bone up on French politics, history, geography, and international relations. Next time she was in a French social setting, she'd have plenty to say. Was this also the answer he wanted? Probably not, but soon she'd be able to hold her own.

ଓ ଓ ଓ

Mark looked around his simple surroundings, a one-room apartment in downtown Cavaillon, France. He'd unpacked his suitcase into the ancient-looking armoire and cooled off with a splash from the small sink in the miniscule bathroom. The kitchen was in a corner of the room, with two burners and a half-size refrigerator. That should be plenty for his three-week stay.

He'd been glad to see a small wooden desk near an outlet, which would encourage him to keep up with his work at least once in a while. He'd scaled down his obligations before leaving Virginia and felt no twinge of guilt. Not only had he not taken a substantial vacation in over a year, he considered this mad adventure, as Logan jokingly called it, a potential investment in his future. Or else the hinge to an entirely different one.

He crossed the room toward the tall, French windows covered by a lacy white curtain and opened them. Sounds of the city filled the small space, the rumble of conversation, the honk of a car. He was on the third floor, which afforded a decent view of the town.

Since it was his first trip to France, everything was worth a studied look, even the pert, painted shops and apartments across the street and the busy residents walking on the sidewalks below, their musical language rising in staccato notes to his window. In the distance a rocky foothill covered with green tufts of trees guarded the town.

He opened the window wider and stepped toward the wrought-iron lattice covering the lower part of the opening. He dropped his shoulders and breathed deeply, allowing himself to relax after a morning of train travel from Paris then Avignon followed by the process of settling in. "Thanks for bringing me here safely, Lord," he murmured as a mild breeze poured over him from the open window. "I pray you'll guide whatever is supposed to happen here." He closed his eyes for a few seconds and tried to draw strength according to the promises of his faith.

Finally, he was in Cavaillon, where at last he'd see Lauren on her new turf.

Two hours later, after a brief rest and some exploration of the town, Mark located the *Chez Jean-Pierre* restaurant. What an original name, he'd scoffed to Lauren when she told him about it during one of their rare phone conversations. In a way, he was glad she hadn't been in touch over the last week or so since he'd decided to make the trip. His tone might have given something away to her and he was fairly certain she would have ordered him not to come.

The restaurant, a melon-colored stucco with a big sky-blue door, was attractive, with flower boxes and wrought iron curling at each window and a terrace in back. He could barely make out a few large beige umbrellas and a garland of lights behind the building.

He looked down at his watch. Five fifteen. He wasn't planning to intercept Lauren just yet. He first wanted to see the place, get his bearings, plan a strategy. The restaurant didn't open until seven, but he might see her going in or coming out. He planned to stay hidden for now, like some kind of stalker, until he felt more confident. He didn't want her to see him just before her shift, anyway. Didn't want to throw her completely off balance at a moment when they wouldn't have a chance to talk.

From where he sat on a bench across the street, he saw two or three employees, perhaps in their late twenties, push through the front door of the restaurant. None of them resembled the picture of Jean-Pierre that Mark had etched on his mind. Finally, a man who might be him came out through the front door with a purposeful, slightly impatient stride, and went toward the terrace. He seemed like the type who could be a self-important restaurant owner. The man glanced over in Mark's direction. Mark made a point of looking down at his phone. Maybe the guy hadn't noticed him, or maybe it wasn't even Jean-Pierre. Mark's stomach twisted with tension. He should get a good night's sleep before contemplating any action.

Mark's eyes grew heavy. His two-hour nap in the train from Paris was wearing off after his overnight flight. He'd only wanted to glimpse the place first, but as he stood up to leave, he saw her. Lauren coasted down the hill on a bike toward the restaurant. She dismounted and locked it on a nearby rack. He smiled when he noticed that her hair was a mess. She must have her chef garb in the backpack she wore. Fortunately, she didn't see him and disappeared inside the restaurant.

Something thumped and stirred inside at the sight of her. He was perspiring. Was this a crazy idea, coming all the way to France to spy on Lauren and hopefully win her back? She might refuse to see him or tell him to go home. And what about Jean-Pierre, his adversary, his competitor?

The late-afternoon sun was still high in the sky and the shady plane trees beckoned. He found another bench further from the restaurant and pulled out his phone, hoping to find moral support. He wasn't disappointed.

There was a text from Logan. "Have you safely arrived? Have you seen Lauren or Jean-Pierre? Don't keep us in suspense, dude, this is the stuff of romantic movies!"

Mark smiled and it softened the tension grinding away at his stomach. He knew Logan was rooting for him, praying for him. Mark texted back, "I just scoped out the restaurant and I saw Lauren. She didn't see me. I may have seen Jean-Pierre, but I'm not sure. I'm thinking of challenging him to a duel but will probably wait until tomorrow."

Mark turned off his phone and a deep sigh followed. Tomorrow he'd likely laugh at his own joke. At the moment, though, he felt weighed down by something, either fatigue or despair. Or both.

Chapter Seven

"Here is your *Figaro* and your copy of *Le Monde*." Madame Carnot placed the newspapers on the wooden kitchen table where Lauren sat drinking a bowl of hot chocolate. "At your request, I borrowed them from Madame Savin next door, and she thought you'd like this *Paris Match* too, though I don't know why you would want this."

The woman's short stature and plump middle made her look like a cute, grandmotherly box, walking around the kitchen chattering as she did every morning. Lauren grinned at the mental image. This particular "box" had bluish-gray hair and silver-rimmed glasses to match, always wore light red lipstick that frequently stained her front teeth, and never stopped talking.

Lately, Lauren was grateful for this, since her comprehension of fast-talking French was growing, as was her understanding of world affairs in the French universe. The *Paris Match* magazine wouldn't be a bad idea, either, since knowing about French film stars and other celebrities would only enhance her conversational abilities. She'd never been the least interested in these things before. She wasn't now, either.

"Merci beaucoup, Madame Carnot, for your efforts. You are very kind and you take good care of me," Lauren told her with sincerity.

Madame Carnot stopped and gazed at Lauren, her hands clasped at her waist. "My dear child, it is my *pleasure* to help you. Since my children are so far away, I have no one I can help, no one to talk to. It is my pleasure."

Lauren set her magazine down, guilt stabbing at her. She hadn't taken the time to listen to the woman, considering her constant chatter as a nuisance. "I'm sorry to hear about that. Where do your children live?"

"My son lives in Switzerland and my daughter in Thailand. They visit me sometimes, but I miss them and my grandchildren. My dear husband died eight years ago. I visit with my neighbors, though, and that's a comfort. You are a comfort, too."

Lauren swallowed and smiled. "I'm glad. You are very kind. My first day here, you said that sometimes Jean-Pierre helps you with things."

The woman nodded. "Yes, he weeds my garden once in a while. I don't know how he finds time to do this, running a successful restaurant. He brings me fresh melons and things from the marché when he goes."

"How do you know Jean-Pierre?"

"My husband and I were frequent customers at his restaurant. He gave my nephew a job for a little while. He's a nice man, Jean-Pierre. A little hot-tempered, but very kind. And that son of his, he has so many problems, but Jean-Pierre has finally decided to be a father to him. He's a good man. I don't know why he never married anyone. He's over forty. Perhaps he will marry you!"

Lauren gave her a weak smile. "I don't know him very well yet, but you never know."

"Why don't you go to the back porch to read your magazines? The sun isn't too hot just yet." The woman finished sponging down the tile counter and wiped her moist hands on her apron.

"Good idea." Lauren ran water into her empty bowl and slipped out the back door, newspapers and magazines in hand. A round café table with one metal chair sat near the back door. In the corner of the yard, tall sunflowers stood at attention as if welcoming her to their space. She settled into the chair and let the toasty sunshine lick her face and warm her shoulders for a moment before getting to work.

She spread out the newspaper, but her thoughts were spooling back fragments of her conversation the day before with Jean-Pierre. He'd told her, *Be who you are*. Why would he say that? Wasn't she being herself, expressing the real Lauren that she was deep inside? Or were there things inside she still pushed down, afraid to let them out?

Too uncomfortable, too difficult to discern if there was even an answer. Her gaze fell back to the newspaper. Maybe it could distract her from difficult personal questions.

The headlines led her to even more disturbing events in the world. She read the bold print of an article relegated to the bottom of the front page. The Syrian war had new victims: families, children, the injured in a hospital that had been bombed.

She sighed, her teeth clenched. Some conflicts seemed to go on forever, and the human misery was unfathomable. Couldn't anyone intervene and set things right? They'd discussed it at dinner with Luc and Fabienne, but only briefly. Of course, everyone thought it was awful, but since it didn't affect them and they felt helpless anyway, that's as far as it went.

The next article had to do with unemployment and fraud and the next was about some kind of trade conflict with China. She pushed them aside. Was she trying to be what Jean-Pierre wanted her to be? Being informed was useful, but what was going to matter for her, being able to converse at a dinner party? Was this what mattered? Shouldn't she choose the issues *she* cared about and pursue those? Maybe that was the first step in being herself, finding a cause or calling she could dive into with all her heart.

℩ ℩ ℩

Today would be the day. Well-rested and well-fed, thanks to a convenient café on the first floor of his building, Mark felt his typical optimism return to him. The day before as he faced the restaurant, the sight of Lauren and possibly Jean-Pierre, he wondered what he was doing as his boldness and hopes slid down into his shoes.

As if bestowing a blessing on him, the sun bathed the streets with golden light and reflected off the trees and a gentle breeze in the low seventies lifted his mood even more. It wasn't the time yet to visit the restaurant, so he explored several of the streets surrounding his lodging. By midday he was beginning to get a mental grid of downtown. On the western edge of the city a block of short mountains kept him oriented.

At three o'clock, he set out toward the restaurant, four blocks or so to the northeast. His stomach began fidgeting with nerves that became an all-out grind as he approached the corner where he could already see the tile roof of the restaurant. When the building came into view, his phone rang. Logan. Relief washed over him, since he really needed a friend just then.

"Great timing. I need some moral support."

"Hey, what's up over there? Have you talked to Lauren?"

"Not yet. She doesn't know I'm here yet. I didn't talk to her yesterday but I hope to today. I'm not sure what time she starts her shift. I'm showing up early so I can intercept her as she's going in."

"Sounds like a good plan. Hey, man, if she doesn't appreciate all your efforts, maybe she isn't worth it. Just saying."

Mark found the same bench where he'd parked himself the day before and sat down to wait. He knew that Logan wished he'd just move on but was supportive all the same. A real friend. "I hope she *does* appreciate that I came all the way over here. I used to be better at predicting her reactions, but not anymore. She's becoming a mystery to me."

"What time does the restaurant open?"

"Usually, it doesn't open until around seven, but the staff gets here a few hours early. I'll walk over and see." Mark looked either way and jogged across the street to look at the small sign on the door. The grinding in his stomach tumbled down to deep disappointment. "Oh no, they're closed today. It's Sunday. I'm going to lose the whole day. Coming here is the best way to get in touch with her."

"Can't you just call her? If she's changed her number, you can look her up on your phone log. She's called you since she's been in France."

"Sure, I have it, but I really need to see her in person." Too easy for her to hang up on him.

"Got it. Hey, sorry about the restaurant being closed since I know you're ready to get this little confrontation out of the way, but somehow it will work in your favor in ways you don't know."

"I hope you're right. And yes, I really want it out of the way. I want to know what my next steps will be."

"Patience, Bro. You're not the only one planning things here. Someone is directing your steps."

At that, Mark had to smile. "Good reminder. How's Dina? Tell her she can't have this kid until I get back."

Logan laughed. "Okay, I'll tell her that. Don't worry, she's not due for another month. You'll be cutting it close, though, especially if the little guy comes early."

Mark squeezed his lips together. As much as he wanted to be a good friend to Logan, just then he couldn't think of anything but his mission in Cavaillon. "Keep me posted and I'll do the same."

The following day Mark took a canvas bag he'd bought at the airport and followed the morning noise for two blocks toward the Monday market. As he approached the colorful stands, he liked it already, the energy of this tradition that had probably been going on since the days when France wasn't yet a country.

He surveyed the colorful array of fresh vegetables spread out like a painting on a long table. Here it was, his first encounter with a French person aside from his apartment contact.

The middle-aged woman behind the stand asked him something. He smiled, said *Bonjour*, and pointed. He'd only had enough time to study numbers and basic greetings, so he pointed to the zucchini and said, "deux," then repeated the process with other vegetables until he had filled his bag. The woman continued saying things to him, but this time with a good-natured grin. She seemed to understand how out of his element he was.

The noise at the market began to pick up as men and women arrived with their canvas totes, straw baskets, and wheeled bags. Some arrived with spouses, children, and dogs on leashes. Going to the market must be a family activity as well as a social gathering, judging by the shoppers emitting enthused greetings as they met in small clusters.

Over the rumble of conversation, shouts from vendors cut through as they attempted to draw buyers. He'd avoid the supermarkets as long as possible. That should be easy, with all of the fresh choices before him. A little further down the block he could see stands with clothing, kitchen gadgets, and oriental rugs.

The previous day he'd hedged against his disappointment by continuing his tour of the town and discovered an old synagogue with an opulent interior, despite an ordinary façade he'd almost missed. He also happened upon some ancient ruins near the tourist information bureau, which was closed. He'd try to visit later in the week to get his bearings in Cavaillon.

Once he stocked up on fresh food for the next few days, he'd try the restaurant again. He should have success today. Walking into the restaurant while Lauren was on duty didn't seem to be a good idea, especially if she was in the kitchen, but he wasn't sure how else he could talk to her in person.

Last stop, fish vendor. His apartment was stocked with basic cookware so even if he couldn't grill it, he could make a meal. Mark stood in line for several minutes. When it was his turn, he was about to repeat his numbers strategy, this time with fish, but shouting broke out behind the stand between an older man and a younger employee who was about twenty years old. They were in each other's faces shouting in French while the woman who waited on him looked on, appearing embarrassed.

Seconds later the boy tore off his apron and plastic gloves and stormed off. The older man joined the woman and they discussed the occurrence in staccato French, their hands gesturing wildly.

The man turned to Mark and spoke in French, perhaps uttering an apology. Mark felt the need to say something to the couple. "I'm sorry about your employee," he told them in English.

Shaking his head, the man said something loudly in French, perhaps a curse word. Then in English, he said to Mark, "This boy help me to clean the fishes. They are not always clean when I receive them and now I have no one to help me. When the marché is busy, I cannot do this."

Mark glanced down the row of fish, neatly presented with their price tickets. He'd been cleaning fish his whole life, up until a few years ago. One of those things dads and sons sometimes do after a fruitful day at the lake, and he was privileged to be one of them. "I can help you." He surprised himself by his own words. Just to fill in for a day or two, to give some relief to the beleaguered fishmonger. "I know how to clean fish and I can help you for a few days until you find someone." Mark smiled at the man to show his sincerity. He thought of Logan, who'd probably double over laughing.

The man's bushy black eyebrows went up. "*Vraiment*? Merci, Monsieur. You are very kind. This will help me and I will find a new boy soon. Can you help me Thursday evening? We have another market then."

"Yes, I will come back then and help you." It might create good will and give him something helpful to do while he waited for Lauren to respond to him. That might take a while.

And in the meantime, he'd found a job.

ය ය ය

When Lauren saw that she was still early for her shift, she made another loop around the perimeter of the downtown on her bike, coasting by the Hôtel Dieu and down the wide Avenue Gambetta, while the breeze and motion pushed her hair behind her. She reveled in the late afternoon sunshine, thankful for a bit of extra time to enjoy it. The weather had been ideal since her arrival, except for a few hot days. The bike she'd gotten second-hand at the marché had almost become a part of her body. Whenever she was in Cavaillon and not on an errand in another town, she loved using it for transportation instead of a car.

Up Rue Raspail, across the road by the synagogue, then onto Michelet, she finally slowed down and then stopped her bike in front of *Chez Jean-Pierre*. Of course, she'd be a bit sweaty before her shift, but it had been worth it.

She breathed heavily as she pulled the bike into the rack and attached two locks, then reached for her bag. She turned and noticed someone crossing the street in her direction. As he neared, she noticed the man looked a lot like Mark, the same gait and height. He'd often been in her thoughts since her arrival, as she tried to make sense of her feelings for him and their past together. But now she must be hallucinating.

As the man reached the curb, she stilled, saw him with startling clarity, the same dark, wavy hair and hazel eyes she knew so well. Her mouth dropped open. Disorientation was quickly followed by frustration mixed with surprise. "Mark? What are you *doing* here?"

He smiled then and stopped about four feet in front of her. "Hello, Lauren. It's good to see you. I hope you don't mind that I came. I wanted to see your world, this place you love so much." He waved a hand toward the town. "I missed you, too."

Anger flushed through her. How infuriating that he stood there as if they were in a coffee shop in Virginia, as if she hadn't crossed the ocean alone to find herself. "You just can't leave me alone to find my way, can you?" Her voice came out in a shrill tone that made her wince. She saw Mark wince too.

His smile fell. He shook his head and said evenly, "Lauren, listen—"

"I know why you came. You want to pull me away from Jean-Pierre. I should never have told you about him. I thought I could trust you as a friend, but I guess I was wrong." She regretted the harsh words and tone that spilled out before she could stop them. But his interference was maddening.

"Is it so wrong that I wanted to see you? To see your life here in France? I'm not going to stay long, I promise. Just a couple of weeks or so. I'd like to see you sometime. As a friend. Just a friend, no pressure. Please?" Mark held out his hands in a pleading gesture.

Lauren stood, her arms crossed, fuming. A friend. Who was he trying to fool? He just couldn't give up.

Couldn't give up. Something softened inside her, curling up tender edges toward her heart. He wasn't giving up, but wasn't pressuring her either, he'd claimed. Still, she needed time for the frustration to stop coursing through her veins, for her heart to stop pounding. To take in this disruption to her peaceful French life. She shook her head and grimaced. "I'll think about it. I have to work now." She turned and left him standing on the curb.

Chapter Eight

A new day, a new marché. Mark leaned back on his heels between fish-cleaning tasks and observed his newest location, Velleron. He liked this market even better than the one at Cavaillon. Certain elements were similar in every market, the noise, the energy, the colorful palette of vegetables, fruits, and flowers stretched out on long tables under awnings that were set up or taken down in a matter of minutes. In this particular market, everything was sold directly by farmers. He hadn't expected to start his new job so soon, but here he was, smelling like fish and covered with scales.

His new employer, Didier, had called the previous evening and told him that he needed him sooner than expected, the following day, in fact, at the market of Velleron, a town about fifteen minutes' drive to the north of Cavaillon.

"Five more kilos of *cabillaud* and three of *daurade* just for the next hour," said Didier as he pulled several fish from a large cooler and slapped them on the broad table where Mark worked. "We keep the others on the ice until more people come in the evening."

It wasn't difficult work, since Mark knew how to clean fish, but it was messy and smelly. Despite the disadvantages, it afforded him the opportunity to hear French spoken and take in the atmosphere at the market, which he was enjoying more and more. It was easy to see why Lauren was so enchanted with this country, and he'd only been there a few days.

While Mark worked, his thoughts circled around his encounter with Lauren the previous day. He hadn't been surprised by her anger, but discouragement still beckoned him. Maybe with time she would soften. She *had* said she'd think about it, and he could always phone her in a few days to see if she was ready to see him. The Lauren he remembered didn't hold on to anger for very long. He hoped the new Lauren would be the same.

As he finished scaling the first *daurade* and pulled another fish from the pile, he looked up and saw her wandering across the aisle between the cheese stand and the onions. She didn't see him and might not, since he was behind the counter under the shade of the awning. Her hair was swung up into a ponytail and dark sunglasses perched on her nose. A woven bag already bulging with produce hung on one arm.

Mark was debating calling out to her when she turned in his direction and stopped, as if unable to believe her eyes—for the second time in twenty-four hours. She slid her sunglasses up on her head and approached the fish stand.

"Mark? Is that you?" This time instead of anger, shock registered on her face.

"Hi, Lauren," was all he could think of to say. He felt self-conscious in his soiled white apron covered with fish guts.

"Well, that's twice in one week you've absolutely amazed me." A small smile tugged at her lips. He took heart.

He grinned back at her. "I figured I needed a new career, you know, midlife crisis. No, really, Didier here is a man short, so I wanted to give him a hand for a few days until he can hire someone else."

She shook her head, still looking incredulous, her eyes wide, lips slightly parted. Then she said, "That's nice of you. Listen, Mark, I want to apologize for yesterday." Her gaze lowered and flickered back up again.

A glimmer of the old Lauren. Mark's spirits lifted.

"I—I was really surprised to see you and it seemed so—" she gestured with her hands as she searched for words. "It seemed so *interfering*, or something. I don't know, you *followed* me here. How did you think I'd respond?"

"I understand your frustration. And your surprise. I'm not trying to badger you, Lauren. You know me, I'm not going to do that. I really did want to see this place from your perspective, to understand what attracts you here. I wanted to see it for myself, and I have to say, so far, I love it."

"Really? I'm glad." Her smile widened just a little.

"And I wanted another chance to just hang around, be friends. Even if we never get back together, I'd like to stay friends and I really wanted to be here with you just for a little while. I know it's probably not convenient for you, especially with Jean-Pierre, but I hope you'll indulge me. Before long, I'll be gone again." He wondered if he was babbling but couldn't stop himself. It might be his only chance to get through to her.

She was silent a moment. Then, "You make it sound as though Jean-Pierre had nothing to do with your desire to come here." Her voice admonished lightly. She shook her head. "You don't have to answer that. What do you want me to do?" Her voice was quiet as her green eyes searched his.

Mark relaxed his stiff shoulders. "I want to be able to call you sometimes, meet for coffee, take a walk. As friends. No pressure."

"How long are you staying?"

"I've planned on three weeks."

Lauren nodded. "Okay. You can call me. We'll see after that." She finished with a smile.

Mark grinned. "I promise I won't be a pest. Just want to be your friend." As he spoke, he saw a man behind Lauren approach, the same man from the restaurant.

The man was handsome, tall and well-built. His stride made him look important, arrogant. He wore a woven scarf loosely around his neck and had a large, square bag hanging across his chest, giving him a thoroughly European demeanor. Mark could understand why Lauren might be attracted to him, and he suddenly felt an unfamiliar tug—a claw of jealousy gripping him from the inside. Mark drew up his shoulders, preparing for a confrontation.

"*Qui est-ce*, Lauren?" the man asked her, hitching his head toward Mark as he stood close behind her. Too close. The claw dug deeper.

Lauren turned to him and said in English, "Jean-Pierre, this is my friend Mark. Remember I told you about him? He's visiting France."

So, she'd told him. Jean-Pierre knew who Mark was. In that moment he wasn't sure whether or not he was glad. The man knew his history with Lauren, that they hadn't been just friends.

Jean-Pierre sized him up with his eyes. "You came to France to get her back?" He shook his head and a derisive chuckle escaped his throat. "Don't dream. She has made her decision."

Mark was at a loss for words. He wasn't sure that Lauren had made a final decision. At least he hoped not. He saw her stiffen with discomfort. He knew her well enough.

He cleared his throat. *Take the high road, Mark.* "You must be Jean-Pierre." He kept his voice bright, unintimidated. "I've heard about you, too. Nice to meet you. I came to enjoy your magnificent country."

Jean-Pierre looked startled. Maybe he hadn't expected a compliment. From what Mark understood about the French, they loved their country and appreciated when others recognized its value. Maybe Mark would get points with Jean-Pierre, or at least diffuse conflict.

Again, the arrogant flick of the man's head, indicating the fish stand. "I'm sure that your work in America is better than this."

Lauren turned to him and touched his arm. "Mark is helping out because the *poissonier* is short-staffed."

Jean-Pierre looked unconvinced. He turned to Lauren and asked, "*Tu es prête?*" which Mark guessed was asking her to leave with him.

She nodded and said, "Good-bye, Mark," though her gaze told him he'd speak with her soon. He smiled at her warmly, nodded to Jean-Pierre and shifted his gaze back to his codfish before Jean-Pierre could launch another challenge.

ର ର ର

When Jean-Pierre took Lauren's arm possessively, she fumed but waited until they were out of Mark's vision before snatching it back. "Tell me, Jean-Pierre, why are you acting as though you're fourteen years old?"

He stopped and stared at her. "What?"

"You heard me." She felt like her blood was simmering up to the surface. "That was my friend, and you were rude to him. Yes, in the past he was my boyfriend, but you didn't have to act nasty to him. You could have been cordial and mature, and it wouldn't have killed you."

He still hadn't moved and seemed unable to respond for seconds. "Maybe you are right," he finally said. "I was surprised to see him and I thought of the fact that you loved him once. It was an automatic response."

Lauren crossed her arms. "Too bad your automatic response wasn't to be *kind*. That would have been better." She turned and marched ahead, leaving him behind.

He jogged to catch up to her. "Don't be angry, *Chérie*. He should not have come. Why did he come, if not to create a problem for you?"

She whirled around. "Are you sure it's me you are concerned about? Let me be clear with you, Jean-Pierre. I don't *belong* to you. I am my own person. I can spend time with whoever I want to. If I choose to spend time with you, I am getting to know you, but I don't belong to you."

Jean-Pierre looked humbled for a moment, a look she'd rarely seen on his face. Her anger softened a few degrees.

"I understand, *Chérie*. You are right, you do not belong to me. But how can I be nice to the man who wants to win you back?"

She let out an exasperated groan. "I am not a trophy to be won."

"Yes, of course you are right. It's an expression. Please . . . please forgive me?"

He reached out and grasped her hands in his, squeezed lightly. The rest of her anger drained away as she looked up into his searching blue eyes, with tiny lines fanning outward. She said, "Yes, I forgive you. But please, respect me as an independent person." She needed to make him understand that she was serious. And irritated.

"Yes, of course. I make a mistake. How long is your friend in France?"

"A couple more weeks. He'll be gone soon." That might be true, but either way Jean-Pierre would have to give her more space.

They drove back to Cavaillon in silence. Lauren grimaced and stared out the window. She wasn't angry anymore, but wanted

Jean-Pierre to think she was in order to make her point. Instead, she found herself thinking again about her encounter with Mark. He had looked disarmingly cute in his soiled white apron and clear plastic gloves, his open expression lacking guile or manipulation. She'd almost giggled at the sight of him, but knew she'd lose her objectivity. Was she glad he wasn't staying in France very long, relieved that soon her life would return to normal?

She wasn't sure.

As Jean-Pierre and Lauren arrived at the restaurant, one of the chefs rushed from the kitchen to the front door to intercept him. "There is a problem," he blurted in fast French. "Marcel isn't coming today. He left a message on the restaurant phone that he had to leave town and won't be back. I don't know why, or why so suddenly. Maybe he found another job or it's because of a girl, I don't know."

Jean-Pierre's face clouded, his eyebrows knit in an angry line. "He is gone and won't come back?" He turned to Lauren. "Marcel is my sous-chef. His role is very important, and we will have trouble keeping up in the kitchen without him." He turned back to the employee. "Merci, Frédéric, I will think about a solution. We will find someone." When the employee had returned to the kitchen Jean-Pierre murmured, "But how to find someone before tonight?" He looked at Lauren. "Would you be willing to help us in the kitchen tonight, Lauren?"

Her mouth opened to speak. She'd hoped to never return to a restaurant kitchen, but Jean-Pierre needed her. "Yes, of course I'll help. I'm already here and you need someone."

Relief washed over his face. He grabbed her by her shoulders and planted a firm kiss on her lips. "*Merci infiniment, Chérie.* You are helping me very much. Do you have a jacket?"

"Yes, I do, but it's at the house." She'd brought it to France with her just in case, but prayed she'd never have to use it. Maybe she'd only have to cook a few times before Jean-Pierre found another sous-chef. She'd pray *hard* for that.

Jean-Pierre moved past her. "For now, I will get you one from the closet, and a toque. It might be a bit large, but it can work for this evening. Then tomorrow you can bring in yours. This works for you?"

She smiled weakly. "Sure. I don't mind helping out tonight until you find someone." But she sure hoped he'd find someone else quickly. She'd really liked the low-stress rhythm of being a hostess, but couldn't very well say so when Jean-Pierre was facing a crisis at short notice. The idea of returning to her chef role in a busy restaurant made her shudder. And one that was seeking a Michelin star rating would likely be more pressure than she was prepared for. Her comfortable French life had turned upside-down in the space of twenty-four hours.

Jean-Pierre returned with a jacket that was clearly too big. She put it on and he folded up the sleeves up around her forearms. "There, that's good. Don't drop your sleeves in the soup, though." He smiled at her and adjusted her toque on her head. "I will let Benoît be the sous-chef tonight and you can help him. This will bring you in gradually. You will learn everything quickly, I know."

Lauren wasn't so sure, and almost repeated that it was only temporary, but ended up silently following him back to the kitchen. She'd only seen it a few times, and briefly. It was spacious and gleaming in the unnatural orderly state that existed just before the dinner chaos hit with an almost violent explosion. She'd lived with that contrast and pressure long enough to brace herself.

"Bonjour, Benoît, Solange." She nodded. "Frédéric, Khaled." She already knew everyone on the kitchen staff. They looked surprised to see her there, but made space as Jean-Pierre oriented her to the kitchen.

For the next several hours Lauren asked a million questions about where to find things, about French cooking methods that might be different than what she knew, and followed orders given by everyone in the kitchen. She felt like a ping-pong ball, responding to Benoît, then Solange, then Jean-Pierre, then Benoît again, then Khaled. On it went into the evening that could only be considered surreal.

"Lauren, the béchamel!" shouted Khaled as he pulled a large pan of pasta from the burner.

She'd been stirring for what seemed like thirty minutes and the béchamel was at the right consistency. She pulled the big pan toward him as he muttered a complaint and snatched it from her hands.

Scowling, she returned to the counter where she continued chopping vegetables for the ravioli primavera and garnishes.

"Lauren, can you check the *rôti*? It's ready to slice now."

She rushed back to where the big roast was settling on the stove after being cooked. Was she supposed to cut it herself? Ask someone else? "You want me to cut this?"

"No, no! Just check it!" yelled Benoît.

In his own corner of the kitchen Lauren heard Jean-Pierre shouting commands, confirming, criticizing. The atmosphere was anything but peaceful, as the dining room had been just a day before. Lauren longed to return there, but knew it would be a week or two before Marcel's replacement could be interviewed and hired.

She sighed, hoping she could hold out that long. Her stress level was ticking higher and higher, like a radiator ready to blow. She fully understood why she hadn't wanted to stay at the Fins and Feathers.

Finally, the kitchen slowed down and she began looking at the clock. This wasn't for her. She'd tell Jean-Pierre the next day. She looked over at where he did three or four things at once, zipping from one table to the next, barking orders at every moment, including to her. That had been almost the only time he'd spoken to her, but she understood. Here he was at his most stressed, most focused. His reddened face showed overload, yet she could tell he reveled in it.

Not her. The sooner she could get out of the kitchen, the better.

Chapter Nine

Mark glanced up from his book and scanned the empty street in front of him. She was late, unlike the Lauren he remembered. Uneasiness needled him. Would she even come?

He'd arrived at the café an hour earlier to get some breakfast. While he drank his café au lait and waited for her, he perused the small book on French beginner grammar that he'd brought with him. He'd been picking up expressions and words since his arrival so he might as well put them together in a logical way he could build on. That day his concentration was fragmented. His eyes kept leaping from the pages to the street to check for Lauren.

A day after seeing her at the Velleron market, he had called her. He knew he ought to wait one more day, but his time was slipping away. He'd been in France nearly a week and he only had two left to accomplish his goal. Scoring a coffee date was an encouraging first step.

"*Salut*, Mark!"

His head jerked up. Thierry from one of the produce stands, waved at him as he strolled by with his girlfriend. Mark waved back and smiled. "*Salut*, Thierry."

Must be Thierry's day off. It was amazing how many market workers he'd met in just two days. Despite his complete inability to communicate intelligibly, he felt warmly accepted by the locals.

The previous day after his shift, Mark had told Didier he had another obligation the following morning and wouldn't be able to work. Didier would gladly keep him busy nearly every day of the week. He'd already had him work at Velleron two days in a row and he was scheduled for the Fontvieille market the following day. If Mark was going to have time to spend with Lauren, he'd have to say no once in a while, since her working hours were opposite his, except when he worked the evening markets.

Mark drained the last of his coffee and scanned the street again just as Lauren coasted into view on her bike. When she reached the café, she dismounted, propped the bike against a tree, and slid into the chair opposite him.

"I'm so sorry I'm late. I have a talkative landlady and she held me up. Not a good excuse, but the only one I have." Her voice was breathless, her cheeks flushed. When a stray lock of hair fell across her face, he wanted to kiss her.

"*Tu es retardée.* Are you impressed?" He tossed her a grin.

She laughed. "I would be if you hadn't just told me I was retarded. I think you meant to say, *Tu es en retard.*"

"Oops." Mark couldn't help but laugh aloud. He repeated her phrase then held up the grammar book. "I was just getting a little studying in."

Lauren's eyes widened. "And yes, I am impressed. You've been here since when?"

"Saturday."

"Five days. How much have you learned?" A playful smile twitched the corner of her mouth.

So glad she asked. "*Puis-je vous aider, madame?*"

She laughed. "Yes, you can help me, Monsieur. I want two kilos of salmon, please! Hey, that was pretty good for just five days. Your accent is decent, too."

"Ah, but I have many talents that you don't know yet." He linked his hands together and offered a lazy smile.

She leaned forward on her elbows. Her green eyes latched onto his. How he'd missed her eyes, dark lashes surrounding sea-green, gazing back at him.

"I thought I knew you pretty well, after two years," she said, "but I did not know you had a talent with language. Or fish-cleaning."

He gave her a Gallic shrug and a flick of a hand that said, 'Well, of course." Yes, he'd learned a lot in five days. It was almost like they were flirting, and he liked it. He especially liked the way she looked disarmed and impressed by his newly discovered talents.

"So, Jean-Pierre let you out for the day?" At his question her smile fell. Bad word choice.

"He doesn't own me," she said stiffly.

"I hope *he* knows that. He didn't seem to the other day." Mark couldn't help but point that out to her. In case she hadn't noticed.

Lauren grimaced. "He was just surprised to see you and came on a little possessive. But I see who I want, and he knows that."

Mark nodded and hoped she'd prove that to Jean-Pierre. "I'm glad you were able to come today. Are you—are you enjoying your visit so far?"

Before she could answer the waiter came to the table. "*Vous désirez, Madame?*"

"*Un chocolat chaud, s'il vous plaît.*" When the waiter left, she looked around. "Are you staying in this neighborhood?"

"I'm renting a flat in that building there." He pointed across the street to a four-story stucco building. "And you? Where is this talkative landlady and how did you find her?"

Lauren smiled. "Madame Carnot. She's sweet, really. Jean-Pierre has known her for a long time and knew she rents rooms in her home."

"So, back to my question. Are you enjoying your time here?" He was afraid of the answer but had to ask.

She hesitated. At that, he quelled the twinge of optimism.

"I *was* enjoying it. A lot. It's the perfect time to be in Provence. Everything is so lovely, and I was seeing a lot of the region. I've been working as a hostess at Jean-Pierre's restaurant in the evenings, and that was really fun, easy work. But then the other day one of the chefs quit and Jean-Pierre asked me to fill in."

"Uh-oh."

"Exactly."

"I do remember that restaurant kitchens are not your favorite."

"I thought I'd left that pressure behind in Virginia."

Mark leaned back in his chair and crossed his arms. "But you *do* still like to cook, right?"

Her eyes narrowed. "Yes. Are you getting at something?"

He shrugged. "Just encouraging you to brainstorm ways you might be able to cook without having to work in a restaurant."

She nodded. "I'll think about that. What I did with Le Bon Voyage should have been a perfect fit. I don't know why it wasn't. After a couple of years, I lost my passion for it."

He didn't respond.

Lauren shifted in her chair, looking suddenly agitated. "I know what you're thinking."

Just then the waiter returned with a steaming mug of hot milk and a small pewter pitcher of liquid chocolate. She looked up. "*Merci*."

"I know you know what I'm thinking. I think of it often, so I won't bring it up."

With deliberation she poured the chocolate into the frothy milk and stirred gently with the tiny spoon. She seemed aware of his intense gaze on her. Without looking up at him she said, "People lose their passion sometimes, but it doesn't necessarily indicate a pattern."

"I didn't say anything. You'll figure out whatever you're supposed to." Above all, he didn't want to pressure her. She already knew where he stood.

Lauren sighed and looked away. He thought he could see tears glistening in the corners of her eyes, but maybe it was just the summer light reflecting off the overhanging leaves. The Lauren he remembered was unable to cry, but he could see emotion welling up in her face and the tightness of her throat.

After a moment she turned back to him, her face a mask, composed and bland. "How were you able to get away from your practice?"

He fully expected the shift and today was only their first meeting, so he wouldn't push. "I was long overdue for a vacation. Besides that, since I'm my own boss, I can arrange things as I want." He fiddled with the plastic wrapper of the cookie that had accompanied his coffee. "Work has slowed down some, now that tax season is over. I brought some work with me, but haven't really done anything yet, other than answer some emails. I'm not too stressed about it."

"I can tell the Provence rhythm suits you." She took a deep sip of her hot chocolate. "Mmm. I've got a weakness for this stuff."

"I'm loving it here so far. Despite cleaning fish. Actually, that gives me the chance to meet some of the locals. Of course, it's only been a couple days, but my impression is that they're nice. It helps that I'm one of them, I guess. I mean, a market worker. They seem in a class all their own. Very down to earth farm people, merchants."

"Of course, they'll like you," she said matter-of-factly. "You're friendly, even if you can't talk to them yet."

"How else do you think I landed a job my third day in France?" He gave her a wide grin. "So, what else are you doing today?"

"Actually, I'm off today. And very glad about that. I'll do some catching up on groceries and laundry and take a long ride on my bike to de-stress from the kitchen."

Mark nodded. *Take a risk.* "I'm available all day too, if you want to take a walk before you do your chores. We could climb up St. Jacques Hill on the west side of the town. I've been wanting to go up there and see the trails and the chapel."

She leaned back and widened her eyes, looking impressed for a second time. "In addition to getting a job, learning French, and befriending the locals in the last five days, you've learned your way around Cavaillon. You continue to amaze me, Mark. As if just coming all the way to Provence was not enough."

Warmth flickered inside him. He couldn't take credit for it all, but was thankful she'd noticed. Maybe Logan was right about God guiding his steps. But he wouldn't count his victories too soon.

Lauren drained her chocolate and ran her tongue over her lips. "I'll be meeting Jean-Pierre later on. He wants to go to Aix-en-Provence for the evening, so I don't have time for Saint Jacques today. Though we could do it another day. We *could* take a stroll around town. I'll show you around. There's a lovely 18th century synagogue you should see. When the Jews were being expelled from cities all over France during the 14th century, Cavaillon welcomed them here."

He'd already seen it but wouldn't tell her that. He said, "Sounds fascinating."

ભ   ભ   ભ

The restaurant was hushed and bathed with a flickering dim light from candles on every table. Though it was a weeknight, the tables were full of patrons and more of them waited at the door. A gentle hum of conversation floated through the intimate space, lifting up to the wooden beams on the ceiling.

"This is a very good place. They have *two* Michelin stars." Jean-Pierre's voice was quiet, as if he were telling Lauren a highly prized secret.

Lauren didn't know how to respond to that but guessed the meal would reveal what a two-star restaurant was like. She didn't quite understand a restaurateur's drive to get a star, as long as the food was good and the whole dining experience was exceptional, as it already was at *Chez Jean-Pierre*.

"I wonder if you are too worried about the star, Jean-Pierre." She reached for the carafe of chilled water and refilled her glass and his. "I mean, your restaurant is wonderful. I have eaten the food and I've observed the atmosphere. Isn't that what really counts?"

He shrugged. "Maybe in America. Not in France. It is like a red label, a sign of high superiority, and everyone knows about this. We have these things in France. You know the Label Rouge for meats and other foods and the Appellation Controllée for wine and champagne. It's like a contest where only a few can win." The candlelight reflected planes and shadows on his face, but she thought she detected a veil of anxiety in his eyes.

"I'm not sure I agree with you." Lauren leaned her elbows on the table. "Anyone with a wonderful restaurant and a faithful, happy clientele can win. And most people don't even know about the Michelin stars." Lauren smiled to encourage him but felt sad inside. The lifelong pursuit of passing recognition by a few people hardly seemed worth it to her.

The sommelier arrived with a bottle of wine Jean-Pierre had requested and prepared a sample for him to taste. "Monsieur LaGrande," he said, almost with a reverent bow, and proffered the sample. Apparently, Jean-Pierre was known even here in Aix-en-Provence, nearly an hour away from Cavaillon. Jean-Pierre swirled the dark ruby liquid in the glass, took a deep sniff, then a sip. He nodded up at the sommelier who then poured two glasses and wiped the neck of the bottle with a small towel.

When the man left Lauren lifted her glass and said, "Welcome to the Restaurant Olympics."

"*Exactement.*" Jean-Pierre lifted his glass to hers. He looked especially handsome that evening. Gone was the windblown look of his hair tied back by sunglasses or pulled into a small ponytail. Now every hair was combed into place. His shirt was crisply ironed and hung evenly on his broad shoulders. She wondered if the extra effort had something to do with Mark's presence. The thought tickled into a private grin, which she hid behind her glass.

Jean-Pierre didn't seem to notice. "It's a shame that we were a day too early for the big marché in Aix." He wiped his mouth on a cloth napkin. "The small one we saw was adequate, but tomorrow is the very important one, I'm sure you have seen."

"Yes, I've been there before, but not yet on this trip. I'm sure you would have sent me there eventually to pick up provisions." If only she could keep going to the markets instead of working in the kitchen. Bad reminder. Her stomach clenched. She'd have to talk to him about it.

"Maybe your friend will show up at that one." There was mischief in his smile. "He is traveling around with the *poissonier*, making the rounds to the markets, though I'm sure that is not what he planned to do before he came."

"I don't know what he planned." Lauren was glad Jean-Pierre had brought up the subject of Mark. It had to be addressed sooner or later. She smoothed her linen skirt and folded her hands on the table. "He said he wanted to see France, since he had never been here. And since we're still friends, he wants to see me sometimes. Maybe see France from my perspective."

Everything she said was the truth, almost from Mark's own lips, but she'd left so much out. A history and deep roots she shared with Mark. Their previous closeness. At the thought of him a surprising puddle of warmth formed in her stomach and fanned up. She hadn't felt that in a while, but there it was. If only she knew what it meant.

Jean-Pierre shook his head and sipped some wine. "No, he is not here just for this. I know the heart of a man, I am one. He wants to convince you to return to him and to America. Be careful of him. He will try."

Lauren wanted to laugh. Never in her life had she considered the need to be careful of Mark. "Yes, he's very dangerous," she said gravely. "You seem to forget, Jean-Pierre, that I am a woman with my own mind. He won't kidnap me and carry me back to the U.S. I make my own decisions. I'm not dating him, but I am friends with him."

"Are you dating me?"

His question took her by surprise. Her relationship with him did resemble exactly that. The way he held her hand, kissed her at times, assumed they would spend time together on their days off. Is that what she intended to happen so soon?

"You are hesitating, Lauren."

"I—I am trying to answer your question. Yes, I am dating you. I am getting to know you better, and I am enjoying it. But I don't want it to move too fast. I hope you understand this."

He nodded. "I understand. It's okay like this. You are dating me, as you Americans say, but not seriously. And I am getting to know you as well." He reached out his hand and she clasped it, feeling his large, warm fingers close around hers.

Lauren let out a breath, only then aware she'd been holding it in. Her shoulders relaxed and she smiled. "Good, I'm glad we are in the same place. We have no pressure." She was especially relieved by defining their relationship in more casual terms. That's what she wanted anyway, but now with Mark in France, she knew she couldn't focus only on Jean-Pierre.

Jean-Pierre leaned back in his chair and stared at her, as if thinking of what to say to convince her. Instead, he released her hand and reached for his wine glass again, took a sip. Put it down. "Why did you fall in love with him before? And why don't you love him now?"

"I—uh, well it was over two years ago. Almost three. He is kind and genuine. He's smart and ambitious. He's a CPA. You call that *expert comptable*. We have a shared faith. That's important to me." She wanted to slip in this fact and allow him to ponder it, since he was, after all, trying to win her over. She was willing to be the bait for such a cause. "We talked easily and almost read each other's minds sometimes." She found herself grinning at a distant memory where they'd finished one other's sentences several times in the same conversation, and ended up laughing until tears flowed. Another wave of warmth slid over her.

Lauren stifled her grin and focused on her wine glass, a glowing garnet in the firelight. "He's a good man, too. He's compassionate. Has a lot of hobbies and interests." It was so easy to describe Mark's good qualities. Anyone would think she was stupid to let him go, and she was sure many of her friends thought she was. But she had to find that missing piece. *Had* to.

"He sounds so perfect, I cannot compete with him." Jean-Pierre looked away, seeming suddenly grumpy.

Lauren reached out and touched his arm, then slid her hand down to grasp his again. "Jean-Pierre, you asked me what I had liked about him, and so I told you. I only answered your question, but I'm not necessarily ready to go back with him. There's a reason I'm here with you instead of in the States still dating Mark."

Jean-Pierre seemed mollified by her explanation and squeezed back, adding a crooked smile which made him even more handsome in the candlelight. "I think I am jealous of your friend Mark."

"That might be something you and he have in common." She grinned at him. "But don't forget, I am here now with *you*. So, let's not talk about him anymore." She hesitated a moment then said, "On another subject, have you found someone to take Marcel's place in the kitchen?"

"I have announced the opening in the appropriate circles. I interviewed someone yesterday, but he was a clown. I am trying to find someone of the right level of competence, and it is not easy." The grumpy frown returned.

Lauren sighed. She was sorry to have brought it up when he was already feeling insecure. It was difficult for him to be short of someone in such an important role. Though she sympathized with him, it was clear that her service in the kitchen wasn't going to end as soon as she'd hoped. She wouldn't say how much she disliked it when he was doing his best to find someone.

For now, she'd do her best to enjoy the present and her evening with a handsome Frenchman in a two-star restaurant.

Chapter Ten

The acrid smell of sliced onions stung Lauren's eyes. She blinked then shut them for a few seconds. Next to her cutting board sat a large bowl of cut vegetables in a rainbow of colors, bright orange carrots, blue-green broccoli, diced green and purple onions, and peppers in red, green, orange and yellow. She didn't mind this part of her job, since it refreshed her in a much needed and therapeutic way. As she cut the fresh vegetables with a razor-sharp knife, a mild breeze and a stream of late afternoon sunshine ferried in through the open window. The juice that beaded out of each one added a fresh, sweet fragrance to the air.

The restaurant wouldn't open for another hour or so, but the prep work had to be done two hours in advance. After that, bedlam would break out and the hours that followed would require a feat of stress-management and endurance. Friday nights were especially busy after a long work week, she'd noticed. In the kitchen, tempers became short, and everything seemed a life-or-death emergency. Lauren mentally prepared for her heart rate to rise and her tension to increase. She prayed that tranquility would be measured out to her to keep pace with her need.

She wasn't made for this life, but a week after her dinner with Jean-Pierre in Aix-en-Provence he still hadn't found a suitable chef.

In the meantime, he'd promoted Benoît to be the temporary sous-chef, rather than trying to find an experienced one to hire on short notice, and now sought someone to fill Benoît's previous role. Several experienced candidates had come to interview, but she never saw them again. More than once, she wondered if Jean-Pierre's standard was too high.

"Lauren, cut these too." Khaled shoved a large bowl of white mushrooms and another one filled with brown and black ones toward her on the metal countertop.

"*Please* cut them," she said under her breath as she reached for the colanders and turned toward the sinks. The kitchen staff was friendly outside of the kitchen, but all warmth evaporated on the other side of the white swinging door, despite her privileged relationship with Jean-Pierre.

She'd been in France for just over a month and her last two weeks had been spent in a role she said she'd never do again. She should tell Jean-Pierre of her feelings, that she hadn't come to France to experience the same stress she'd just left behind, but she knew he still needed her. Maybe if she told him she was unhappy working in the kitchen, he'd be willing to hire someone more quickly. But would that amount to manipulation? Or would she simply be taking care of her own needs, and was that okay? She wasn't sure, so didn't say anything, yet prayed daily that he would tell her he'd hired someone.

In the previous week she'd seen Mark twice for coffee and once at the Velleron market. Each time he was relaxed and friendly, as well as non-pressuring, which she appreciated. In the same period, Jean-Pierre had taken her out to dinner twice, pampering her with top restaurants. He'd insisted on a bike picnic the previous Sunday. She had the feeling he was trying to fill her free hours so she would spend them with him rather than Mark.

She refused to see Jean-Pierre the coming Sunday, since she would be meeting Mark for a hike up St. Jacques Hill to on the western side of the town. She debated hiding her plans from Jean-Pierre but wanted him to know that she didn't belong to him. She could spend time with whoever she wanted to. Though he'd said nothing, she could tell by his grimace and the furrow on his forehead that he wasn't happy about it.

After finishing the mushrooms, she took all of the scraps and mushroom stems to the bin, which was already full. Her prep work was caught up for the moment, so she closed the plastic bag and hauled it from the can to take it outside. She left the building and the sunshine felt toasty on her skin. She could only savor it for a few minutes, but was glad to be outside, even if it meant toting garbage to the dumpster in back of the restaurant.

As she approached the dumpster, she saw a flash of movement, someone darting behind it. She tossed the bag into the open dumpster and peered behind it where a young boy was crouched. Even though she knew someone was there, she still jumped back in surprise when she saw him.

The boy also looked frightened, so Lauren knelt toward him, posting her elbows on her thighs. She said in French, "Don't be afraid." She noticed he had something rolled up in his shirt, probably from the garbage can.

He said something in another language. Arabic. Lauren was accustomed to hearing it, having spent time in France as well as traveling in Middle Eastern countries. "Do you speak English?"

The boy nodded and pulled himself up, still glancing about himself with dark, wary eyes. His olive-skinned face was smudged with dirt and his dark hair needed a good wash. He answered her in halting words. "I speak a little English. I'm sorry, I am hungry. I don't come back." He straightened and backed away, and as he did, he appeared taller than Lauren had thought at first.

"Wait, don't go." Lauren held up a hand to beckon him. "Maybe I can help you." If he were hungry, she could find something to give him. Maybe he was homeless, or a runaway.

He stopped, looked at her with suspicion. "No, it is good, I go away."

"What is your name?"

The boy considered her a moment, then said, "I am Tarek."

"How old are you?"

"Twelve."

"Almost a man." She'd hoped to get a smile from him, but he looked at the ground, still clutching in both fists the food rolled up in his dirty shirt. "Where are your parents?"

"I think they are dead." His voice was soft. He looked away from her. She noticed his Adam's apple pulse, as if he held his grief down in a tight knot inside his throat.

A wave of sorrow clenched inside Lauren's stomach and moved up to her neck. "Oh, no. You aren't sure?" Her throat felt dry. She swallowed.

"We—we are from Syria and a bomb fall on our house. My mother and my brother, I don't see them again. I think they are dead. My father, we come to France. When I arrive here, I don't find him."

"You were separated from him?"

Tarek nodded. When he lifted his eyes to hers, she was struck by the hollow and tragic emptiness there, older than his years with experiences he should never have had. "My uncle too," he said. "I am with my father and my uncle, and I cannot find them. We are on a big train and too many people. I don't see them. I am alone now. I do not know they are alive."

Lauren shook her head, at a loss for words. "You are hungry, Tarek. I will help you." She glanced back at the kitchen door. Someone would soon wonder where she was. She turned back to Tarek and lowered her voice as she squatted down on her heels in front of him. "Listen, Tarek. I work here at this restaurant and sometimes we throw away food that people don't eat. I can save some food for you. Will you come back tomorrow?"

Traces of distrust remained on the young boy's face, but he nodded. "I will come."

"I don't know what time I can meet you, but I will put some things into a bag and put them behind that tree." She pointed to a thick poplar behind the restaurant. "Come after five o'clock, okay?" For two weeks she'd observed the waste a busy restaurant could produce. Finally, it would be used for a real need.

"Thank you, Madam. *Merci.*" He backed up, watching her, then scampered away, just as Frédéric called for her.

Lauren dropped her shoulders as she watched the boy disappear. Her throat was tight and ached. Her eyes stung from unshed tears that refused to flow. From the article that she'd read about the war, she knew only a small trace of what this child had been through. She could do nothing for the crisis there in his country, but she could do something for him. She could help him. She *had* to help him.

છ   છ   છ

Mark stopped climbing and found he was breathing heavily. He drew his wrist across his perspiring forehead. "The guy at the tourist office didn't mention how steep the climb was to St. Jacques Hill." He opened his water bottle and offered some to Lauren.

She shook her head. "I have some, thanks."

"I didn't think I was out of shape." Felt good in the shade. A soft caress of a breeze dried his perspiration.

"I don't think you're out of shape. You're just not used to climbing. Most of your exercise must be horizontal, not vertical." She grinned. "Look, we're near the top."

He lifted his head and saw an arch of white stone, which he guessed was the top of the chapel. They had been hiking for only about twenty-five minutes, climbing on stone steps built into the hill as well as trails of foot-worn earth. Lauren didn't seem to be huffing like he was. He figured all the biking she'd done in the last month had paid off. Whatever discomfort he might experience that day, Lauren had agreed to spend it with him, and that outweighed it all. A wave of contentment ballooned inside him.

Soon, a white stone chapel came into view, plain on the outside, but with clean lines and arches. The stone piece he'd seen from a distance was a curved frame encircling a bell with a thin metal cross on top. He guessed it was the Provence version of a steeple.

The trees fell away as they approached the chapel, a lone sentinel atop a limestone cliff. They followed a stone path toward the building and after another swig of water, they went inside. Cool stones emitted a chill and a layer of silence which enveloped them like a damp glove. The inside was as plain as the outside, narrow, with wooden benches and a simple stone altar. "Do you know any of the history of this church?" A thin reverberation from his voice returned to him.

"No, I don't. Only that it was built sometime prior to the fourteenth century. So, it's pretty old."

"I'll say."

The visit didn't take long. Mark felt relieved once they were outside and the sunshine baked the chill from his skin. They followed a dirt path that led to an overlook which guarded the city of Cavaillon below.

"Wow, look at that." Lauren approached the edge of the cliff and gazed out over the town of Cavaillon, which spilled out for miles in front of them. "I guess this is why people make the effort to come up here. You can see the whole valley and town."

Mark caught up to her and took in the view. He pointed to the valley below. "And from down there you can see this chapel. Have you noticed that?"

She nodded and smiled. "It's a good landmark."

For a few minutes of silence, they soaked in the view from above the strands of buildings and their gray and orange tile roofs, the structures seemingly scattered on top of one another. He could barely make out roads like ribbons separating the city blocks. Threaded across the town, tufts of trees looked like heads of broccoli from so far away.

Mark had made them a picnic from delicacies he found at various stands at the market the day before. A chunk of goat cheese, some dried fruit and fresh apples, a bit of deli meat for sandwiches—he'd learned it was called *charcuterie*—and two miniature pies that looked almost too good to eat from the local *boulangerie*. "Are you ready for a picnic? There's a good spot over there." He hitched his head toward a mound of grassy earth close to the cliff.

They sat down on the shady spot, where they had a wide-open view of the valley. "This is a good spot." Lauren slid her sunglasses up on her head and stretched out her legs, leaning back on her arms.

"Ready to eat yet, or do you just want to enjoy the view a little longer?"

"In a few minutes I'll be ready. Right now, I'm taking it in. We're not really that high, but it's nice to be up here and see the town spread out."

She was sitting only a foot or so from him. Her wavy hair fluttered gently around her face, touching her shoulders. It had been so long since he'd been this close to her, even longer since he'd held her in an embrace or had her snuggle onto his lap like she used to do. During those times, he'd always wondered if she hungered for lost nurturing from childhood as she let him cradle her within his arms. Whatever the reason, he always loved it when she did that. Now it was no more than a fading memory.

He sighed. Would he ever have that privilege again? Since his arrival in France, he sometimes felt like he was making progress at winning her back. But then he'd remind himself that at the end of his trip, she could easily tell him she wanted to remain friends, that nothing had changed. She might even tell him she'd chosen Jean-Pierre. He had to face that possibility and rein in his hope.

"Being here reminds me of that camping trip we took with Don and Allie on the Blue Ridge Parkway. Remember?" Mark cocked his head in her direction.

A soft smile curved her lips. "Yes, I remember. It rained that one night and Allie and I got soaked. That's how we found out our tent wasn't waterproof." She turned her head to grin at him as she remembered. "You guys didn't rescue us, though, because you were already asleep. Amazing she and I didn't both get pneumonia."

Mark laughed. "You should have woken us up. But you did invest in a new tent after that, didn't you?"

She nodded. "Of course, I did. Haven't used it that much since, though. That was back when Allie and Don had just started dating. And now they're an old married couple with a baby."

"Imagine that."

Something in his tone must have touched a nerve because she shot him a glare. "I'm not going there."

Mark held up his hands in self-defense "I didn't say anything. Just noting that it was pretty clear to me they were going to get together." Of course, they'd said the same thing about him with Lauren. A stab of disappointment took an edge off of his contentment. He stared out across the roofs spread out below. "What about Bree and Travis? Did you see her before you left the States?"

"Yeah, I stopped by. And what can I say, they're newlyweds. How do you think they are?" She laughed. "I saw *that* coming, thank you very much. For a while I didn't think Bree would go for it, but it all worked out." She added softly, "Sometimes it does."

Sometimes for some people. Would it work out for them? Mark crossed his arms across his bent knees. He couldn't even make a wild guess. His spirits drooped a few degrees further. A new subject was needed. "How are things at the restaurant?"

Lauren sighed and looked unhappy. "Not so great. Jean-Pierre has been interviewing for a couple of weeks and hasn't found anyone. I like working with food, as you pointed out the other day, but the atmosphere—it's just too stressful for me. I guess if I were in charge it would still be busy but I'd handle it differently. Everyone gets caught up in the necessity for all the customers to be deliriously happy and end up treating each other harshly."

Mark pressed his lips together. He should just keep his mouth shut, but couldn't help it. He'd always been honest with Lauren, and she with him. "Why do you feel obligated to stay, Lauren? You didn't come here to work for Jean-Pierre. You already knew you didn't like kitchen work, so you didn't need that experience to learn from."

She turned and looked at him, silent, her head nodding slightly. Her green eyes fixed on his, but he could tell her mind was churning. Finally, she said, "You're right, of course. But I know he needs someone now and I'm already trained." She shrugged. "He asked me so I said yes."

"But that doesn't obligate you for your whole visit. You've given him two weeks, which is already quite a lot. His loss of a chef is a shame for him, but he's likely been through that before. He'll find someone. He's taking the easy way by asking you, though he must know you don't like working in the kitchen." He was out on a limb now, and maybe she would think he was trying to influence her against Jean-Pierre. Yet it was the truth, and he hoped to help her see it. "You should tell him you don't want to do it, that's not why you came here. If he doesn't like that, well, it will tell you something about him, won't it?"

She sighed deeply and looked back out at the Cavaillon vista. "What I should have done when he asked me is tell him I'd only do it for a week to give him time to regroup. Not knowing when it will end is what bothers me."

"But it's your *choice*, Lauren. You came here on your own. He doesn't control you. Are you afraid of Jean-Pierre?"

Her head snapped back to him, her brows furrowed. "No, no, I'm not afraid. I'd hate to let him down. But I know what you're saying, it's not my responsibility. And you're right, it's not. But now, there's Tarek."

"Who?"

"I was on the verge of telling Jean-Pierre about my feelings. But then a couple of days ago when I took trash out, I saw this boy hiding behind the dumpster. He'd taken some food out of it. He's a Syrian refugee. He—" She swallowed and shook her head. When she turned to him, he saw moisture in her eyes and her lips were tight. "He's lost *everything*, his mother, his brother, his home. He broke my heart. You wouldn't believe what he's been through. I have to help him." She swallowed. "I saved some food for him from what wasn't eaten or what will get thrown away. There's a lot of waste at the end of the day, so I left some of it in a bag for him. I want to do that for a little while, so I can't leave the restaurant just yet."

Yes, that was the Lauren he remembered. He understood now. Mark leaned toward her. "I can help him too. At the marché at the end of the day the merchants want to get rid of the stuff no one has bought rather than haul it home and have it rot in the next couple days."

She smiled now. "Oh, that would be great. He'd have some fruit and vegetables too. It would be more balanced for him."

Mark grinned. "He'll be eating pretty well, then, between Jean-Pierre's and the marché. Or you could just let me get things at the marché and quit the restaurant. There would still be plenty for him."

"Maybe." Her smile fell. "He's lost his father and uncle, too. They are probably alive, but he was separated from them when they arrived in France. I don't know if there are any services that can help find them."

"We could look for something in Cavaillon. You would know better than I would where to start, but maybe there's some kind of social agency that helps people."

"Good thinking." Her face was solemn as she placed her hand on his arm. "Thank you, Mark." Her gaze caught his for a moment too long. He felt heat on his neck and warmth from her hand on his skin.

"Of course, I'll be glad to help. Sounds like this kid really needs it." Her description of Tarek had stirred him, but he was also glad to be able to spend more time with her as they tried to help the boy.

Finally, she pulled her knees up and encircled them with her arms. "How about that picnic? I'm starved."

Yet a haunted look remained on her face.

Chapter Eleven

Lauren folded the jacket into a neat square and slid it into the canvas bag on her bed. She reached to take the toque from the dresser and caught her reflection in the mirror.

Green eyes stared back at her above a resigned frown. "You don't look very happy." Her whispered pronouncement floated through the still room. When had she lost the lightness and joy she'd had in her first two weeks in France? She had to talk to Jean-Pierre. She had to leave the restaurant. And soon.

Was it only the restaurant? Her reason for coming was to try to "find" herself. She let out a hollow chuckle at the cliché. Right, find herself. She wasn't necessarily any closer to knowing what she wanted to do, though she knew with certainty what she didn't want.

The restaurant cast a long shadow across each of her days. Bumping alongside these thoughts were those that ricocheted back and forth between Mark and Jean-Pierre. Several days earlier when she'd spent time with Mark, she'd detected in herself an unmistakable hum of attraction toward him, warming embers, though not a raging fire. He had surprised her in so many ways, beginning with his arrival in France. He'd made that decision, aware that her heart had cooled toward him, aware of Jean-Pierre in the same city. And yet he'd been willing to cross the ocean. To clean fish for her sake. A spontaneous grin spread across her face and lit up her eyes, for a moment, chasing away her somber expression.

What was going on in her crazy emotions?

Would she feel the same warmth for Mark if they were back on familiar ground in Virginia, back in accustomed routines? Would her attraction again betray her by turning fickle? She wasn't likely to trust those feelings anytime soon, giving Mark premature hope. She wouldn't risk his heart again unless she was sure.

And Jean-Pierre. Her thoughts were getting muddier by the day. Her evenings in the kitchen had gradually slipped a film of chill over her feelings for him. She and Jean-Pierre were now linked to a difficult work setting instead of picnics, bike rides, and visits to herb farms.

Of course, that was unfair. She knew that relationships required tedium, conflict, and daily life in addition to excursions and restaurants. But this was *his* work, which he loved. It wasn't hers. She was merely helping out. If he knew how it affected her, he'd surely find another chef, and very quickly.

Lauren glanced at her watch. She still had almost thirty minutes before she had to be at the restaurant. She slipped on comfortable shoes able to support her standing for many hours, then wandered to the window. She didn't have a city view, but on the other side of a low fence she could see a playground and a school yard. An hour ago, there was a cacophony of shouting, laughter, screaming. All was quiet now.

Her thoughts went to Tarek, who might have played in such a yard a couple of years ago, before life turned him into a young scavenger. She sank down on the bed and reached to the bedside table to take the article Madame Carnot had given her two weeks earlier. She almost couldn't bear to read it, and in fact, only skimmed it, for fear the details were too raw, too brutal. The once-beautiful city of Aleppo, ground to dust, its residents killed or forced to flee. It would never be the same. Her throat ached again and her eyes stung, but tears didn't flow. If only she could cry, she could release the pain that built up each time she thought of Tarek.

"Think of something *cheerful*." She couldn't go to work feeling depressed and weepy, since her shift would be hard enough as it was. Her thoughts went back to Virginia, where life had been simpler. "Bree!" Lauren jumped up and scrambled for her phone. She'd hadn't called Bree in over two weeks. It would be morning there, so her friend might be available.

Bree answered on the second ring.

"I'm so glad you answered. I'm sorry I haven't given any news in so long."

"I hoped it was because things were going so well." Bree's voice was light with a lilt more apparent than the year before, when she'd been plagued by anxiety. That seemed to be history now. "You have a lot to summarize, my dear friend. How are things with Jean-Pierre?"

"First, how are you and Travis? Are you settled into the new house yet?"

"Getting there. We're almost completely settled in. Now, tell me how *you* are doing. I asked you first." Bree giggled. Lauren felt as though she were right there next to her, and wished she were. She could use a hug right now.

"I can't wait to hear everything." Bree's voice was breathless.

Lauren sighed. "There's quite a lot to tell. First, Mark is here."

"What? Mark?"

Lauren smiled as she pictured Bree scrunching up her nose when she heard something odd or surprising. "Yes, he's been here about two and a half weeks. He hasn't said this to me, but I think he came to get me back."

"Obviously. The man's in love and has never given up on you. What's it like to see him again over there?"

"It's been good. We spend time together once in a while, just as friends. I'm actually starting to feel a little bit more for him, like some of my love is coming back, but I don't trust myself."

"Relax and give it time to grow again. You'll know. How did he manage the trip with his work?"

"He's considering it an extended, overdue vacation, but has brought some work along, too. He's due to leave in a few days, but he hasn't mentioned it."

"Maybe he's planning to stay longer. What about Jean-Pierre?"

Lauren summarized Jean-Pierre's attentions and the work pressures she'd fallen into since her arrival. "I'm not feeling objective anymore about Jean-Pierre. I want to get out from under this pressure, not just because I don't like it, but so I can see things more clearly with him."

"You could just tell him, couldn't you?"

Lauren glanced back at her watch. She needed to wrap up the call. "I should. Mark said the same thing. But now there's a new wrinkle. I met this boy, a Syrian refugee, and I want to help him."

"Oh, you do have a lot going on, Lauren. What can you do for him?"

"At the moment I just bring him food from the leftovers at the restaurant. I'd like to keep doing that for a little while. Jean-Pierre doesn't know about that, of course. Mark wants to help too. The boy's name is Tarek. He got separated from his dad and uncle, so we're trying to help him."

"I'll pray that you can. Could you try to bring him here? That'd be a lot of red tape, I bet."

"Yes, it likely would. It crossed my mind, that if his family can't be found, he can make a new life in the States. He speaks a little English." Lauren glanced at her watch again. "Oh, Bree, I have to leave for work now. I'm sorry to have to cut it short, but I'll call you soon."

"Okay." Bree's voice was soft. "I wish you didn't dread going to work. That's how you felt at Fins and Feathers. I wanted you to have a fun time in Provence. I hope you can sort everything out with Jean-Pierre and Tarek. And Mark."

"Thanks. I'll keep you posted on all my drama."

When Lauren arrived at the restaurant there was already a conflict underway in the kitchen between Frédéric and Solange. Lauren busied herself and tried to stay out of their way, but kept glancing through the window to see if she could spot Tarek.

Jean-Pierre came in and started barking orders. He seemed more nervous than usual. He looked across the kitchen and made eye contact with Lauren, then gave her a small smile, though it didn't reach his eyes. Something was wrong.

The tension did seem higher than usual. When she had the chance, she sidled up to Jean-Pierre and asked in a low voice, "Is everything okay?"

He glanced around and whispered, "I have heard a rumor that perhaps the Michelin inspector is going to visit tonight or tomorrow. You remember I told you they don't announce themselves."

Lauren nodded. "It should be fine, though. No need to do anything different. You can't top excellent, can you?" She smiled at him, hoping to lighten his mood.

He gave her a wry smile with tight lips. "I wish I could think like you, Lauren. You see things in the right way. I like how you do this. Maybe it is your religion that helps you. But I have worked all my life for this moment."

"Jean-Pierre, you have *already* succeeded, don't you see?" Though she was whispering to him, she allowed bold insistence to enter her voice. "A Michelin star isn't going to make a great restaurant greater. It already *is*."

He shook his head slightly as if saying she simply didn't understand. She gave him a final smile and turned back toward her work area. She'd never get through to him. Might as well stop trying.

As the evening wore on, she heard his voice slice through the kitchen numerous times, evidence of increased tension. "Lauren!" This time it was directed to her. "Tables five and six need to be plated! Now! They are waiting."

She shot a look back at Jean-Pierre, and scurried to the counter where plates already waited. That had been Khaled's job the day before, so she hadn't paid attention. Suddenly it was hers. In a flurry of dishes of varying sizes, the evening rush was plated and sent through the swinging doors. Gradually, periods of silence increased. Lauren relaxed her stiff shoulders and went to the refrigerator for her bottle of water.

Normally, the after-rush lull lasted only about five or ten minutes, if it happened at all. She took the opportunity to move toward the doorway and slip outside. From the doorway where she stood, she saw Mark kneeling by the dumpster. Beside him she could see Tarek as well, though he was partially hidden by the shadow of the dumpster. It seemed they were having a conversation. Mark glanced up and saw her. She gave a slight wave just as she heard her name from the kitchen.

"*J'arrive!*" She turned and dashed back into the kitchen. "Coming!"

"What are you doing outside? Come in, we need all hands here." Jean-Pierre's face was red and glistened with perspiration. Something clicked in Lauren's mind. She couldn't give him any more time, only a few days, perhaps, before telling him she had to leave. Mark was right. She didn't owe this to Jean-Pierre.

She got busy plating the Coquille Saint Jacques and steamed garlic green beans but was startled by Jean-Pierre yelling at someone outside. She craned her head to look out the window and saw Jean-Pierre outside waving one arm. Just then Tarek scampered away. Mark was no longer there, thank goodness. Lauren leaned against the counter. Now that Tarek had been seen, she had to change her strategy. She would have to change it anyway, since she was determined to leave soon. Very soon.

Several minutes later as calm returned again to the kitchen, Jean-Pierre found her at the sink rinsing serving spoons and ladles. "*Chérie*, I am sorry," he whispered close to her ear. "I shouted at you, and I was impatient."

She stopped rinsing and stood still for a moment before looking up at him. "You are correct, you shouldn't yell at me or anyone here. We work for you, but you should treat everyone with respect."

He nodded. He lowered his eyes briefly and pressed his lips together. "Yes, you are right."

"And you should also not yell at children. That boy out there might be hungry and homeless." She'd said too much. She hadn't wanted to give away her involvement with Tarek but was incensed at Jean-Pierre's reaction to the child. She hoped he wouldn't guess.

"You saw the boy?"

Uh-oh. *Be careful. Lauren.* "I just saw him out the door when you did." It was true, just not all the truth. "I am guessing he is homeless, but I don't know." True again. She didn't know where

Tarek stayed. But she knew his days hanging around *Chez Jean-Pierre* were finished. She hoped she'd be able to find him again.

"Then I am sorry for him as well. Please forgive me, *Chérie.*"

"I forgive you, Jean-Pierre." She hesitated then turned around to face him. "Jean-Pierre, we need to talk. I don't want to work in the kitchen. It isn't a good fit for me."

"I know you don't. I try to find a new chef. I think I found someone, but I need to speak with him again. Very soon, Lauren."

Lauren hesitated. "Okay, if you're close to hiring someone, that's fine. I don't want to work here anymore, but I don't mind staying out front as hostess."

He looked down at her, the stress painted on his face like a mask, yet his blue eyes reached out, asking for time and understanding. "Thank you, *Chérie.* Thank you."

ଓ   ଓ   ଓ

The internet hadn't been working well all week in Mark's temporary apartment. In the meantime, he'd found an internet café a few streets from home. It was noisy with high school students and job-seekers, but he'd managed to get some work done, work he'd neglected and almost forgotten about. It was from that other world. A smile crept across his lips as his eyes roved around the café, his new office where he came regularly now after morning shifts of fish-cleaning.

Along with his work, he'd neglected Logan, who he hadn't phoned in about a week, though they'd exchanged a few emails. Dina was holding steady, but first babies sometimes came early and often late. He'd heard that somewhere, he wasn't sure where. Maybe his brother Chris, who had two of his own. Fortunately, Logan answered his phone.

"Hey, Mark. Good to hear from you. I was wondering when you'd call again."

"Sorry, dude, things have been crazy. I told you I had a job at a fish market. I work almost every day at different markets around the area. And I try to see Lauren when she'll let me squeeze into her life."

"You must be making progress. You sounded pitiful that first day, but I hear the old Mark in your voice." Logan chuckled.

"At this point I'm not sure whether I am or not. We hang out together sometimes, and I get the feeling she's warming up again. But no guarantees yet."

"Just be patient. I'm sure she appreciates what you've done so far."

"Yeah, I think she does. She's been roped into working in the restaurant for this guy she came to see. She's doing him a favor but can't seem to tell him she wants out of it. I hope that'll eventually work in my favor."

"Maybe she'll get tired of him or see his worst side at the restaurant."

"I think that may be happening. How is Dina? Any baby yet?"

"Not yet. She had a checkup yesterday and everything is on schedule for about three weeks from now, unless he comes late."

"Good. I'm sure she's ready, but I plan to be there."

"You're due back in a few days, though, right?"

"Uh, I was. But I think I'm going to have to extend. There's a new situation. Lauren met this young boy, a Syrian refugee. He's been separated from his relatives, and she really wants to help him. I do, too. So, we're going to try to find his father. I'll probably need a couple more weeks."

"Are you able to do some work from there?"

"I've been working on some cases today. I haven't done too much since I've been here, other than emails, but spent all morning on it. I'll make a few phone calls later on, when the time difference is more favorable. I'll be okay for a couple more weeks."

"I hope those two weeks make a big difference," Logan said. "I'm rooting for you and praying for you, of course."

"I know. Thanks, Logan. It means a lot. And I really need it."

Mark's need to extend his trip was clear to him and had hovered in the back of his mind all morning as he worked. Between Lauren and now Tarek, it clearly wasn't time to leave. Maybe Lauren was making some movement toward him. He knew that it could go in the wrong direction, but he was determined to give it just a little bit longer. And he wanted to help Tarek in whatever limited way he could. If he were honest, he simply wasn't ready to leave France under any circumstance. He hoped two weeks would be enough.

Mark's phone rang. "Hey, Lauren. What's up?" She'd called him at least twice since he'd been in France. He hoped it was a good sign.

"Hi, Mark. Do you have time to talk?"

"Sure. I'm at the internet café on Garibaldi near the park. Just getting some work done."

"I know the place. See you in a few minutes?"

"Yes, I'm at a good stopping point." Or else he'd make one for her. Was something wrong? She sounded wound tight and ready to snap. He hoped it was only his imagination.

Twenty minutes later he saw her coast up to the curb and dismount from her bike. She pushed open the glass door of the café and slid into a chair across from him. He was right, she wasn't doing well. He could easily tell by her expression.

"Is this normal restaurant stress, or is something bad happening?"

135

She smiled then and relaxed her shoulders. A shoulder-length braid was swung forward over one shoulder. He noticed a light smudge of eye shadow, which she didn't always wear. Was it for him? A ripple of warmth rose up at the thought.

"You know me pretty well." She smiled at him, but her smile was subdued. "I'll tell you what's happening, but please, tell me first about your conversation yesterday with Tarek. I saw you talking to him at the dumpster."

Mark leaned back and shut his laptop. "Do you want anything to drink?" She shook her head. "Well, I came to the restaurant around five-thirty, as you saw, to try to meet him. I told him I was a friend of yours and we wanted to help him. He was fairly open with me. He said he's been getting the food the last few days and he's grateful."

She nodded. "That's good. I'm glad he's getting it. I was thinking we could find a refugee center and go tomorrow to see what we can do, since I'm off."

"Good idea. It's on my list to check online to see if there's a place we can visit."

"So, what else did you talk about with him?"

"I asked him where he was staying."

"That's good thinking, because I had no idea."

"He sleeps in a park near the tourist office. There's a small park there with bathrooms. The police patrol sometimes, so he hides when he sees them."

"It would be good if we could find him a normal place to stay. I could always ask Madame Carnot if she would mind, but I hesitate to do that. Many French people, especially the older ones, fear a new influx of foreigners. And she's pretty tight with Jean-Pierre. I wouldn't want him to find out about my involvement with Tarek before I quit the restaurant."

"Maybe I can find someone from the marché who can put him up for a while."

She suddenly gave a deep sigh and put her head into her hands for just a moment. When she lifted her head, he saw concern in her eyes. "Jean-Pierre saw Tarek last night."

"He did? What happened?" Mark felt the tension rise in his chest. He didn't want to tangle with Jean-Pierre on his own turf or create problems for Lauren.

"He shooed him away. He didn't see you, though. It was after you left."

Mark let out a breath. "Does he know Tarek is getting food from the restaurant?"

Lauren shook her head. "He didn't seem to know. I told him he shouldn't shout at children, nor at his employees. He was in rare form last evening."

"Shouting at everyone? More than usual at any rate?"

Her mouth quirked. "Yeah, more than usual. He thought there might be a Michelin inspector there, so he was on edge."

"A what?"

"You know, Michelin stars that are awarded to exceptional restaurants? They come without being announced. Like food writers who come incognito and do reviews. Well, French chefs get really wrapped up in that like it's their life mission, so Jean-Pierre is vying for a star."

Mark shrugged. "Whatever. *Chaqu'un son truc.*" To each his own.

Lauren's eyes widened and, despite the solemn conversation, she broke into a laugh. "Where in the world did you learn that?"

Mark gave her a secretive grin. "I have my tutors. I've learned a lot of practical expressions. And then there are other things they teach me at the marché that I choose not to say in polite company."

They both laughed. So much like old times it almost made Mark's eyes sting.

"Not sure why everyone wants to teach foreigners the worst words. Anyway, now that Jean-Pierre knows Tarek was hanging around the restaurant, he'll be on the lookout for him. Tarek might be afraid to come back, so I'm so glad you found out where he stays. We need to find him a decent place to sleep, at least. And let's plan to visit an agency that might be able to help him." She pulled her chair back and reached down to pick up her canvas bag.

"I hope we'll find one." Mark looked up at her as she stood. "If we don't, we could stop by the police station and maybe they can refer us."

"Can we meet tomorrow at about ten?"

"I'll meet you in front of this café. Hope everything goes well tonight."

She sent him a weak smile that said she doubted it, then left the café. He watched her as she mounted her bike and pedaled up the street.

Chapter Twelve

"How did you sleep, Lauren?" Madame Carnot reached for the French press. "Do you want some coffee?"

"Oh, yes. I didn't sleep well. Thank you, Madame Carnot."

She'd slept quite badly, in fact. During her waking moments of the night, she kept seeing Jean-Pierre's angry face, Tarek's fearful one. And Mark. She saw him breaking into a smile or his brow furrowed with concern when they talked about Tarek. When he'd told her that he planned on extending his stay in France, relief had coursed through her. She realized she wasn't yet ready to be alone or to be without his comforting presence.

"You're not working today, are you?"

"No, thankfully. It's nice to have a day off." She wouldn't say too much about her feelings working in Jean-Pierre's restaurant. He already knew how she felt, in any case. It was a relief to have told him. He wouldn't be surprised when she told him it was her last day. Whenever she decided that would be.

Fortunately, Madame Carnot went into the next room to water her plants. Lauren didn't have the mental energy to listen to her this morning. She leaned on the counter as the coffee steeped. Through the window the early morning light was just breaking through the mist, backlighting the trees in the back of the small house.

How had her life gotten so messy? This trip was supposed to help her discover her next steps, to give her some ideas. And to clarify her feelings about both men now pursuing her. "Where are you leading me, Lord?" she whispered in the semi-darkness of the kitchen as she gazed out the window. The day was already bright and promising, the thin line of bright fury against the horizon having mellowed into a cornflower blue expanse.

An hour later Lauren was on her bike feeling the breeze whip through her ponytail. The sensation lifted her spirits. The route to the café where she'd met Mark the day before was a nice, downhill coast. From almost a block away she saw him waiting for her at a table outside on the terrace. She coasted down toward the curb, pressing the brakes lightly until she stopped, then hopped off, and leaned the bike against a tree.

"Hi." She sat down across from him at the small café table, gave him a smile. He wore a dark gray cotton tee-shirt, which set off dark hair that had gotten longer. She'd always liked it that way, and noticed how it curled around his ears. A hint of stubble shadowed his jaws. Warmth pooled inside her, and she turned her gaze away. He was, after all, a handsome man. But she didn't want to send him any messages or be misinterpreted. Especially since she didn't know her own mind at that moment. Her feelings, well, they were a bit more obvious to her, but her mind hadn't caught up.

Lauren pulled a swatch of paper from her canvas bag. "I found this address with a satellite office for OFPRA, which is an acronym for the office of refugees. I'm glad there is one here. It's a good place to start."

"How did everything go last night at work?" Mark's dark eyes found hers. There was concern there.

She shrugged. "It was okay. Less drama. Jean-Pierre was better-behaved. More patient. I didn't see Tarek. He must have been properly scared off."

"Probably. But we'll find him. We can stop by the park after we finish at the refugee office and try to connect with him. Maybe we'll even have some information by then. Something to give him hope."

Lauren smiled but didn't feel it. "I don't know if I told you that the night before last when we had our tense evening at the restaurant, I told Jean-Pierre clearly that I didn't want to work there anymore. I told him it wasn't a good fit for me."

"That's good. I'm proud of you. When will you be able to stop?"

She hesitated. "He assured me he'd found someone he wanted to interview again, and it would be soon. So, I guess I caved in and said okay."

"You could have told him you'd work through the weekend and then be done. Could you do that?" He was pressing her, but gently. Not letting her get away with her own cowardice.

"I could. I should have. Why do I always say *I should have* with him? Don't answer that. I don't even know. I don't owe Jean-Pierre anything." She sighed and looked away to a young woman passing by pushing a baby carriage. Why did she hesitate to state her needs with Jean-Pierre? She just needed to tell him and be done with it. She'd do it tomorrow. And for the next twenty-four hours she wouldn't think about it. She'd just enjoy being away from the kitchen, being with Mark, and doing something productive for Tarek.

"Ready to go?" Mark's voice broke into her thoughts.

She nodded and stood. "It isn't far. We'll walk."

They walked together in silence for about fifteen minutes. Finally, a low beige building came into view, quite ordinary except for a gently fluttering French flag extending up above the roof.

Lauren checked her address. "This must be it." They entered the building and were immediately surrounded by throngs of people and a clatter of voices. People of many nationalities, some in turbans, in African robes, Arab robes, head scarves, or in European clothing—they were lined up waiting for numbers. In a large room beyond them which Lauren could barely see, more people waited in rows of chairs.

She sighed and raised her eyebrows at Mark. "We might have to wait a long time."

"It's okay. It may be the only time we have to wait, and we'll get some valuable information, hopefully."

They filed into place at the end of the line. Mark stood close behind her. She could almost feel him against her, and his warmth and calm gave her comfort. They didn't have a choice about waiting, but at least she wasn't alone. Fortunately, Mark had thought to get the boy's last name.

An officer at the head of the line spoke to those who reached the front, then they proceeded to a machine where they pushed a lever for a numbered ticket. Ten minutes later when Mark and Lauren arrived at the head of the line, a police officer stepped toward them and asked them the purpose of their visit, perhaps to direct them to the correct service.

Lauren turned to him. "We are trying to help a Syrian refugee, Tarek Nazari, find his father and uncle. He is only twelve and he has been separated from them. He's just a child."

The agent hesitated then said, "Go to window nine and wait there." He indicated the place with an upward jerk of his head.

Lauren gave him a grateful smile. "*Merci.*" Looks like they wouldn't have to wait behind everyone in the next room. They approached the window where a woman was already being interviewed. After several minutes, the woman got up and left. Mark and Lauren sat down in front of a middle-aged blond woman with dark glasses. Despite the slash of red lipstick, she looked pale and weary, although it was only ten-thirty in the morning. A name plaque in front of her read *Françoise Lafitte.*

Lauren repeated her request to the woman and she wrote down Tarek's name. "Do you know when he arrived in Cavaillon?"

"About three months ago," said Mark in English, which Lauren translated to the woman.

"What is his father's name?"

Lauren wrung her moist hands. Of course, the dossier would be in Tarek's father's name. Or his uncle's.

"Hassan." Mark spoke, again surprising Lauren. Thank goodness he had thought to ask Tarek pertinent questions, which she had not.

For the next several minutes the woman typed on the computer keyboard in front of her, looking into the screen and then typing again. "Hassan Nazari. Tarek Nazari. I'm not finding either of them in my data base."

Lauren's courage sank. "He's not there? Is there any other way we can find his father and uncle?"

The woman pursed her lips, looked again at her computer and gently shook her head. "It is possible that the information has not yet been updated."

Mark leaned forward. "Can you keep his name on file as well as his uncle and father's? They might show up looking for Tarek and then we can connect them." He and Lauren exchanged a glance. She nodded at him. *Good thinking, Mark.* At least one of them had his wits activated that morning.

"Yes, we will keep his information." The woman looked directly at Mark and spoke in English. "People are coming and going all of the time. We may discover his relatives soon in the future."

Lauren leaned forward. "Is there anything else we might do to help? Any other agencies in the area that are working with refugees?"

"Yes, there are several churches working with them. They help with their needs and sometimes help them resettle into a new life. I will give you the address of one of these. It's called Eglise Evangélique de la Bonne Nouvelle." She leafed through a stack of papers on her desk and pulled one out, wrote on a sheet of paper, then slid it across the desk. "Here is their address. They might be able to help you."

"Thank you." Lauren scribbled her phone number on the bottom of the paper and tore it off. "Here is my number if you find anything about Tarek's relatives. I will know how to find him."

As they left the noisy building Lauren stopped on the sidewalk and turned to Mark. "I'm so glad you thought to ask him all those demographic questions. I didn't think of anything but getting him some food."

"I guess we each have our strengths, so we'll work well together." He smiled at her and she wanted to hug him. "I know that visit didn't give us any solid answers, but we shouldn't give up. It's only a first step."

She sighed. "I was thinking that this was our only option but maybe it's not. Maybe the church can help. I agree that we shouldn't give up, even though I feel discouraged right now. I don't understand why they don't even have his name, if they arrived in town three months ago."

Mark's hazel-brown eyes found hers as he placed his hands high on her arms. "Don't forget, that was an estimate from a twelve-year-old, which is all we have to go by. He might be way off in his date of when they got here, or maybe they arrived in France but didn't get here to Cavaillon until more recently. I think leaving his father's name with the office was the best thing to do. They could find him one day, sooner or later. The father is likely looking for his son, too. We just don't know where."

Lauren pulled the paper the woman had given her from her bag and read it again. "Church of Good News. That's what the name means. I sure hope so." She stuffed the paper back into her bag. "Could we go visit this church now? Do you have time?"

"Yes, of course. Is it here in Cavaillon?"

She nodded. "It's not too far. Ready to walk again?"

"Sure." He held his arm out as if to escort her and they laughed. It felt so comfortable to be with him. So familiar, so steady. She curled her fingers around his arm and kept them there as they walked.

Mature plane trees cast a dappled shade over the sidewalks and a soft breeze cooled the otherwise hot morning. "Were you able to get any food for him at the marché yesterday?" she asked.

"I sure did. I got some fruit, mostly, and managed to even get some runny cheese."

"He might not like the cheese, but it'll be protein for him. Now that he's here in France, he'll have to acquire a lot of new tastes." Lauren smiled. Tarek was certainly getting a French buffet in recent days.

"I couldn't find a baguette at the marché for the cheese, so I bought him one at a boulangerie near my apartment. When I went to the park, I didn't see him, so I left it in the spot we'd agreed on so he'll find it."

Lauren shook her head. "You think of everything, Mark. I knew you were detailed and efficient, but maybe I guess I'd never observed it before in such a practical way."

Mark seemed at a loss for words at her compliment, his face pinkening slightly. She wanted to hug him again as he simply smiled back at her with a shrug.

They walked in silence for a few more minutes until they reached a storefront church building. "I hope someone's here." Mark stopped and peered into the window. "I hadn't thought that being a weekday, they might be closed." He went to the front door and pushed it open. He looked back at Lauren. "Let's see what we find."

She followed him into the dimly-lit space. She could see rows of chairs and a wooden cross in the front of the room behind a wooden pulpit. A musty smell surrounded them in the silence. On the wall behind the pulpit were wooden letters. *Jésus, Lumière du Monde.* Jesus, light of the world. Lauren smiled at the sign. Felt good to be there. She called, *"Bonjour, il y a quelqu'un?"*

She heard a rustling of papers then footsteps from somewhere in the back of the building. Soon a stout, older woman with salt and pepper hair emerged into the sanctuary. "Hello, can I help you?" she asked them in French.

Lauren recounted Tarek's situation. "Is your church doing something for refugees?"

The woman nodded. "Yes, on a small scale. We have helped several families with their transition to living in France. We give them housing, accompany them to their residence appointments at the police or *préfecture* and we hold French classes here on Mondays and Wednesdays. We are a liaison with the OFPRA office if they have people to resettle here in Cavaillon. Many of our church members are engaged in helping them."

"Tarek needs a place to stay, first of all." Mark's voice echoed in the empty space. Lauren translated for the woman.

"I will bring his situation up to our group and see what might be available for him. Please give me his name and your contact information and I will let you know what we find. He is welcome to come to French class next Monday if he is ready. My name is Madame Bénétreau."

"I'm Lauren and this is Mark."

The woman nodded with a soft smile. She and Lauren exchanged phone numbers. As Mark and Lauren turned to go, she spied a stack of brochures about the church near the door on a wooden stand and grabbed one. She slid it into her bag. A neglected task for her personally, finding a church, but here she was. God through circumstances had brought her to them.

"Thank you, Madam Bénétreau. I appreciate what you all are doing for the refugees. And I am looking for a church too, so I'll visit soon." On impulse she took a second brochure. "For a friend." She'd give it to Jean-Pierre.

The woman beamed. "You are both welcome here anytime. I hope we are able to help your young Syrian friend." She pushed open the heavy front door for them and light pooled into the darkened hallway.

As Mark and Lauren left the building the late morning sun encircled them with warmth. "That was positive, don't you think?" Lauren shaded her eyes against the sun as she looked up at Mark.

"Absolutely. I was encouraged by the whole morning. We've made a start, and who knows where it will go? God has His hand on this little guy."

Lauren grinned. "You're so optimistic. But I'll have to agree on that one. This church will be a great resource for him, to connect him with other people and help him get settled. Who knows, he may even become a Christian one day. And, I hate to say it, if his father can't be found, maybe he could settle with one of the families at the church."

"I think they'll find his dad sooner or later, but this will be good in the interim as well as for a backup."

They turned to walk back the way they'd come, back toward the old city center. "Want to go to the park now and see if he's there?" Lauren hitched her backpack higher. "We can tell him the latest."

Fifteen minutes later they skirted the large parking lot in front of the tourist bureau and slipped into the adjoining park. Lauren scanned benches and trees along the path.

"There he is." Mark hitched his head toward the right and Lauren saw Tarek leaning against a tree peeling an orange.

The boy looked up in fear as they approached then a timid smile crossed his face. His eyes, the color of coffee beans, seemed alert and intelligent. His hair stuck up in several spikes on his head and needed a good wash. Lauren noticed his clothes were dirty and a rip along one side exposed his ribs. She made a mental note to find some clothes for him.

She approached and leaned her hands onto her thighs. She smiled and said softly, "Hello, Tarek. Can we join you?" Lauren squatted down beside the boy and Mark sat down on Tarek's other side.

Tarek held out a piece of orange to them. Mark chuckled and held up one hand. "No, Tarek, it's for you. I hope you like it."

"What is your name?" he asked, looking from one to the other.

Mark laughed. "I guess we forgot to tell you, didn't we? Tarek, I am Mark and this," he held a hand out toward Lauren, "is Lauren. We are your friends. We want to help you find your family."

Tarek small mouth twisted into a half-smile that wasn't reflected in his eyes. There, only hopelessness and loss emerged. "I hope. Mark. Lau-ren." He tried out each unfamiliar word and looked back at them for reassurance.

Lauren grinned. "That's right. We found a place where you can learn to speak French when you are ready. Maybe they will also help you find a place to sleep."

A strangled look crossed Tarek's face and he shook his head. "My father will not find me. He will not know—"

She placed her hand on his bony arm and stifled a shudder at its frailness, as though it could break any second. How long had he been living in parks and eating from trashcans? "Tarek, your father will not be able to find you in this park. We are working with the refugee office and also with a nearby church. They are both trying to locate your family. Until your father is found, you should stay in a real house and sleep in a real bed. Do you want to do that?"

Understanding passed across his face and the haunted look lessened only slightly. "Yes, thank you. If it is possible."

"It will be easier for them to find you if you are in a real house." Mark leaned forward. Tarek nodded then, seeming convinced.

The metal gate of the park squealed and they all looked up. A uniformed park officer sauntered down the path toward them, looking left and right for infractions or anything else unusual. He would surely find Tarek's presence unusual.

"Quick, let's go sit on that bench there and Tarek, go into the men's restroom." Mark whispered to him as he stood to his feet and helped Lauren up. "We'll distract him or just sit there on the bench."

Tarek slipped into the restroom and Mark and Lauren sat down on a nearby bench. When the officer had passed, she called a cheery, "*Bonjour, Monsieur.*" The man touched his hat, eyes fixed on Lauren, and continued. Once or twice the officer glanced back at her. "Looks like you have a fan, Lauren. I can understand that." Mark grinned.

Ten minutes later when the officer had finished his rounds and left the park, Mark got up and called into the men's room. "It's safe to come out, Tarek."

The boy emerged and came to the bench. Lauren patted the space beside her, and he sat down stiffly. "We will continue to bring food here and Monday at noon either one of us or both of us will come back here to let you know if there is any news. Okay?"

The boy nodded, a stoic frown on his face. When his eyes filled with tears, Lauren felt a gripping pain expand in her throat. "Are you okay, Tarek?"

He nodded and looked away as several more tears traced a path down his cheeks. He leaned against Lauren. "I—I think about my mother." Tears came faster now, and a sob escaped his throat.

"Oh, Tarek." Lauren wrapped her arms around his bony shoulders and held him against her chest. "I know you miss her." Her words emerged softly as her own eyes stung. She blinked several times. When Tarek pulled away and looked up at her she said, "I—I lost my mother, too. I was a little older than you are."

He stared at her for a moment before the tears started flowing again. After a moment he calmed and leaned back, seeming physically drained and empty of hope. Lauren stroked his dirty hair. She didn't care that she'd have to wash everything when she got home. A lump remained in her throat like a chunk of coal she couldn't swallow.

"We'll find your dad if we can, Tarek." Mark leaned toward the boy. "We'll do everything we possibly can."

Tarek nodded again, calmer after Lauren's embrace. He'd probably needed a good hug for months.

As Mark and Lauren stood to leave the boy looked up at them. "Thank you. Mark and Lauren."

"I'll see you tomorrow, Buddy. I'll bring your food by."

"Budd-ee?"

Mark laughed. "That means friend. I'll see you tomorrow, my young friend."

Then the closest thing to a real smile they'd yet seen emerged on Tarek's dark, tear-streaked face.

They left the park and crossed the parking lot to the sidewalk leading back into town, walking in silence. Lauren felt as though her insides were being wrung out, twisted with grief for the young boy who had lost everything.

"Want some lunch now?" Mark asked. When he saw her face, he stopped and touched her arm. "Are you alright, Lauren?"

"I—I can't—" How could she explain? A sinkhole was opening inside her.

She spotted a nearby bench and collapsed onto it. Mark was immediately beside her, his arm a strong band around her. She could feel his warmth seep into her as she leaned against him. "I feel so much sadness for this little boy. I can't express it. I mean, I'm *unable* to express it. It's like, all this tragedy and sadness is stuck right here." She touched her throat.

Mark's eyes were as gentle as his voice. "You can let it out, Lauren. You know you're safe with me, and you need to do it."

She nodded, unconvinced. If he only knew how hard it was to let it out and how much she wanted to. She must be going crazy, just like her mother had. Is this what her mother had felt? Trapped inside her own body with emotions she couldn't verbalize or cry to the surface? No wonder she'd ended her life. The thought made Lauren sit up straight. *Oh, God, don't let me go crazy like her.*

"What are you thinking, Lauren? That you aren't allowed to cry? That you will be too vulnerable if you do? It's okay. I cried for Tarek more than once since meeting him."

She met his eyes. "You don't understand, Mark. It's all bottled up inside and can't come out. I'm afraid of going crazy."

Mark slid both arms around her and pulled her to his chest. He held her there for several seconds, gently stroking her hair. She leaned into him, feeling his warmth course through her, feeling safety in his arms.

A moment later he pulled back and kept one arm around her shoulders. He peered into her face, locked her eyes with his. "Lauren, you are *not* going crazy. I have known you for three years and you're emotionally stuck, not crazy. I'm not telling you anything new. We've talked about this." There was an intensity in his voice and on his face that made her stop. Listen. "You're afraid to let any emotion go. You need to think about *what* you're afraid of. Think about it, Lauren. Take the time to ask yourself that question and see what answers you can find."

"I will." She would. Now she needed to escape the severity of his gaze and the magical draw of his nearness. Just then she wanted to burrow into his chest and never leave, but she couldn't. She wouldn't give him false hope in her moments of weakness. She looked back at him, forcing a bright tone and peaceful expression. "Can we go eat now? I'm really hungry."

On Mark's face she saw sadness. He shook his head slightly and stood. "French Pizza?" he asked, and held out one arm.

Chapter Thirteen

"It's time to take a break, Mark," said Didier with a smile which flashed silver from a capped tooth. "The crowd is thinning out."

"*D'accord.*" Sure, gladly, he'd take a break. He'd been on his feet for too many hours at the Apt weekly market, and they ached. People came from miles around to visit Apt's award-winning market, sample the produce, and enjoy the festive atmosphere. The lines that day had been continuous. Those who weren't locals were tourists who had read about the market in a tourist book, or those renting cabins in the nearby town. He'd probably never get the scent of fish out of his fingers.

Didier had seemed grateful for Mark's continued help, especially when Mark told him he'd be extending his trip. His idea of cleaning fish to temporarily lend a hand had expanded to several weeks already. He didn't really mind, since it kept him busy in the mornings. Then in the afternoons he had time to take things to Tarek or catch up with his clients at the internet café.

He'd had no trouble collecting unsold produce past its prime to give to Tarek. Most of the vendors were glad to get rid of it, or willing to do it for Mark because they liked him. Some were eager to help a boy in need, though he didn't always explain the circumstances.

Each day when Mark made his delivery to the park, if Tarek was there, his face would widen with surprise and delight, as if he were being given a new bike or a game. It was just food, something Mark had taken for granted all his life. *Just food.* Mark shook his head and swallowed the sudden lump in his throat.

He had a few objectives during his half-hour break. The first one led him through rows of produce stands to the textile tables just beyond. In that section one could find clothing, accessories, rugs, bed linens, table linens, and curtains. Almost everything one could need that was made of fabric.

On Mark's first day at the Apt market, he'd seen a large bin of children's clothing piled up like rags. He returned to the bin now and rummaged through the pile. Most were wrinkled, but looked clean. Maybe they were used, maybe not. It didn't matter. He'd have to estimate Tarek's size. The kid seemed small for his age and very thin. That was changing with the steady supply of food, Mark noted with a smile. He held up several pairs of pants and examined them, mentally imagining Tarek's frame. He did the same with shirts and shorts. He'd likely need pajamas too, if he were to go live with a family or with his own family. Hopefully.

"For your child?" a vendor asked him after he'd sorted through the clothes for several minutes.

"A friend. Twelve years." Mark's French had grown a bit in the last month, but he still had a long way to go. His comprehension far outpaced his speaking ability.

"*Il est petit?*" The vendor held his hands out to mime a small size.

"*Oui.*" Mark collected the items and paid for them. He wandered to another stand that sold cheap games. He stared for a moment at a paddle ball set. It had probably been a long time since Tarek had played with anything. He'd likely forgotten how to be a child. Playing wouldn't come to mind if bombs were falling on his house and destroying his neighborhood, his family, his life. Mark reached out and took the paddle ball set and chose a rubber ball as well.

At another stall were piles of toiletries of all kinds in plastic packs of twos and threes. Mark selected some soap, a pack of small towels, a toothbrush and toothpaste. They would be as important as new clothes for Tarek. He'd ask Tarek later if he wanted to come by his apartment for a shower. Such simple things hadn't been available for a long time. Mark murmured, "Please help us help Tarek find his family, Lord."

As he wandered through the other stalls in the ten minutes remaining of his break, he perused some old books and admired rainbow bouquets of flowers he'd love to give to Lauren one day. He sighed and wondered if Lauren would remain emotionally blocked. Was that the reason she'd backed away from him over a year ago? Or was he simply not God's choice for her? If he were not, he wanted to get that message from God and soon. Then he'd go on with his life. In the meantime, here he was. He prayed for Lauren as well at that moment, something he did frequently.

He returned toward the fish stand and spotted a familiar man a few stands away. Jean-Pierre. He was relieved to see that Lauren wasn't with him. The man stood far enough away that he wouldn't likely see Mark, but Mark still slipped under an awning into the shadow. From his hidden place, he observed for a moment. Jean-Pierre seemed chummy with several of the vendors, waving his hands, smiling, laughing, scowling. Totally in his element, the successful restaurateur.

Mark didn't know if Jean-Pierre was still a competitor or not. Lauren had been closed on the subject and it made Mark uneasy, since he still didn't really know where he himself stood with her anymore. His mature adult mind told him it was silly, but next to Jean-Pierre, he felt somehow inadequate.

He'd mostly conquered those feelings in the last ten years, feelings that had infected him during his childhood in the shadow of an uber-talented older brother. Those feelings had grown to a full-blown disease during adolescence. Following that difficult period, it didn't get easier, since Finn went from being the talented one to the talented *and* exotic one, at least in his own mind. His parents loved all their sons equally and were proud of them all, but somehow Finn drew everyone's admiration during family gatherings and holidays as they listened to his latest exploits of photography around the world. He'd recently been approached about doing a documentary movie. Even Mark's French adventure would never top Finn's stories.

"That's just dumb," he muttered to himself. Of course, it was no basis for self-esteem. Just a little twinge that reminded him that he needed to go back to who God said he was and who he'd made him to be. Repeatedly.

൙ ൙ ൙

Isle-sur-la-Sorgue was too far for Lauren to take the bike that day. She was still tired for that effort, though she likely could if she had plenty of sleep and mental clarity.

Jean-Pierre had loaned her his car so she could go there to get more black truffles and some herbs. It wasn't really a big market day, but she knew where to find them. Whenever she went to the canal-threaded town, she was drawn to the sounds of rushing water one could hear from almost everywhere, and it calmed her. Made her want to stay for hours.

She looked at her watch. Time to get back and prepare for her evening at the restaurant. Hopefully there wouldn't be but a few evenings left to endure. Jean-Pierre had said nothing more to her about the new chef he was interviewing and she wondered if he or she had been ruled out and they were back to zero. If that were the case, it wouldn't change her mind about leaving. She hoped he wouldn't work his charm and convince her to stay past the weekend. She had to stop putting his needs before hers.

After the last month, she had to admit that Jean-Pierre was still attractive and exciting to her, but each day it seemed more apparent that they were going in different directions. He wasn't a believer, though he might be one day. His dedication to his restaurant wasn't a problem for her, but his obsession with Michelin stars might one day be.

Lauren headed toward the parking lot with her bags of truffles and herbs—chervil, sorrel, and dill. On impulse she grabbed some herbes de Provence in a small burlap bag and added them to her collection. She was about to cross the street when she saw a blond woman in a bright orange apron humming and sweeping outside a storefront called *La Boîte de Délices*. The cheerful orange, pink, and yellow stripes of the awning and artful display in the window caught her eye. Jars of mustards and jams, tins of tea, and boxes of candies were arranged on weathered painted boxes among flowers and branches for a natural effect that was both cluttered and perfectly coordinated. She stopped and said to the woman, "Your display is lovely. It is very artistic."

The woman stopped sweeping and turned, a broad smile on her face. "Oh, thank you. You're very kind. It's my own style of artwork, I guess. I don't paint or sculpt, but I do like to arrange a nice window display." She followed her statement with a musical laugh, though she hadn't said anything particularly funny. Lauren had the distinct impression that she completely enjoyed her work even down to the sweeping.

"Is this your shop?"

"Yes, I opened it about two years ago. Mainly, I do catering but I also sell specialty items like these foods and crafts that are made by local businesses."

Lauren hitched her bag higher on her shoulder. "Catering? Hmm, that's interesting. I'm a trained chef myself, but I find that, even though I like working with food, the pressure of a professional kitchen isn't right for me. Catering sounds fun."

"Oh, it is." The woman's face lit up and her smile spread further. "It's much better for me than a professional kitchen, because I am my own boss and I'm not directed by the chef, the customers, or anyone. I create a menu according to the needs of the occasion. I even decorate for the event, which my clients really love. To tell you the honest truth, I love that part as much as preparing the dishes."

Lauren grinned. "How perfect, since you have a gift for decorating too." No wonder the woman hummed while she swept. She'd found both balance and enjoyment in her work, something Lauren had not yet done. Catering was something she could try one day. It was similar to what she'd done with Bree, but without the myriad responsibilities alongside.

"My name is Claire." said the woman.

"Lauren. From the States, as you can probably hear in my accent." She held out her hand and the woman shook it.

"You speak French very well. I can hear just a touch of an accent, and thought you might be German or Alsatian." Claire set her broom against the building and turned back to Lauren. "Once in a while I need some extra help with a catering event. Would that interest you?"

"Yes, I'm sure it would. I'm working at a restaurant in Cavaillon at the moment, but I won't be there too much longer." Lauren rummaged in her bag for a piece of paper, something she'd done several times already that week. She wrote on the paper. "Here is my phone number. Please let me know whenever you need some help. I'd be happy to come."

"Thank you, Lauren. Here is my contact information, too." Claire extended a business card that, naturally, was colorful and well-designed. "I'm sure I'll need to call you soon. I have an engagement party, a retirement, and a few baptisms coming up soon."

"Sounds wonderful. All happy occasions, it seems."

"Ah, yes. That's another reason why I love catering. It usually surrounds a happy event. I look forward to working with you sometime soon, Lauren."

As Lauren returned to Jean-Pierre's Citroën she pondered the idea of catering. Doing an event with Claire would give her a taste to see if it might be a fit.

An hour later she arrived at *Chez Jean-Pierre* with her provisions and her chef clothing just as a layer of despondency settled over her. She tried to ignore it and went to Jean-Pierre's office. The door was ajar, and the office was empty. His desk was covered with stacks of papers and receipts. Did he do all his own accounting too? No wonder he often seemed stressed. She rummaged in her purse and found the church brochure she'd taken for him and set it on his desk just as he came in.

"Bonjour, *Chérie*." Jean-Pierre suddenly stood behind her. He looked at her with a quizzical expression, likely wondering why she was there, since she'd never been in his office before.

"I—I just came in to give you this." She held up the brochure. "Remember the day we went to Ménerbes and you said you might be interested in attending a church some day?"

"Ah, yes. I remember." He smiled at her. "Thank you for that. We can go there together."

She smiled in return and began to move toward the door when he stepped toward her. He stood close to her and wore a sober expression as he looked into her eyes. "I miss you, Lauren. I feel we have not spent very much time together in recent days."

That's because I'm always here, was on the tip of her tongue to say. She should. But didn't. Why? Still, she didn't know why she often held back her opinions, her needs. "I miss—" she began then shrugged. She wasn't ready to tell him she missed *him*. She missed the life she had when she'd first arrived in France. "I miss the things we used to do together. The rhythm of life . . . before. Do you have news about the Michelin man? I mean—" she laughed aloud as she pictured the pudgy, white trademark of the tire company. "Michelin is tires too, I guess. I mean the star man." Now she sounded ridiculous, but he knew what she meant.

"Oh, him. Yes, I think he was here this week and we have had a good week, no problems in the kitchen, so maybe he will give me a good review. I try not to worry about this."

"Liar. You worry all the time, Jean-Pierre." Lauren shook her head with a chastising smile.

"Yes, I'm afraid, too much." His voice was quiet. He reached out and pulled her close then and brushed her lips with his. A tremor went through her, but it was weaker than it had been the last time, a week or so ago. Mark's face came into her mind.

When he pulled back from her, she added, "And the new chef?"

Jean-Pierre laughed. "Are you all business today? We could always talk about us instead."

"I ask because I'm planning to leave my job in the kitchen very soon. I told you—"

"Yes, I know. You told me you want to leave. But I will still see you, *non?*"

"Of course. Though I will eventually have to go back to America. I don't know when."

"Maybe never?" A playful smile pulled at his lips. He drew her forward and kissed her again, more deeply this time. "Perhaps I can convince you to stay—"

"Jean-Pierre, the oven—oh, excuse me." Frédéric stopped abruptly and backed out of the door. Lauren could feel her face burn. She and Jean-Pierre usually maintained a professional distance while in the restaurant. Bad timing.

"I am coming, Frédéric," he called as he released her arms. He turned back to her. "We will continue this conversation maybe Sunday, if you are free. I will take you to the Verdon Gorges. They are lovely, you will see."

She smiled weakly and followed him out of the office to the kitchen where she busied herself with prep for the evening dinner service and strove to avoid eye contact with Frédéric.

Nearly four grueling hours later, which had, thankfully, passed like a blur, Lauren leaned against the counter and breathed deeply. A very busy Friday night was over. It had been more crowded than usual, thanks to a new menu item, roasted quail with sorrel sauce and black truffles. She'd been able to taste a mouth-watering bite during her break, but it didn't make up for the stress the evening had caused her.

The other employees were cleaning and finishing desserts during the lull just before the after-theatre crowd would arrive. She still had a long night ahead of her. Jean-Pierre strode into the kitchen from the dining room with a scowl on his face. Some new annoyance in the dining room, no doubt. He headed toward her and his scowl remained. She lifted her eyebrows. "Everything okay?"

"Lauren, I would like to speak with you. Perhaps we can step out to the terrace for a moment, since there are no patrons there now."

Her eyebrows shot up again then furrowed, but she followed him dutifully through the kitchen back door.

When they were outside, he turned slightly away from her and stroked his chin a couple of times, as if gathering his thoughts, choosing his words. "Lauren, I know this is not your favorite job to do and I was happy that you were able to help, but I have learned something that makes me most unhappy."

She stared at him, waiting, while her heart began to pound like a tympani drum inside her chest. She'd never seen him with eyes so cold, a frown etched like stone.

"Frédéric has told me he saw you giving food—*my* food—to that young urchin boy I chased away a few days ago. I want to ask you, is this true?"

Lauren felt the blood drain from her face as the heat filled her neck. "I would *never* give away your food, Jean-Pierre. You should know that about me. I gave only trash to the boy, scraps that were going to be thrown away. That boy was hungry but we throw away food here every day."

Jean-Pierre shook his head and stared at her. She felt a chill emanating from his hard gaze. "So, it's true. I cannot believe it. I trusted you, Lauren. I don't understand how you can betray me like this." His face was ashen, closed.

Panic gripped her then. She said, "Jean-Pierre, I did not betray you. Did you hear what I just said? It was *garbage* I was going to throw away. Food from peoples' plates, bread that was stale. Why throw this away if it can feed a young boy, save him from hunger?" She had to make him understand. "Do you really think I would have given away your good food that you bought to serve people? Of course, I would never do this!"

Her explanation didn't seem to faze him, and this fact replaced her vexation with anger and frustration. He wasn't listening. He preferred to listen to Frédéric.

Frédéric had seen her taking food to Tarek. Was he only now telling Jean-Pierre about it because he saw her embracing the boss? If so, why should he even care, unless he was jealous of her relationship with Jean-Pierre, desiring a privileged status for himself? Or else wanting to make trouble for her simply to be spiteful?

"Jean-Pierre, I told you that this boy, this *child*, was hungry. I learned that he is a refugee from Syria and has lost everything. He lives in a park because he was separated from his father. A little boy. Imagine if it was your son who was hungry."

His head jerked back to her. "Do not speak of my son."

"Why not? If your son was hungry, wouldn't you want someone to give him table scraps if they could?" Before he could answer, she continued, fueled by the indignation that rose up into her throat. "Do you know that there are over seven-*hundred* thousand people who used to have normal lives like yours and mine, but who are now *refugees* all over the world? Do you know they have lost *everything*?" Her voice had become louder and several of the kitchen employees hovered around the door to listen.

"I see, Lauren, where your loyalty lies. With the boy, with the refugees."

A frustrated groan squeezed out of her throat. "And I see that *your* loyalty is with Frédéric, not me. You are not listening to *me*, Jean-Pierre." She lowered her voice. "Listen, I came to France because I like you and wanted to get to know you better. Then I agreed to work at your restaurant to help you, because you needed help. Doesn't that count for anything?"

"You never wanted to work here."

"True, I told you that. I'm not happy in kitchen work, but I wanted to help you. But you don't care about that because I gave trash to an orphan boy who was hungry." She stopped and shook her head, watching him. "What kind of man are you, Jean-Pierre? Do you care about your restaurant more than human beings? Does human suffering do nothing for you?"

He drew up his shoulders. "Don't try to make me guilty of the war, Lauren. I had nothing to do with this. I am doing my best to run a quality business and have given my life for this."

"So, what do you have, Jean-Pierre?" Her voice became soft. She would give up trying to convince him. "A restaurant with a star. Great. No relationship with your son, no contribution to the suffering of people, no lasting impact. I see very clearly now that we have nothing in common. *Nothing.*"

"You are not Mother Theresa, Lauren. Don't make yourself out to be better than me."

"I am no better than you and I am certainly no Mother Theresa. But I do what I *can*. I saw this boy's need and it touched me. He lost his mother. I felt sad for him and wanted to help him find his father. And also, not starve to death."

As she spoke, she undid the buttons of her jacket. She wriggled out of the sleeves and shoved it into his hands as he stood there grimacing at the ground. Without another word she turned and went into the kitchen. She saw Frédéric wiping down the stainless-steel counters, pretending to have heard nothing of her row with Jean-Pierre. She pulled off her toque and threw it at his head. He flinched as the wad of stiff fabric grazed his face. "Are you happy now, Frédéric?"

Without waiting for an answer, she pushed through the swinging kitchen doors and out the front door of the restaurant into the summer night.

Chapter Fourteen

Mark and Tarek stood together on the corner in front of Mark's apartment building and waited for Lauren to arrive. Tarek smelled like fresh soap and his dark hair, still moist, was combed back from his face. Mark had even trimmed it so he'd look less like the Artful Dodger. He wore the new clothes that Mark had bought for him, following a long and much-needed shower in Mark's rented flat. The clothes almost fit. Sort of. They had an appointment with Madame Bénétreau at the church. A new door in Tarek's young life was about to open. And he looked like a rabbit about to bolt.

"Feel better all cleaned up and wearing new clothes?" Mark smiled down at the boy as a wave of tenderness mixed with sympathy flooded into him.

Tarek nodded, a shy smile almost emerging on his face. "I am afraid now," he admitted, and cast a beseeching look up at Mark.

Mark leaned over, his hands on his knees, until he was almost eye-level with Tarek. "There's nothing to be afraid of, Tarek. This lady is very nice and she wants to help you. She knows that you're waiting to find your dad, but you need a place to live until then. She is going to talk to us about a family that you might be able to stay with."

Tarek nodded but said nothing. He blinked and swallowed, blinked again.

"And when your dad does find you, both of you are going to need some help from other people until you get settled. Make sense?"

The boy nodded again. "Yes. Thank you." His voice was soft and he seemed younger than his twelve years, but doing his best to grow up quickly.

Mark could certainly understand the kid's anxiety. Living with total strangers, being dependent on them, not speaking the same language, and doing all of that in a totally new culture. And at such a young age. Seemed pretty overwhelming, on top of worrying about his father's whereabouts and if he was even alive. It was too much for any child to have to bear. But this solution was better for him than sleeping in the park, eating scraps, and wondering what would happen next.

"Another thing, Tarek. If you stay in a home that has an address and a phone, once your father is found, you can find each other more easily. Like Lauren was telling you the other day, your dad can't find you if you're in the park with no address." Creating a connection between Tarek and the church was even more important with his and Lauren's imminent departure from France. At least he hoped that Lauren was planning to return to the States. He wasn't allowing himself to mentally entertain any other scenario.

As he searched Tarek's face for understanding he heard the scrape of gravel and a squeal of brakes as a bike rolled to a stop. He stood up and turned and was relieved to see Lauren dismount and lean her bike against a tree.

"Hi, guys," she said. Her cheeks were flushed and her brown, wavy hair emerged from a straw brimmed hat and tangled across her cheeks. She looked calm, more than the last time he'd seen her, and wore a short casual dress which, as usual, looked chic and earthy at the same time.

She approached them with a smile and looked down at Tarek with admiration. "You look great, Tarek. I like your new clothes." Tarek returned a tentative smile with hooded eyes. To Mark she said, "Mrs. Bénétreau said they might have a family in mind for him, but they won't be there today. It's a first step, though."

"Absolutely. Maybe she wants to get to know him first. Or they might have some kind of procedure they have to follow."

"I'll lock my bike and we can walk there together." Her cheerful tone was probably meant to uplift Tarek, but Mark wasn't sure it had worked. He still looked like he was being taken to his execution. Mark laid a hand on his shoulder as Lauren pulled the lock through the spokes of the bike and fastened it to a tree.

They crossed the empty street and headed up the hill in the direction of the church. Mark and Lauren walked on either side of Tarek, without words, wanting to surround him with support.

The streets of Cavaillon were calm that day and a gentle breeze shifted the branches overhead. Mark longed to talk to Lauren about something other than Tarek, to dig deeper into her world and thoughts. Ever since they'd met, he'd always been able to talk easily with her, but these days, he strode a delicate path, striving to avoid anything she might interpret as pressure. "Do you have to work tonight?" A lame start, but it might get her talking. He looked at her over Tarek's head, predicting an affirmative response accompanied by either a groan or a whine.

"No, I do *not*." She tilted her head and gave him a coy smile.

"Wait, you mean he let you take a Saturday night off? Isn't that, like, Michelin Star Day?" Unbelievable. Something must have happened. Maybe she'd finally stood her ground with Jean-Pierre.

She flicked the straw hat from her head so that it hung on a string down her back. His fingers itched to pull the rogue strands of hair behind her ears, but she did it herself. He couldn't believe how cute she looked just then, but for sure she didn't know it.

"I quit." A grin spread across her face. "You wouldn't *believe* the blowout. I'm done." She looked satisfied and resolute.

At her words, Mark stopped on the sidewalk, feeling something akin to joy expanding like a balloon in his chest, but schooled his face to show only surprise. "Done with the restaurant *and* with Jean-Pierre?" He almost held his breath.

"Yes, finally. One of the kitchen staff told Jean-Pierre I'd been giving food to Tarek. He confronted me during a lull in the evening. I let him know it was just scraps and stuff that we'd be throwing away, but he got it into his head that I had betrayed him. Can you imagine? He didn't even care that a boy was hungry."

"So, he fired you?"

"No, better than that. I walked out." Her voice sounded triumphant, and when her feet started moving again, Mark and Tarek fell into step with her. "I realized he and I don't have any business being together. We have little in common. Certainly not the same values. But he was so persuasive. At times, I felt like I couldn't even be myself."

Mark stifled a huge grin. She might interpret that as a victory grin, although her news didn't guarantee him anything more than he already had. At least his competitor was out of the picture. For that, he was immensely grateful. "Good, I'm glad. You seem more peaceful."

She nodded, a gentle smile on her lips. "I am. At least that part of the puzzle is solved."

Her words were both reassuring and, well, not, since *he* was part of her puzzle that was unresolved. He refused to dwell on that.

"How far is the church? I can't remember how long it took us the other day."

"We're almost there. Just past the next corner near the Tabac store."

Soon they arrived at the storefront church. Lauren pushed the glass door open and they entered the darkened space. Madame Bénétreau was already waiting for them and approached from a lighted section of the sanctuary. "Bonjour, my friends. This must be Tarek." She leaned down and spoke softly to him. "Hello, Tarek." She turned to Lauren. "Does he speak French?"

"No, just English. In the present tense."

"Welcome, Tarek," the woman told him in English. "We try to help you. Come in, please."

They left the sanctuary and filed into a brightly lit room that looked like an office, where a teapot and cookies awaited on a wooden table surrounded by folding chairs. "We'll sit here," she told Lauren. "My English is not perfect, but I will try my best to speak with him. I will ask him just a few questions."

Mark looked at Tarek, who sat stiffly on the wooden chair, as if preparing for an inquisition. He was quiet, likely summoning up the inner adult he had been forced to become. Lauren must have noticed, because she reached out to touch his back. The boy's dark eyes found hers and looked back at Mark. Lauren was smiling at him and in a soft voice, she said, "It's going to be okay, Tarek. This is a good thing."

Tarek nodded, then turned his attention back to Madame Bénétreau.

"I have only a few questions. I don't want Tarek to be too nervous about anything." She leaned forward and smiled at the boy. "Tarek, my name is Madame Bénétreau. This building is a church and many people in this church actively help refugees and other people who need help. We will try to help you." She paused, waiting for a nod of understanding. "Would you like a biscuit? Here, they are very good." She proffered the plate to him, and he timidly pulled a cookie off the plate.

"We are working with another agency in town that is trying to find your family. Until they find your father, you can stay with one of the families from our church. I have some of your information already but wanted to ask you where and how you were separated from your father. Were you already in France when this happened?"

Tarek looked at Mark as if asking permission to speak. Mark nodded at him, smiled what he hoped was a reassuring smile.

"I am with my family in Syria. The bombs are falling in the city." Despite the tragedy of his words, Mark had the impression Tarek had recited his story to many authorities since leaving his home, which couldn't be easy for the kid. "My mother and my brother are dead. The bomb fall and they both die." He stopped, swallowed. Blinked rapidly. "I go to Turkey with my father and my uncle. We are the only ones left in the family. We go to France with a . . ." he looked to Mark.

"Airplane?" Mark imitated the wings of a plane with his hands.

Tarek nodded. "Airplane. We go to France. We are in France but we not take the train with my father."

"You got on the wrong train?" Mark asked him gently. He nodded. "In Paris, or somewhere else?"

"Not Paris. I don't know."

Madame Bénétreau said, "It may have been in Nice when they were separated. Do you know where you were separated from your family, Tarek? In what city?"

Tarek shook his head.

She waved a hand dismissively. "It doesn't matter. It's the job of OFPRA to find them and know how to bring them together." She leaned forward again. "Tarek, I am sorry about your mother and your brother. It's very, very sad. But we will try to find your father. I will help you as much as I can. You will stay with a very nice family."

Mark was watching Lauren, who nodded agreement with Madame Bénétreau. When she did, he saw a glint of tears in her eyes. He hadn't seen that in—well, ever.

As they got up to leave, the woman gestured Lauren and Mark aside. "The poor boy has been through so much." The rims of her eyes were pink with unshed tears. "We do have one family I have spoken with about him staying with them, but they are expecting a baby. They are praying about whether or not to take Tarek. If they decide against it, I will bring him to my home. I'm a widow and I have room."

Mark and Lauren exchanged glances. "That would be wonderful, Madame Bénétreau. You are very kind."

She shook her head slowly. "It is the normal thing to do. The humane thing. He's just a child. I'll do whatever I'm able."

"We feel the same. Thank you for everything. You'll be in touch?" Lauren asked the woman.

Lauren's sad smile gripped Mark's heart. But he liked the way she said, "We."

"By tomorrow I will let you know something." Madame Bénétreau accompanied them to the front door.

When they emerged back onto the sunny sidewalk, Mark turned to Tarek. "That wasn't too bad, was it, Tarek?"

Tarek shook his head. "The lady is nice."

"Yes, she's very nice. You'll meet other nice people at the church and they'll all like you a lot," Lauren told him as they walked.

They reached the park gate and Mark pushed it open for Tarek. It seemed strange to be taking the boy back to the park when he seemed so close to having a real home. But it wouldn't be long. "Too bad I don't have space in my room for you, Buddy. I'll come by tomorrow afternoon, like usual. We might have some news for you by then."

The boy nodded and a ghost of a smile appeared on his lips before he slipped through the gate.

They watched him vanish in the depths of the park then turned to each other. Mark said, "What's next?" He knew Lauren didn't have to work later. If she didn't want to see him, she'd have to find another excuse. Maybe she'd want to hang out in Cavaillon with him. Hike, have coffee. Even visit a laundromat. It didn't matter what. Mark quelled his hopes as he awaited her response.

Lauren glanced down at her watch. "I need to do a few things, but if you want to, we could meet for dinner later. I could come by at seven."

If you want to? He'd been waiting for three weeks for this. A day *and* a dinner date with Lauren. The excitement inside reminded him of the first time he'd asked any girl out, but he assumed a calm, friendly mask. "That would be perfect. I'll do a little catch-up with my clients this afternoon and I'll wait for you downstairs at seven."

Lauren leaned over to unlock the bike. She mounted it and gave a final smile to Mark. "See you later." She pulled her straw hat back to her head, tightened the strap under her chin, and started up the hill. Mark stood watching her until she was out of sight.

ભ ભ ભ

As Lauren's feet pedaled uphill, she thought about Tarek's skinny body passing through the gate and disappearing down the path to the "home" he'd occupied for the last several months. Despite his thorough cleaning and new clothes, his gait seemed like that of a child who'd been splintered by life and completely broken. He wasn't yet convinced that moving in with a family was a positive step that would take him to a more stable life, whether or not his father was located.

If only she could bring him with her to her temporary house. There was room, but she could guess what Madame Carnot would say. Though she was a kind woman, many people were distrustful of foreigners in need, as if they were all thieves. Lauren would dare to ask, if another option were not so close on the horizon.

Lauren felt the pressure of unshed tears behind her eyes as her bike climbed the Garibaldi hill toward Madame Carnot's house. The unaccustomed feeling was made worse by the ache in her throat, the overwhelming sadness threatening to engulf her.

This was getting out of hand. What was happening to her calm, controlled response to whatever came her way? People knew her as even, level-headed Lauren, and sometimes as *blocked* Lauren, or bland Lauren, which was less flattering.

She certainly hadn't been blocked the night before when her frustration pushed her to break off with Jean-Pierre and storm out of his restaurant. It was a shame that Jean-Pierre felt she'd betrayed him. She wouldn't want that to be the last memory he had of her, after all the time they'd spent together. But she'd tried to reason with him, and his implacable stubbornness, his determination to think poorly of her, well, it just lit a fire under her. It was over and she was relieved. She did miss seeing him, but she'd get over it with time.

She couldn't think of that now. Now was for Tarek. She'd focus her energies on helping him. As much as she wanted to keep calm and controlled so that they could find the best course of action for him, she couldn't keep the tragedy of his situation from weighing her with almost crippling sadness. At least Mark was there with his calm logic and an obvious attachment for the boy. She had to admit his presence was a huge comfort. A comfort she had missed.

When she pushed the cheerful blue door of Madame Carnot's house, she didn't see any sign of the woman. Lauren was relieved, since she desperately needed to be alone to make sense of her tangle of emotions, of Tarek's pain and her jumbled feelings about Mark and Jean-Pierre. She bounded up the stairs two-by-two and closed herself in her room just as a few tears spilled out and tumbled down her cheeks.

A few more tears came as she thought of Tarek and all he'd lost. Images of a young boy playing soccer in a field filled her mind, and it could have been only days later when he stood on the same field, watching bombs fall and destroy the only neighborhood he'd ever known. She pictured his mother lying in a heap, covered in blood, perhaps missing limbs. Then without warning, those images morphed into her own mother stretched across the bed, a lifeless stare fixed onto her peaceful but pale face. A cruel, scribbled sentence, "I'm sorry," on the swatch of paper beside her.

Tarek was a lost child. But she, too, had been a lost child.

Before her mother's death, her father had frequently been gone with his work. After her death, a kind neighbor watched out for them and invited them over often. One day a year later her father explained to his daughters that he was taking a job in Indiana, and they would go live with Aunt Kate, her mother's half-sister. In the months that followed he'd made weak promises to come bring them to live with him, but it never materialized. Lauren had never clicked with Aunt Kate, and the feeling was mutual. Alone at age fifteen. Orphaned, for all practical purposes. A year later she was invited to a church where she discovered Christ, who became a life raft for her.

So, why was she falling apart now? Was it a good thing that she was feeling this all so deeply? Mark would say she was getting unblocked, but it felt like a painful foreign country to her.

Finally, the tears subsided. She lay on her back and stared at the ceiling, a whisper of calm tumbling over her like a veil. She listened to the quiet, occasionally broken by a dog's bark, a child's cry, a car passing.

She'd *cried*. Not too much, so at least things didn't get out of hand. When was the last time? She couldn't remember. For years she'd been aware of the grief, frustration, and sadness bottled up, sealed off and stored neatly in a forgotten place. What was normal for other people was rare for her. At times, she was glad she had such control, since giving into sadness was risky. Emotions were messy. She'd seen that with her mother.

Lauren pulled herself upright and looked at her watch. She still had plenty of time to do her errands before meeting Mark. Thinking of Mark caused a surge of warmth to swell inside her. He was the most secure part of her life right now. He accepted and loved her unconditionally. It was almost as if—as if she still loved him. Did she? Was her love for him coming back, or had it never left?

If she didn't figure out her feelings for him fast, he'd likely move on and she'd lose him forever. Sure, they'd tell each other they'd always be friends, but realistically, he'd slowly fade from her life as he built a new one with another woman.

A claw of despondency grabbed at her, and for once, her deep well of sadness didn't come from Tarek, but the prospect of one day losing Mark to another woman who adored him as he deserved. Why did that feel so bad? If she wasn't ready to move forward with him, he should find someone else. She ought to want that for him.

Lauren shook the thoughts forcefully from her mind. These rabbit trails wouldn't help her at all. She wanted an indisputable proof of her feelings for Mark, not just dread of losing his friendship. She could not string him along with false hopes. It would be plain wrong.

A few hours later Lauren stood on the cobbled street at the foot of Mark's building. The summer night was balmy, and the sun hadn't fully set. It felt like a date. A date with Mark. In France. She smiled.

She was a few minutes early and sat down on a nearby bench to observe the sounds and scenes of early evening. Clusters of people in work clothes walked by from time to time. The temperature was ideal, and a soft breeze caressed her bare arms. She felt fully alive.

"You look fresh and lovely."

Mark's voice startled her. Her head jerked up and she grinned at him. "Sorry, I was daydreaming. Thanks, though." She stood up. She *did* feel pretty that night in a new turquoise sundress with a small leaf pattern, an indulgent purchase made that very afternoon in a cute boutique she'd wanted to visit downtown. Of course, she wasn't trying to impress Mark. Just going out for the evening. She *had* taken a fair amount of time with her hair and make-up, though.

Mark wore a deep blue short-sleeve dress shirt and khaki pants. He was casual, but neat and suitable for a dinner out and . . . she paused and looked away . . . quite attractive. Something hummed inside her.

"Daydreaming about spending time with me, I hope. No need to answer that." He grinned at her and extended a hand. "Ready?"

She was getting used to holding his arm lately. They never did that while they were dating, but she liked it. They walked together like other dating couples she saw, looked just like them, walking close together, laughing at silly observations as they went.

"Did you finish your errands today?"

"I did. I also had time to read in the back yard."

"Good for you. I think quitting the restaurant is the best thing you've done since you got here. You always seemed so wound up and tense, but not anymore."

She was glad he'd noticed a change in her. She felt somehow different, if nothing else, emptied of accumulated grieving for Tarek, and maybe a little bit for herself. And of course, relieved to be out of a job. Silence from Jean-Pierre. No surprise there.

"Here's a nice place I've been to before." She cocked her head toward an inviting brick storefront restaurant with a dark green awning, a warm light spilling out the windows onto the sidewalk. "Want to try it? Looks like they have a terrace in back."

"You came here with Jean-Pierre?"

She shook her head. "No, I had lunch here by myself one day. I haven't tried it for dinner."

"Well, okay, then. I'll go." They laughed and he held the door open for her.

The maître d' sat them at a cozy table on the terrace. Seeing Mark over the glow of a flickering candle, she felt a flutter of attraction in her stomach, which all made it exactly like a romantic date. How normal everything felt being with him, yet how different. She hadn't overlooked her own swelling attraction to him over the last couple of weeks. That evening in particular all her senses were alerted to him. In the candlelight his shadowed face looked tan against his dark, wavy hair. He seemed relaxed and confident. Was she falling for him all over again? Could she even trust her feelings? They'd betrayed her before. What if she followed them and they bottomed out later? She would end up hurting him even more than the first time.

She looked at his familiar, steady hands in the candlelight and wanted to reach for them. Of course, she'd have to rein in her burgeoning desires. That was one thing she did really well, after years of practice stuffing inconvenient emotions into neat, tidy boxes and forgetting them in the closet of her mind.

The tall waiter in the starched white apron brought their meals, and the aroma made Lauren's mouth water. "Mmm. This smells delicious. This is *gratin dauphinois*." Lauren pointed to her plate. "The potatoes are cooked in cream and garlic. Some recipes cover it with cheese, and some don't. There's a little touch of nutmeg, too. That's the secret ingredient."

"Sounds and smells wonderful. I'm sure you don't miss restaurant cooking. Eating is another story." Mark smiled and studied her over the rim of the water goblet. "I know you're about to find your niche. I can feel it."

"I have an idea." She felt a rush of excitement and leaned toward the table. "Wait till you hear. Just yesterday I met a woman named Claire at Isle-sur-la-Sorgue and she is a caterer. She told me she'd let me know if she needed a hand one day. I'm free to help her and try it out, now that I'm no longer tied to the restaurant."

"I'm glad you have something new you can try." Mark's voice softened. "Any misgivings? About Jean-Pierre, I mean?" He spoke as if he was treading on delicate ground.

"Not really. I liked him, but I think deep inside, I knew we weren't made for each other. He was exciting for a while, different. But we have very different values. He pursued me, but sometimes I imagine that if we were married, he wouldn't be as attentive or kind. Just a hunch. Anyway, I didn't like that he had no interest in helping Tarek and almost accused me of stealing from him."

"After all this time, he had no clue about your heart."

Lauren stilled. That's right, Jean-Pierre hadn't a clue. But Mark got her completely. *Completely.*

"I—I cried today," she blurted, sounding like a child. But she'd really wanted to tell him. "A little bit."

Mark's eyes grew round, his eyebrows lifted. "Really. That's wonderful, Lauren. A breakthrough, I'd say. What brought that on?"

Suddenly she felt self-conscious. "It was, well . . ." She stopped. Gathered her thoughts. "Tarek was the trigger. He's so tragic, and his situation is so unbelievably sad. So, it was him, then I also started thinking about my mom. I guess my mind made a link between him losing his mom and me losing mine. All the memories came back kind of fresh and raw. I usually try to avoid them, but there they were."

Mark nodded, looking thoughtful. "All the memories you tried to shut down. You can't heal that way, Lauren. I think you know that. You have to face those painful experiences and grieve them, even now, more than fifteen years later. I think that's why you've been blocked. But it seems like you've started to break out."

She nodded. He was probably right, she'd been blocked. Maybe still was. He'd said it before, but now it resonated. Despite that, she didn't want to talk anymore about it that night. Maybe having a good cry on a regular basis was therapeutic, but she didn't want to live that way, indulging in crying spells like others go to the gym. In any case, hadn't her faith given her perspective on all of that? She went for years without talking about it, and here she was, talking to Jean-Pierre, to Tarek, and now to Mark.

"I haven't asked you what's going on back in Virginia. I know you've been here for a few weeks but seems like we're always busy doing things for Tarek, so I haven't caught up on your life."

Mark smiled sadly, likely thinking that again, she was backing away from facing her past. And he'd be right. But she wanted to enjoy the evening with him, to savor the food and the summer night, hear the sounds of the evening, watch the sun slowly melt into the horizon, as snatches of French conversation and laughter spun up toward the trees overhead. She wanted to absorb this moment, not dwell on the past. And she wanted to just enjoy being with Mark, newly exciting, newly handsome to her.

Mark leaned back and wiped his mouth on the cloth napkin. "The biggest news, I guess, is my friend Logan is about to become a dad. Remember Logan?"

"Of course. It hasn't been that long. This is their first child, I guess."

"Yes, it is. They're excited, but it seems the kid is running a bit late. That's perfect for me, since I'm not there to be Uncle Mark just yet."

"Can't rush that one, regardless." Lauren shrugged and grinned at him over her wine glass.

"Work is the same. My practice has grown with a couple of really big clients. I did a lot of work in advance to be able to come here and not feel stressed out, but I'll need to go back fairly soon."

She felt a thump inside. Of course, he had to go back. She only hoped she knew her plans before he left. And Tarek needed to be settled. Mark had been such a comfort helping her with Tarek, fueled with the same level of commitment to help the child.

Mark added, "Not much else I can say. You know me, boring Mark."

"Why do you say that?" She reached out and touched his arm and let her fingers slide down to his. A tingle rippled up to her wrist. "It's not at all true. I know you aren't fishing for compliments. You really believe it, and I don't know why."

He shrugged with a tight-lipped half-smile. "Maybe that's why you left me."

"Mark, I told you it wasn't you. Of course, it's not you. What you call 'boring' is stability and maturity. You're solid and stable,

Mark. You're just the kind of person I need—" Lauren caught herself. What had she said? Just when she didn't want to give him hope she'd done just that. But it was true. He was perfect for her and she knew it. That was what was so maddening about all this. She slid her fingers away from his.

Mark's small smile spread to a grin. "You said it, not me." He leaned forward and locked his gaze with hers as his hand found hers again, clasping them in his. "Lauren, it's so clear for me. I pray every day it will be for you. We're meant to be together."

She let out an embarrassed chuckle. "I was trying to set you straight in your complex about being boring. You are *not* boring in the least. You compare yourself with Finn, and you shouldn't. I wouldn't have dated Finn. He's full of himself."

"He is a little bit, I agree. But with good reason. So, you were only trying to set me straight in my self-esteem?"

Lauren squirmed. "I don't know. You have so many qualities. Mark, you're a great guy, truly. I'm the one who is messed up."

"Lauren, I think you're less messed up than you were. Maybe ten or twelve percent less." A spark of mischief danced in his dark eyes.

They both laughed and the sound tumbled through the night air. What was happening inside her? She almost agreed with him that they were meant to be together. Almost, though she stopped just in time. She couldn't be impulsive with his heart. She had to be sure.

Chapter Fifteen

Mark's gaze wandered around the sanctuary as the church service completed its second hour. His head was buzzing from hearing so much French. At first, he'd tried to pick up snatches and he'd enjoyed being able to identify a word here, a word there. But it went too fast and he couldn't keep up.

On the walls hung colorful banners with Bible verses in French and on the stage sat an electric piano, two guitars in stands, and a djembe drum. The music had been so good he was compelled to tap his toes and clap. It had struck him that musical worship was a unifier among all believers worldwide. Some tunes he recognized, others he didn't. But he was well aware of the common focal point of Christ.

Following the worship was the sermon, and there was no getting around it. It was *long*. When he looked around the room at the fifty or so attendees of all ages, the message seemed to be striking a chord for them. Their earnest faces showed rapt attention, their eyes squinted, they nodded, smiled, grinned.

Next to him sat Tarek, who seemed as distracted as Mark was that day. Tarek likely understood nothing of either the language or the Christian setting where he found himself. Shoved under his chair was a duffel bag filled with his belongings, most of which Mark had given him. After the service he'd be moving in with Madame Bénétreau and he looked as though he wanted to make a dash for the door.

Mark glanced sideways at Lauren, who seemed absorbed in the message. He'd have to ask her later for a summary. He could smell her light perfume and it reminded him of when they used to sit in church together back in Virginia. A wave of memories washed across him, leaving a path of sadness and uncertainty in its wake. At least he was here with her in church now. For that he was thankful, even if he understood little. Her hands were folded in a relaxed pose on her lap. He wished he could take one of them and enfold it in his.

Finally, the pastor started to pray in a loud voice, with eyes closed and hands extended in front of him. He said, "Ah-men," and the people repeated, "Ah-men." Then the musicians took up their instruments and there was a final praise chorus. At the end of the song another man went to the microphone and made some kind of announcement, then everyone stood up.

Conversation bubbled up in the room as people began moving around and greeting each other. As Mark and Lauren stood and their eyes locked together for a moment. She gave him a small smile, but quickly she was swept into a conversation with the woman next to her. Mark kept an eye on Tarek. The two of them seemed unsure of what to do next.

Madame Bénétreau wove through the throngs of people until she reached where they stood in their row. She looked directly at Tarek and clasped her hands together. "My young friend, I am very happy to welcome you to my home today. I hope you will be very comfortable there until we locate your father."

Tarek watched her face as she spoke. He blinked but didn't move, except for his Adam's apple, which expressed his unspoken emotion. The woman looked up at Lauren and Mark and told them, "In a few minutes we'll have our last meeting about the dinner, then I will take Tarek home and get him settled in."

"What dinner is that?" asked Mark.

Her face lit up. "Oh, it's a wonderful thing. We are hosting a banquet to raise money for the refugee ministry. There are several good cooks in the congregation, and they came up with the idea last year. It was a great success, so we're repeating it this year." She turned to Tarek and said, "Just a few more minutes for a short meeting. I know you must be bored and hungry. I'll take you home soon." She smiled at him, gave him a quick squeeze on his shoulder, and hurried off.

Mark turned to Lauren. "When will this banquet take place? Before I leave France?"

"This Wednesday." Lauren gathered her French Bible and a small fabric journal from her chair. "They've already done a lot of the planning for it. The tickets will go on sale tomorrow. This meeting is to finalize the details and make sure everything's ready for Wednesday."

Mark tried to hide his disappointment that their morning at church wasn't yet over. He just wanted to hear English again and be alone with Lauren. She'd planned a picnic for them in a nearby park.

The previous day he'd had to face the fact that he couldn't stay in France much longer. Loose ends were developing in his business. He hoped for closure—one way or the other—with Lauren before that date. It seemed to him that they were getting closer again, so he had trouble reining in his optimism. He only hoped that optimism wasn't misplaced.

Fortunately, the planning meeting didn't last too long. The familiar context of food and a meal made the French words easier for him to follow. When they stood up again Lauren said to him, "I hope you don't mind but I volunteered us to help out at the banquet. Is that okay?"

"Sure." He grinned. "As long as I don't have to talk to anyone in French, I'll do whatever is needed." It was an event he could wholeheartedly support, and as a huge bonus, would get to do it with Lauren. "What will we do?"

"I'll help with cooking, as you would predict." She chuckled. "I knew I wouldn't stay out of a kitchen for too long, but this is entirely different. You may be able to serve and clean up. Or even entertain everyone with ninja fish-cleaning tricks." The old sparkle of mischief he remembered glinted in her eyes.

He laughed. "Or I can do stand-up comedy with my attempts at French."

"Even better!"

They laughed again, then both seemed to remember Tarek. He stood still, this time clutching his bag of belongings in both arms. Mark's heart went out to the little guy and couldn't help but put one arm around his thin shoulders. His round dark eyes found Mark's and he saw pain and anxiety there. Mark leaned down and said, "It's going to be okay, Tarek. We'll still come and see you. I'm sure Madame Bénétreau won't mind."

The boy found a small smile. Mark sent a quick prayer that Tarek would feel comfortable with Madame Bénétreau because he and Lauren would likely both be leaving soon. The last thing he wanted to do was abandon the boy and add to his despair.

When it came time to pass Tarek over to Madame Bénétreau, Mark felt hollow, like his work was done and Tarek's fate was still unknown. He swallowed and looked at the ground as he and Lauren left the building.

"What's up?" she asked, bumping his shoulder with hers as they emerged into the warm sun. "You look so sad."

"I don't know, I just got attached to the little guy. I enjoyed bringing him stuff, looking after him. I knew I'd have to say goodbye sooner or later, but I feel sort of unemployed now." He shrugged.

"Me too. But you'll still see him until you have to leave. And you can keep in touch after and get updates from Madame Bénétreau."

He nodded. He hadn't missed the fact that she'd said "you" instead of "we". Was she planning to stay? If she were, she'd have volunteered to keep him updated. Maybe she was going to leave France soon as well. Now that Jean-Pierre was no longer a factor, she might not have any reason to stay. He could only hope.

They started down the sidewalk in the direction of Tarek's park. Lauren shaded her eyes from the sun as she looked at Mark. "The Saint Jacques hill where we hiked before has a lot of areas we haven't seen. I thought we could go back there, if that's okay with you. That way we won't have to borrow bikes or a car."

"Sounds perfect." Or almost, since he remembered the steepness of the hillside. He did feel in better shape now, though. They passed several plane trees and on the smooth trunks, flyers about an upcoming fair were tacked. Tarek might like that.

They walked toward the hill in silence for a few moments. Tarek must now be on the way to or even in his new home by this time. Mark pictured him being shown to his new room, putting away his few belongings in a wooden dresser, arranging the few toys Mark had given him in a closet, sitting down to lunch with Madame Bénétreau. Was the boy still feeling afraid, sent to live with this stranger? He hoped Tarek was relieved to have a home, a bed, but it was hard to discern his thoughts and hopes. What he'd been through was difficult to imagine.

"Are you thinking of Tarek?" she asked.

"Mmm hmm. You?"

"Yes. I wonder how he'll do with Madame Bénétreau. She's so nice, but it's a big change for him."

"Exactly what I was thinking."

"He'll be okay, once he adjusts to everything. One thing I have to do tomorrow is either call or drop by the OFPRA office to let them know his new contact information. That way, once we're not here anymore, they can still reach him."

Mark nodded. So, she *was* planning to leave France. A wave of hope welled up inside him. Maybe he should just come out and ask her what her plans were. She likely didn't know all of them.

"Jean-Pierre texted me earlier."

Words to break his happy bubble. "What did he say?"

"Just that he was sorry he'd blown up at me and wanted to make it up to me."

"Hmm. Nice of him." Mark couldn't keep the acrid tone from his voice. "But it doesn't change anything, does it? You told me you had little in common with him, even if he *is* sorry." More blunt and transparent than he intended.

She shot a glare at him as they walked. "He gets points for recognizing his unfairness." Her voice defended the man who seemed, once again, to be Mark's competitor.

"I wonder if he was thinking of Tarek's need, or just that he was sorry for losing you." Mark knew he should leave it alone, since she could interpret his words as pressure. But he only had a week left with her. They started climbing the familiar steep hill toward the St. Jacques chapel. He'd try to pace himself on the hill this time.

Lauren didn't answer for a moment. From the corner of his eye he saw her shrug. "It was just a text message. I'll have to talk to him to find out what he's thinking."

He wanted to tell her not to let Jean-Pierre put her under his spell again but held his tongue. She wasn't a child. And she wouldn't like his interference, telling her what to do. He'd have to trust her judgment and even more, continue trusting God with her.

When they arrived at the top of the hill, he glimpsed the stone cross of the chapel over the treetops. Lauren hitched her head to the right. "We can go down that trail. There's another nice overlook there that we haven't visited together."

A few minutes later they were settled in a clearing that overlooked a valley on the other side of the hill. A circle of trees gave the impression of an enchanted secret meadow. Perfect place to spend time with Lauren.

"I brought a blanket," she said. "Today I was more efficient than usual."

"I remember you as being very efficient. Always. I'm sure you still are." He helped her spread out the blanket. When he sat down, he noticed she sat close to him and brushed his arm or his leg as she unpacked her knapsack.

She'd prepared sandwiches on baguettes and included fruit, a small, grated carrot salad in a plastic container, a bottle of orange juice, small cups and plastic forks, and what looked like a pastry box. He'd had enough French pastry to be enthused about what was in that box. More than the food, though, he wanted to know Lauren's thoughts about him. About them. After three weeks. He was terrified to ask and uttered another silent prayer.

Mark grasped her hands, warm and soft, in his and said a brief prayer for the meal. He rubbed his thumb over her hand during his prayer, like he used to while they were dating. When he said, "Amen" she squeezed them and locked gazes with him for more than a second. He felt swallowed whole in her green eyes fringed with dark lashes. A tingle of warmth washed over him, but he gave himself an internal warning. Which did no good at all.

After they ate the sandwiches, she slowly unpacked the small pastry box, as if unveiling a national treasure. "I don't know if you've had this one before. It's called an *opéra* and it's decadent."

Sure *looked* decadent. Mark was a fan of chocolate, and he was sure its multiple layers of chocolate cream and melted chocolate wouldn't disappoint. "Mmm. Tastes as good as it looks."

When they'd finished eating the pastry and licking their fingers, they both leaned back on elbows and stretched out to digest. He wanted to talk on a deeper level without scaring her away. How to begin? He'd never had this problem before with her. "You've been here a month or so," he stated. "How would you evaluate your visit so far? Aside from the fact that restaurant work is still not for you."

She didn't seem to be threatened or invaded by his question. Instead, she cocked her head with a pondering look. "I think some of the pieces are coming in, little details here and there. I didn't tell you yet that Claire, the caterer I met, needs my help tomorrow evening. One of her employees is sick. That'll be a chance to try a different food setting. I'm looking forward to that."

He nodded. "Good. Maybe you'll have some impressions that will guide you. Or else help you eliminate it, which would also be a help." He waited, hoping she'd say more. About him, about them.

She didn't but stared at him a moment. "I'm glad you came to France, Mark." Her features softened and her voice was gentle.

Heat rose up inside him. She was only inches away. Was she trying to say something? She smiled softly and leaned toward him to wipe a smear of chocolate from his cheek. Her closeness, the intimacy of the gesture left a hot glow on his face.

When she didn't pull back, he leaned toward her, closing the distance between them. He slid a hand behind her neck and pulled her forward. When he covered her lips with his, her softness and the taste of her invaded his senses. It had been so long. So very long.

Lauren didn't draw back from him. When she wrapped her arms around his neck and leaned into him, he gently lowered her to the blanket and shifted his weight as he continued kissing her, savoring everything about her. She tasted like chocolate and promise, one he'd been waiting for. A small sound of pleasure escaped from her throat as he renewed his kiss and ran his fingers along her cheek.

He pulled back and stared down at her, stroking her hair gently. She stared back for a moment, but the tenderness in her eyes suddenly became cool. She turned her head away as tears glistened in her eyes and fell down her cheeks toward her ears.

Mark stilled, a cold grip reaching inside him. "Is something wrong?"

Lauren struggled to pull herself up. She pulled her knees close, as if suddenly wanting to protect herself. "Mark, I—" She frowned and sighed. "That was lovely, and I've thoroughly enjoyed your visit. I can't deny that I have felt more for you, for our relationship, than in the last year. Something is there and might be growing, but I still don't know that I can promise you anything. I just have to tell you that."

He felt like he'd been slapped. He swallowed hard. Shook his head in disbelief. "Lauren, you felt something then. I know you did. You *feel* something for me. If you deny it, I'll leave you alone."

Lauren looked stricken, her face pale. "Yes, I do feel something for you, Mark. Like I said, it's grown since you've been here, but I can't trust it. That's the problem. I have to be *sure* that my feelings won't do what they did last time. They just faded away. What if we got back together and that happened again? I can't do that to you again, Mark. I just can't."

Yes, you can. He wanted to cry out. Something inside was tearing. All the progress he thought he'd made felt like ashes now, dispersing in the summer breeze, leaving nothing behind but a gray puff of smoke. He'd come for nothing. He'd leave with . . . nothing. But some memories, a heartache for both Tarek and what he would never have with Lauren.

"Lauren, we could always try. Date a while, casually if you want. I'm willing to risk it." He made sure she was returning his gaze, but her face had closed. "But not for long," he added.

"I—I know that to some degree love is a decision. It isn't all about romantic feelings. But there has to be—"

He held up his hand and she stopped speaking. He couldn't bear to hear again how she had lost her passion for him. Her kiss certainly said otherwise.

In the gap of silence, he spoke. "Lauren, I've told you this before. This is the last time I'll say it, I promise. You'll never hear this from me again. You lived through a loss that you've never processed and never healed from. In your unconscious, you're accustomed to drama. It feels somehow— familiar. What you and I had was stable. It wasn't drama. It was real and it was healthy." He almost said "boring", but that was *his* issue, not theirs. "Jean-Pierre seemed exciting to you because he was different and exotic. In the day to day, he'll be more difficult, I guarantee you. I think you'd regret being with him. In fact, you've already had a taste of that."

He stopped. She seemed to have closed off, hugging her knees even tighter as she looked down at the grass. She didn't look angry. She looked deeply sad. Broken. Tears tumbled from her eyes and tracked down her cheeks.

He sighed. "But of course, this isn't about Jean-Pierre. Lauren, I'm leaving this week." Her head jerked back to him and he saw the tragedy on her face. More tears filled her eyes and spilled out. He swallowed. "I came here to be with you and see if we could work things out, but I have to leave now." A sob threatened to fill his throat. He pushed it down even as the despair billowed up inside his chest cavity. "I've waited a year and I guess it isn't meant to be. I was mistaken." His voice cracked as he spoke. He was broken, emptied out.

Mark stood up. Lauren scrambled to her feet, and she faced him. "No, it wasn't a mistake. I loved being with you, Mark." She wrung her hands. "I'm so sorry. I don't know what else to say. I can't let you get your hopes up at this point. I'm still not there yet. I may be one day but I can't promise you anything. It wouldn't be fair."

"I can't wait for you anymore, Lauren." He hated to say the words, but it was true. It had been a year. He had to let go. He blinked away tears that stung his eyes and bent down to pack up the picnic basket and fold the blanket. They walked silently down the hill. Fortunately, she stayed a few steps behind him. She couldn't see the tears that escaped and rolled hot tracks down his cheeks.

Chapter Sixteen

"Please take the potatoes from the oven, Jerôme, and distribute them onto those plates over there." Lauren indicated a row of plates already filled with veal chops. The teenager nodded back at her and slipped his hands into oven mitts. The din in the rented kitchen was considerable, from clanking dishware and ten volunteers from the small church. With such a small congregation they had an impressive ratio of involved members.

For the banquet they'd been able to rent a community hall that had plenty of space and a professional kitchen for a low price. Church members had spent the afternoon decorating the dining room with banners, paper chandeliers for elegant lighting, and maps on the largest walls indicating where most of the refugees in France had originated from. The room was full of town residents who supported the cause. And some who didn't particularly, such as Jean-Pierre, who had come, perhaps, to get back into Lauren's good graces. Or maybe he'd had a change of heart. She was glad that his first exposure to the church was such a positive one. Maybe it would lead him back there once she was gone. And she soon needed to be gone. Answers or not.

"Sophie, the béchamel sauce—it's about to boil. Thanks." The previous day when the designated banquet chef had sprained her ankle, Lauren was the obvious replacement in the eyes of the committee. She'd accepted with pleasure. Not only was it a chance to dedicate her culinary training to a truly worthy cause, but it would also take her mind off of her heartache.

Instead of abating since Sunday afternoon, her sorrow deepened with every passing hour, especially as she looked through the doorway and across the dining room at Mark's sullen face. She knew she'd broken his heart again, made him regret coming to France. That knowledge, in addition to the certainty that she'd lost him maybe even as a friend, was like a knife inside her. And then there was the equally painful possibility that he really *was* the man for her, but her emotional state blocked her from seeing it.

She sighed. If she didn't believe in God's sovereignty in these matters, she'd want to scream.

On Sunday at the end of their walk she'd asked him if he still planned to help with the banquet. He'd woodenly responded, "Of course. I made a promise and I'll keep it. For Tarek." He'd kept that promise by clearing off tables, pouring coffee, water, and wine, washing dishes, sweeping the sanctuary and helping to decorate it, and replenishing napkins. Although she'd been in the kitchen most of the evening, her conscience led her to check on him frequently through the open doorway from the small but well-equipped kitchen. It was a blessing that they weren't working in the same room. He'd been cordial to her since the Sunday picnic, but gone was the closeness they'd shared, exchanged glances, a passing touch of their fingers. Right before the banquet started, he informed her that he had a flight out the following day. He was going home, leaving her—and them— behind.

Despite the despair weighing down in her stomach hour after hour throughout the evening, the banquet appeared to be a raving success. The banquet hall was packed with local residents as well as those from neighboring towns who had a special burden for the plight of refugees. Between the main course and the dessert was the designated time slot for a stirring address by Bertrand Foquet, the head of the church committee.

Lauren had a moment's rest before she had to prepare the dessert, so she stood in the back of the room to listen. She scanned the room for Jean-Pierre and saw him at a round table near the door. He stared at her and flicked his fingers in a small wave. He'd left several messages and they hadn't talked yet, but she had texted him about the event. She nodded and smiled back at him then turned back to the speaker.

"Though France has always received refugees, the number of applicants for asylum in France far exceeds the number that are accepted." Mr. Foquet's voice resounded through the room from the stage. On the screen behind him were heart-rending photos of children and families walking with possessions on their backs or living in squalor in refugee camps, close-up photos of frightened children, of crying infants.

"Once they are accepted, there isn't always a good system in place to integrate them into a new life. These are people from all walks of life, professionals, workers, students, housewives—people like you and me who have lost their livelihood, their homes, their cities. Many have lost family members. When they apply for asylum, they wait months or longer to know if they are accepted, and sadly, most are not. Then they have to begin all over somewhere else. You all know the stories about refugee camps, where thousands of people live in inhuman conditions, just waiting for their lives to begin again. Our mission is to help those who come here to

Cavaillon. They come here from various places, Syria, Afghanistan, Albania, Sudan, and elsewhere. They leave situations of danger and war or political threats. We cannot help all of them, of course, but we help those we can. To do this we need your help. Your compassion, first. Then of course, your financial participation." Ticket prices as well as donations would go toward the refugee fund.

Lauren averted her eyes from the photos. Between the sad situation of Tarek and others like him and Mark, she had more grief than she could handle. If only she could go to Mark and tell him she loved him, that his visit had rekindled her heart for him. She knew in her head that he was good for her and that something concrete *had* rekindled, but she needed to know it wouldn't evaporate like dew on a sunny day. She *did* feel something for him—a lot, lately. But she didn't trust herself, and her confusion and lack of trust formed a dam inside her, reinforcing the blockage she'd carried for so many years.

"Lauren, the meal was fabulous. Everyone says so," Madame Bénétreau whispered to her as she approached the kitchen door.

Lauren smiled at the woman. "Thank you, Madame Bénétreau. Is Tarek doing well at your home?"

"Yes, he is settling in. He is very quiet. Well, it's only been a few days, but I think he is warming up little by little. Mark came to say goodbye to him this afternoon. Tarek was very sad, but promised to write him letters. Mark looked very sad as well to be saying goodbye."

Lauren smiled, feeling an invisible hand grip her stomach. Her eyes burned, but Madame Bénétreau seemed not to notice. "Good, I'm glad Tarek is settling in and had a chance to say goodbye to Mark. It's wonderful that Tarek has a home now." Lauren had given Tarek's new address to the OFPRA office so they could find him. There wasn't really anything else she could do for Tarek besides pray for his father to be found and stop by occasionally to check on him until she herself left France. Tarek would surely miss Mark, who had been a literal lifeline as well as a friend to the boy. She also would miss Mark in ways that went beyond words.

Mr. Foquet was winding down. "Thank you all for your attention this evening," he said. "I hope you are informed as well as touched by the situation of refugees in France. We will serve dessert and coffee or tea now. There is a box on each table for those who would like to give a contribution to our work and there are extra brochures on the tables."

The din of conversation rose again, and Lauren slipped back into the kitchen to supervise the dessert. The next day Mark would leave. He hadn't asked to see her before his flight. He'd given up on them. She didn't blame him. How long could she expect him to wait until she fully understood her feelings for him? If she were completely neutral for him that would be easier than this zone of renewed affection that she didn't know would last. She'd plunged fully into his kisses, savoring them, wanting more of him. Right before she turned away. No wonder he was hurt and confused. She was, too.

Lauren shook her head. She must be mentally ill, just like her mother. How could she not know her own mind, after spending two years dating Mark? Now he'd go and find someone else, and it would be her fault.

೮౩ ೮౩ ೮౩

Mark shifted his weight in the passport control line at Dulles Airport in Washington, D.C. He'd arrived on U.S. soil and he wasn't sure how he felt about it. Didn't matter. He had to go on. He'd had seven hours in the plane to think about it, his efforts, his persistence. Clearly, Lauren wasn't the woman God had for him and the sooner he accepted that fact, the less pain he'd endure. He'd already invested over a year waiting and spent a month in France hoping Lauren would change her heart. He'd previously reserved a ticket for Saturday but didn't see any point staying until then. He decided to fulfill his commitment at the banquet and leave the following morning.

The line inched forward as sleepy travelers dragged their baggage through the roped lanes. Mark felt grumpy and likely looked it too. He hadn't bothered to shave that morning and had put on rumpled clothing to match the way he felt. Maybe that's why no one addressed a word to him during the seven-hour flight. Everything about his appearance sent a warning.

Logan had offered to meet him at the airport, but he'd declined. He needed time to pull himself together emotionally, as well as take stock and tune up his business, his house, and his life. Dina was still in waiting mode with the baby, but she likely wouldn't last too long.

Mark dragged his duffle bag on the floor as the line advanced, too tired to hold it. Some of his fellow travelers glowed from their vacation in Paris or elsewhere and loudly describe various places and incidents. Despite his sadness over how *his* trip had ended, he couldn't deny that he treasured his weeks in France as well. Helping Tarek had been a high point, helping Didier with his fish, getting a taste of the country Lauren so loved. He'd enjoyed the market atmosphere, his new French acquaintances, Tarek. Even Lauren, just being with her and having a friendship again. He hadn't been neutral about her, though, and maybe that had created pressure, despite signs that her heart had warmed up to him again.

When he reached the passport desk the agent asked him, "Was your trip for business or pleasure?"

He wasn't sure how to respond to that and ended up with "pleasure." Close enough.

He dialed Logan. "Just got here to the airport."

"Hey, Mark, great to hear you on this side of the ocean. I'm eager to hear how everything went. We lost touch over the last couple or so weeks."

"Uh . . . Yeah, sorry about that. It went well, except for at the end. I want to see you guys but need to keep it light." His eyes burned. He looked up at the fluorescent lights overhead, hoping they'd sizzle out any temptation to let tears flow.

"Oh." Logan's voice dropped. "Dude, sorry. Sounds like what you wanted didn't happen. Hey, can you come by tomorrow or the next day? Baby's coming any moment, but as long as he's not here we'd love to see you."

"Sure thing." Mark couldn't keep the dullness out of his voice. He hung up and blinked once, twice. Time to go home. Time to move on.

ca ca ca

Glowing candles cast a dancing glow across the elegant table and reflected in the crystal glasses of the guests. Only a few people lingered at the table now, sipping on their digestifs, dirty dessert plates in front of each seat. It was nearly midnight. Lauren and Claire exchanged glances and smiled, a silent congratulations for a successful event. They both leaned near the doorway, waiting for the moment to clear everything. It wouldn't be long now. Lauren's feet ached, but she felt satisfied with the flow and results of the evening. She'd felt the same way the previous Saturday night, when she'd been able to help Claire for the first time.

The women returned to the kitchen. "May as well start putting these things away," Claire said. "Otherwise, it will be an even later night, if we wait for everyone to leave. Once again you did great,

Lauren. You have a lot of intuition about catering. Did you tell me you'd never done it before?"

Lauren's hands were moving quickly, pulling utensils from the dishwasher and loading them into a case of cutlery that Claire had brought. Her unhappy thoughts threatened to keep pace, but she pushed them down. She couldn't afford to let them escape from the carefully sealed box where she'd trapped them. "That's true, I haven't catered before Saturday, other than what I did in my previous tour business." Le Bon Voyage seemed decades past instead of just a year.

"And what do you think?" Claire leaned back against a counter and crossed her arms. Her smooth face was open with anticipation, her blue eyes wide in expectation.

Lauren stopped arranging the silverware and looked up at her. "I really enjoyed our event the other night and also this evening. I like doing the parties. I loved that you organized the whole evening down to the table décor."

"Better than restaurant work?"

"Oh, much better. I'm so glad you asked me to help you. When I came to France, I only knew that I didn't want to work in a restaurant kitchen. But what was the first thing I did? Worked in a restaurant kitchen." She let out a hollow laugh. With a pang she remembered what a mess she'd made since her arrival in France.

"I think you told me your friend persuaded you, right?" Claire's voice was soft.

Claire was easy to talk to and Lauren felt a sudden and uncharacteristic need to spill out her story. "Last year I came to France and while I was here, I met him. He owns a restaurant in Cavaillon, *Chez Jean-Pierre*."

"Yes, I know the restaurant. Not the man, I've only seen him from a distance."

"Since last year he's wanted me to come visit, so I decided to come and see if there was anything to the relationship."

"And? What have you decided about him?" Claire's grin urged Lauren to say more.

"I like him—I liked him more at first. But when his sous-chef quit, he had me fill in as a chef in his kitchen. It created tension, then my old boyfriend showed up—"

"Wait, what?" Claire stood up straighter. "Your American former boyfriend came to France?"

"Yes, he came and surprised me." Lauren grinned at the memory of their stand-off in front of Jean-Pierre's restaurant that first day. He'd stood there looking jetlagged and uncertain.

"Your face changes when you talk about him. I want to know more about *him*." Claire was grinning now.

Lauren covered her cheeks with her hands. "Oh, that's not a good story. It didn't end well." She related some of her history with Mark and the way her feelings for him had gradually faded.

"But he came all the way to France to get you back. Didn't that make you love him again?"

Lauren's mouth opened but no words came out. Finally, "Uh— I'm not sure. That's the honest truth. I have no idea. Yes, I started feeling something for him again, quite a lot, actually. But I don't trust myself, so I couldn't make any promises. He left yesterday." To her surprise tears sprang into her eyes.

Claire looked perplexed but approached Lauren to put both arms around her. She was silent while Lauren cried for a moment. Lauren pulled back and Claire fished a paper napkin from one of the boxes and handed it to her. "You're crying but you also sent him away. I'm confused, Lauren."

"So am I!" Her tears renewed for a moment and she mopped them with the napkin. Her insides felt like twisted ropes. And frankly, this darned crying was becoming an inconvenient nuisance. She couldn't stop it if she tried. Was she finally unblocking? Maybe Mark had been the catalyst, or Tarek, who she'd seen earlier that afternoon as she stopped by to check on him.

"I wonder if you're still really in love with Mark. It seems that way to me."

Claire didn't understand the situation. Mark was comfortable, after two years. But did that mean Lauren should be with him? Was she really in love with him? Was there more to it than familiarity and appreciation for his qualities? She'd said the other day that he was exactly what she needed. "I wish I knew if I was in love with him and if I would *stay* in love with him. Right *now,* it feels like I still love him. But will it last? That's what I'm afraid of, Claire. It happened before."

The woman looked thoughtful. "I see what you mean, why you're afraid. I do think it's common to lose feelings for someone, but it's *not* common to get them back, as you have. Maybe there's a reason for that."

"I never thought of that." It was true. She'd had a definite resurgence of passion for Mark during his visit and she missed him terribly now. She looked down at her hands. No need to mention Mark's theory of her past tragedy causing emotional repression. Lauren took a deep breath. "He's a great guy and I know I'm missing this chance . . . because I can't make up my mind." Lauren gave her a lopsided smile at her lame attempt at humor, but she knew that wasn't the real problem. If it were only a matter of making up her mind, she'd be on a flight right now.

Wouldn't she?

Where had that thought come from? Maybe she was in love with Mark but the last to know it. Oh, Lord. How was she ever going to know? What else could she do? She'd given it time, she'd spent time with another man, she'd prayed until she ran out of words.

Claire turned away and began stacking plastic containers of unused food. "Just think about it. Maybe making up your mind is all you really need to do." She turned and placed a hand on Lauren's shoulder. There was compassion in her gaze. "Lauren, I don't know you very well. I can see that you're sad without Mark, but you looked happy when you talked about him just now. That's pure observation on my part, I'm no psychologist. Though . . . maybe it wouldn't hurt to talk to one, if you think that would help."

Lauren gave Claire a wry smile and wiped her drying tears with one wrist. "I'll think about it." And pray about it. And maybe see a psychologist too.

Chapter Seventeen

The familiar gray front door opened, and Logan's six-foot height filled the space. Before Mark could greet him, Logan swept him into a bear hug and gave him two thumps on his back. "Welcome back, Dude. Come on in. What can I get you?"

"I'll take a beer, if you have it. Good to see you." Despite his heartache, Mark felt warmed by his best friend's loving welcome as well as the familiar surroundings of Logan's home. Initially, Mark had had some trouble readjusting to American life, décor, roads, signs. He found himself looking for outdoor markets, crêperies, boulangeries, people on bikes. Flower shops with colorful plants scattered on the sidewalk, the cheese shop, the boucherie, the lyrical and staccato sound of French conversations floating in the air. The absence of these familiar pleasures and habits deepened the hollow that already weighed down inside him.

He'd put Logan off for a couple of days so he could regroup and sort out his thoughts and emotions. It would require more time, of course, but standing in Logan's hallway just then, he knew there was a path out of the shadows of his sadness.

Since his return he'd tried to skirt around persistent thoughts of Lauren, but still he found himself wondering what she was doing, how she was feeling, and if she had reunited with Jean-Pierre. He'd need to be strict with himself, even brutal, in thrusting those thoughts from his mind. For the moment, he still lacked the strength.

Logan said, "Mind hanging in the kitchen with me? Dina's got a few things to do upstairs. You know, everything takes her longer since she's so—big. She asked me to keep an eye out here." He pulled open the fridge and handed Mark a beer.

Mark pulled a stool up to the granite island and popped off the cap while Logan checked the oven temperature and tossed a few foil-wrapped baked potatoes inside it.

Logan turned back to Mark, leaning his forearms on the counter. His voice was subdued. "I gather things didn't work well with Lauren. No need to go into detail if you don't want to talk about it. We're just here for you."

"Thanks. I know you are and it means a lot to me." Mark cleared his throat then took a swallow of beer. Maybe after a brief summary they could talk about other things. "Things went—well, they actually *did* go pretty well for a while. It seemed like she was warming up to the idea of *us* again. I was optimistic. Probably shouldn't have been. But she has this fear of losing her attraction again and hurting me again. But it's—" Mark waved one hand in the air, "—it's complicated. She has reasons from her past to be afraid of emotion, so there's this whole background—"

Mark shook his head, fearing he'd said too much, starting on a path he wasn't willing to continue. He wouldn't divulge the details of Lauren's past. Part of him wanted to talk about something worlds apart from Lauren Abbott. The other part felt the need to lay out his raw feelings and sift through them before wrapping them in a box for burial.

"So, what'll you do now?"

Mark shrugged and looked up brightly. Forced, of course, and likely not too convincing. "I guess I'll catch up on my clients, my yard work, friendships. I have plenty to do. I've been gone a month." Maybe he'd dig out that phone number for Becky, the woman he'd met during his last dinner with Logan.

"Of course, you'll do all that. But what will you do about Lauren? Is it . . . done?"

The lump in Mark's throat thickened at Logan's words. He swallowed. "Um—yes, I guess it is. I'm sure we'll stay friends."

Logan's dark brows knit together, and he shook his head. "Not sure that's a good idea, at least initially. Once you get some distance from this trip, you know, let some time go by, you'll be able to be friends. I've been through that, the 'let's stay friends' thing with a past girlfriend before I met Dina. It took me a year to fully let go. I wouldn't want to see that happen to you. Might seem brutal, but you'll heal faster in the long run." Logan grabbed two fat vine tomatoes from where they sat on the counter, removed the stems, and sliced them into chunks. He slid them into a bowl already filled with baby spinach and arugula.

Mark looked down at the rim of his beer bottle. Noticed the way the light from the hanging lamp overhead reflected off the edges. Tried to keep the sting from his eyes. Tried not to think of what it would be like to *not* at least be friends with Lauren. To cut off completely.

But Logan was probably right, even though he spoke like a happily married man expecting his first child and light years away from his dimly-remembered heartache. Maybe Mark, too, would be in that place one day, looking back on Lauren . . . *who*? How long would that take, since she still had a mile-deep foothold in his heart?

If she'd been cold or platonic toward him during his visit, it would be easier to close the door and consider it futile. But she'd warmed to him, been attracted again to him. He'd seen it in her eyes. And her kiss, that *kiss* . . . it was genuine. Right before she pulled away.

He hadn't written to her since his return a few days earlier. She hadn't either. There was simply nothing to say. Now he had the daunting task of repairing his heart.

Logan had just finished salting and peppering the steaks when they heard a wail from upstairs.

"Dina? Honey, is everything okay?" Logan shouted.

Then Dina's voice from upstairs. "He's coming!" In an instant, Logan vanished from the kitchen and bounded up the stairs. The sound of his feet thumping on the steps reached Mark in the kitchen. A few minutes later his steps thudded down the stairs again and he appeared with a canvas tote in one hand. He handed it to Mark. "Can you take this to the car for me? I'll go get Dina. Her water just broke. We're going to the hospital."

০৪ ০৪ ০৪

Lauren fiddled with the tassel on her woven purse as she sat in Doctor Renard's waiting room. Around her were worn pastel-colored couches and chairs and the requisite coffee table with magazines. Late morning sun spilled in hazy patches through the white lacy curtains on the tall French windows.

She'd had an early appointment with the doctor. He'd done a physical and taken blood, and she now waited for her test results. She couldn't concentrate, though she'd tried to read an article in a women's magazine. Her thoughts boomeranged around in her head and her heart still ached over what had happened with Mark. She hadn't heard from him since his departure five days earlier. She guessed he was settling back into American life, albeit with a bruised heart of his own. He was moving on to a new chapter without her.

Doctor Renard was a fiftyish man with a thinning layer of white-blond hair, a round face whose ruddy texture reminded her of a ham, and the kindest eyes she'd ever seen. For these gentle, blue eyes she'd been immensely relieved, and felt her tension melt as she began to recount her concerns to him.

She'd planned to talk to him only about her mother's medical condition, but once she started speaking, everything had come tumbling out—her painful response to her mother's death, her teenage means of coping, her loss of passion for Mark, her change of heart for Le Bon Voyage business she'd had with Bree, and her fear and confusion about her ability to commit to anything or anyone at all. With each new revelation her tears came faster and stronger, emerging from a seemingly bottomless crevasse inside her.

Dr. Renard had listened attentively, compassion etched on his face. He handed her tissues, one after another. Afterward, he'd taken a blood sample, at her insistence, since he hadn't thought it was necessary.

Even before Claire's suggestion that she see a counselor, Lauren had decided once for all to find out if she had her mother's "crazy gene". She had no idea if such a thing existed or she was a carrier, or if her mother's particular weaknesses could even be transmitted. In her gut she knew that her mother's illness probably had nothing medically to do with her *own* emotional frozenness, but she'd do whatever it took, step by step, to learn why her life was falling apart. She was ready, desperate, to do it now.

"Mademoiselle Abbott . . ." A female voice pulled Lauren from her tortured thoughts. "Your results are ready. Doctor Renard will see you now."

She pulled herself up from her chair, grabbed her shoulder bag, and followed the nurse back to Dr. Renard's office.

"Sit here, will you, Miss Abbott?" The doctor gestured toward a straight-back chair next to a large corner desk, instead of the examination table on the other side of the room where he'd first spoken to her. He sat down beside her, instead of behind the massive desk covered with files and papers.

Lauren sat down, perched stiffly on the chair's edge. She reminded herself to relax and leaned against the wooden back. Deep breath. Swallow, breathe.

He pulled a document from the stack on his desk and peered over it. Laid it down and swiveled his chair to face her. He leaned forward with his elbows on his knees, hand folded together, and looked at her with a gentle expression, like a kindly father addressing a frightened child.

"As I suspected, there is no indication in your blood sample that there is anything abnormal you might have inherited from your mother. I have also ruled out any thyroid disorder that could mimic symptoms of depression. Your physical was normal. According to your description, your mother had long-term emotional disturbances, including clinical depression, that required much medication and repeated hospital stays." He'd previously stated that if she'd never had any symptoms similar to her mother's, she was probably not a candidate.

Lauren's muscles relaxed and she gulped air into a deep well inside her as relief coursed through her. She nodded. "That's good news, that I haven't inherited anything, um—like that." She attempted a smile she didn't feel.

Dr. Renard's face was solemn. "What you've told me about your response to her suicide suggests that, as a young teenager, you coped the best way you could. You didn't have therapy, no family structure except for the aunt you told me about who wasn't very nurturing. You found comfort in religion and the church. But that may have intercepted your mourning process. I wonder if all these years, you've been afraid to express your deep feelings about your mother, and this has affected other deep emotions, such as those for your boyfriend."

Lauren opened her mouth to speak, and nothing came out. She'd heard something similar before, from Mark, from Jean-Pierre. When she found her voice, she asked him, "What do you mean about my faith intercepting my mourning process?"

Dr. Renard cocked his head to one side. "When you were telling me the story of your mother, you said once or twice that God had helped you with your grief and that He showed you how to find joy. I don't doubt that your faith has helped you and that you have joy in it. That is legitimate. I myself believe, so I know what you mean. Yet, we can sometimes short-circuit the healing process by thinking we *shouldn't* feel grief or sadness. We end up stuffing those emotions down and calling it faith or joy. What it really is, Lauren, is repression. The grief hasn't gone away, it's been closed off. And if it hasn't gone away, that means it is still there, but hidden."

She nodded. Swallowed. She'd always thought her pain had simply faded away, replaced by maturity and the present. Was it simply buried under layers of emotional concrete? She shifted in her chair, feeling a cramp of discomfort. Wasn't that more or less what Mark had said to her? But this time his words, and those of Dr. Renard, were penetrating like insistent, massaging fingers pressing into her denial.

Her emotions were in turmoil, yet her mind had to know answers. "How do you think this might have caused me to lose my positive feelings for my boyfriend and for my business?"

Dr. Renard leaned back in his chair and stroked his chin. "My opinion? I think you are very afraid of emotions. You are afraid of all emotions, and your fear doesn't distinguish between positive and negative. You're afraid, at some level, that if you let go and *feel*, you'll end up like your mother. Not suicidal, necessarily, but losing control of yourself."

Lauren's breath hitched and her throat tightened. Her eyes filled and her voice emerged as a ragged whisper. "Really?"

Doctor Renard nodded gravely.

"What do you think I should do?" She blinked rapidly a few times.

"I can't tell you exactly. If it were me, I'd meet with a counselor at some point. But in the meantime, try to feel everything you can. Make an effort. Think about your mother, as painful as it may be. Process the feelings you have about her. If feelings of grief come, embrace them. Then go about your life. Embrace emotions, don't run away from them. And trust God with your feelings, because He created them."

She sat still for a moment, her thoughts whirling around in her skull. Tears filled her eyes again and as they spilled over, she smiled. "Thank you, Doctor Renard. Thank you so much." She stood.

He stood up and faced her. "If you still have doubts, you can have some genetic testing done once you return to the states." Dr. Renard walked to the door and held out his hand to her, which she gratefully shook. "I wish you the best. All you need to do now, Lauren, is heal. And go enjoy your life, all of it."

After letting herself out through the front door of Dr. Renard's Avignon office, Lauren strolled slowly, deliberately through the city's medieval streets for an hour, observing the picturesque charm on every corner, feeling the balmy summer breeze, and mentally sifting through what the doctor had said to her. A layer of calm and a filmy, light emotion she almost couldn't identify—hope—settled over her. Thankfully, she didn't have the crazy gene, but she did have some work to do on herself. She'd tried to avoid the past for too long. She needed to look at it square in the face and admit the ways in which it seeped through her protective cracks, contaminating the present. Then she'd be able to move on. Whether that led her back to Mark one day or not, she had to climb out of the shadows of avoidance. She needed to emerge into the sunlight of fearless confrontation and healing.

The train ride back to Cavaillon wasn't long, and reminded her of the first time she'd made the trip six weeks earlier. She'd been knotted with anxiety and anticipation at the thought of a reunion with Jean-Pierre. It seemed like ancient history now. They hadn't talked yet about their conflict or their relationship, but she already felt a sense of closure there. Her heart had already moved on.

When she descended from the train at Cavaillon and crossed the footbridge toward the other side, she could see in the distance the upper arc of a Ferris wheel gently turning, with tiny, distant silhouettes of people swinging their legs from their seats. She'd seen the posters tacked to tree trunks the week before. The summer festival had come to life.

The rest of the afternoon lay before her and she missed seeing Tarek, so she mounted the sloping sidewalk in the direction of Madame Bénétreau's home. Hopefully, he'd be there.

Lauren rang the bell of the metal gate outside the woman's house. Minutes later the front door opened, and she emerged, a distraught expression pulling her normally cheerful features down. "Oh, Lauren. You're here, but too late to say goodbye to Tarek."

"Goodbye? Did he find his father? What do you mean, where did he go?" That would make her day even better, to hear that Tarek's father had been located, but Madame Bénétreau was shaking her head. When she lifted her face, Lauren saw tears in her eyes.

Panic gripped Lauren's chest. She reached out a hand and touched the woman's shoulder. "What happened?"

"Oh, Lauren. I don't understand the government. Doesn't make any sense to me. I got a call this morning from the refugee office and they told me they were sending Tarek to a *foyer* in Lyon, to live with other boys in his situation. Like a group home or something. Someone came to get him an hour ago."

"Oh no!" Lauren's hand flew to her mouth. "Why would they do that when he had a stable home with you?" Tears sprang to her eyes. Another trial for poor Tarek. She blinked and shook her head. Her grief churned into frustration and anger.

"I don't know, something about the office in Lyon having more resources to locate missing relatives, or something like that. I kept telling them they could phone me with any updates, that they didn't have to have him physically there." The woman was wringing her hands. "He has been through so much. This is the last thing he needs."

Lauren placed her hand on Madame Bénétreau's arm. "Maybe they made a mistake and we can get him back here. I agree, it's no easier for them to locate his father if he's there than if he's here. I'll go to the refugee office tomorrow morning and try to make a case. Was he upset when he had to leave so soon?"

Madame Bénétreau lifted her hands helplessly. "I don't know. He's very stoic, that boy. He's been through too much. He was just getting settled here, starting to talk a bit, but he was only with me for a week when he was taken away."

"I will do everything I can to get him back. This is the best place for him until his father can be found. I'll talk to the same woman I did before at the refugee office. I'll go first thing tomorrow morning, since it's late now."

"Thank you, Lauren. Please let me know what they say. My heart goes out to him."

"Mine too." With a parting smile and watery eyes, the women clutched each other's hands and said a tearful goodbye.

Lauren returned to the street baked by the late afternoon sun, a heavy weight inside her, replacing her previous wave of peace. She almost regretted giving Tarek's information to the refugee office, but knew she hadn't had a choice, if he were ever to be reunited with his father. She longed to talk to Mark, tell him what had happened. He was so calm, so often saw the big picture. He was the only other person who cared about Tarek like she did. But she'd probably burnt her bridges with him. Maybe forever.

She let out a long sigh. She needed to focus on Tarek now. "Lord," she whispered as her feet kept moving, taking her across town with no particular destination. "Please watch over Tarek. There was a reason you allowed him to come to France and allowed me to meet him. There's a reason he ended up connected to this church. I don't know what you are doing in his life, but I thank you for it. Please bring him back."

A sob cut off her final word and her eyes blurred. "And thank you that I don't have the crazy gene, and please guide my path to getting unblocked. I know you can heal everything in me, no matter how deep down it is. And show me your will regarding Mark. Please." By the time she finished her prayer her voice was barely a whisper and a new wave of tears had begun a path down her cheeks.

Lauren continued walking even as tears blurred her vision. Her eyes already burned from crying that morning in Dr. Renard's office. Well, apparently, she wasn't finished yet. She must be making up for all those years she repressed her feelings. *Try to feel everything you can*, Dr. Renard had advised. Now was the time to reach down and touch her deepest sorrows, since she was overwhelmed with grief for the boy.

Lauren spied a small park and slipped inside the gate. She sat down on an empty bench in the deserted park and leaned back, allowing the pent-up sadness to surge out. Her tears flowed silently. She pictured Tarek with strangers, as she had been, alone and confused, feeling like a lone leaf in the wind.

Like Tarek, she'd been forced too young to lose the nurture a child needs. She'd bypassed her own childhood as she watched her mother's mental health swing up and down, as she tried to predict and modify her feelings and behavior accordingly. When she finally arrived at Aunt Kate's apartment, a dry socket in her gut and two suitcases in her hands, she'd hoped for a welcome, for understanding. Instead, in a cold, dutiful home, she'd felt fully the orphan on the day she arrived and every day after that until the moment she came to Christ.

As she sat on the bench in the small park, she grieved those years and the ones before with her mother, when the only thing normal was a fluctuating level of chaos. She grieved the loss of relationship with her sister, Michelle, and the emptiness and solitude that she had felt most of her life. They could have comforted each other, but Michelle's coping style took her to a wild life that left Lauren behind.

Mark and Doctor Renard had been onto something. She'd stuffed the pain from those experiences down deep. It would take a while to dig them out and it wouldn't be easy. She'd made up her mind to go there so she could heal and have a future.

When at last her tears subsided, she felt hollow and washed-out, and her eyes felt like sandpaper, but a wind of peace stole over her again, deeper than it had following her visit with Dr. Renard. She sat still for a few minutes. The hope flickered inside and grew as the moments passed. Her thoughts led her to Mark. She should have agreed to a trial basis with him, at least. Too late now.

Or maybe not. She could no longer deny her feelings for him. They were back in full bloom, stronger than ever. Whether she could trust them or not was another issue. As Claire had said, maybe she only needed to choose to walk in his direction.

She pulled a tissue from her canvas bag and mopped her face. As she did, she became aware of the laughter, music, and the clamor of the festival echoing from a few blocks away. She let herself out of the park gate and followed the noise and the Ferris wheel, still visible over the treetops. By the time she reached the ticket gate, noise enveloped her.

Lauren paid her admission and fell into step with the flow of the crowd. The tang of roasted sausage and the cloying sweetness of sugar and pastries filled the air. In every direction there were splashes of color, booths, crowds in summer attire, umbrellas and awnings. She observed everything carefully, as one seeing it all for the first time, absorbing it with all of her senses. For a moment she imagined what it would be like to be a child in that place. What would she want to do? She hadn't had much of a childhood, so she wasn't sure. The Ferris wheel looked scary, but fun.

Lauren waited a short time in line for the wheel to stop and its passengers to disembark, then mounted the seat that stopped in front of her. She settled into the seat, attached the seatbelt, then held her breath when the wheel began to groan into motion. As it lifted up gently, smoothly, she let out her breath and continued breathing deeply to still her fear.

Fear gave way to wonder as the town became smaller the higher the Ferris wheel climbed. Cavaillon spread out like a carpet before her. Apartments, churches, stores all appeared like a model of a city, or toys in a playroom, and trees like tufts of broccoli and lettuce. She gasped in delight as she identified her house, Jean-Pierre's restaurant, the streets she often traveled on her bike.

Soon she was at the top, and with a rush of emotion, her eyes filled again for the dozenth time that day. For the first time her tears were tears of wonder and joy and sudden blinding certainty that God was carrying her in the present and into the future. She was safe in His arms through the uncertainties of life and emotion. Still safe, up high or low, risking or not, expressing all that was inside her, joy, grief, all her humanness. She was safe.

Taking the risk to live fully wherever God was leading her was similar to riding the Ferris wheel to the top, in a way. She'd been uneasy, no, fearful at first, until the fear was replaced by awe at the beauty, the panorama that put smaller fears into perspective. It was a privileged view she would never find if she continued clinging to safety far below.

She was finished with that. She would no longer preserve a false sense of safety from hiding from fear and denying her feelings. God was big enough to handle all of that and more. It was time to step out, trembling or joyful, to embrace the future.

Chapter Eighteen

Lauren shifted her weight and adjusted her canvas tote bag higher on her shoulder as she waited in the line at the refugee office. The line inched forward slowly as people waited to take a number. Maybe it seemed slower to her than usual because she was anxious to make a plea for Tarek to be returned to Cavaillon. Her eyes roved around the room and into the adjoining one. There seemed to be even more people requesting asylum than there had been the day she'd come with Mark. Hopefully, she would be able to say or do something that would enable Tarek to return.

"Madame? The reason for your visit?" The uniformed official addressed her as he had the first day when she reached the head of the line.

"*Bonjour, Monsieur.* I would like to speak with Madame Lafitte, who I spoke to before about a young Syrian boy who is separated from his family. Yesterday the boy was taken out of a stable home and transferred to a *foyer* in Lyon. I believe he will be better off here in his home until his father is found."

"How old is the boy?"

"He is only twelve. He was staying at the home of a woman here in Cavaillon. I very much want to bring him back here. He has suffered a lot." She didn't know if that would add weight to her plea, she'd try anything that might help.

The man's brow furrowed. "Madame Lafitte, you said?"

She nodded, a thread of hope sweeping inside her. "She's at window nine."

"Go, then, to window nine and wait there to speak with her. Maybe she will have information about the boy, since action was taken on his case only yesterday."

"Merci beaucoup." First step accomplished. Now, if only Madame Lafitte saw things in the same light or even had the ability to do something. She hoped they weren't all powerless before callous laws.

A thought stopped her. Even if that were the case, there was one more powerful. Her shoulders relaxed. Yes, God was more powerful than even the French government. A small, stubborn smile emerged with that truth.

Lauren waited for what seemed like thirty minutes near the same cubicle where she'd met Madame Lafitte the first time. The woman was talking to a family—a man in one chair with a toddler on his lap, a woman with an infant on hers, and another child who must have been six, chewing on his fingers, standing behind his mother's chair. They all looked beleaguered and weary. Lauren sent a silent prayer for the family. She could only guess their story, how far they'd come, how long they'd traveled, what they'd lost.

Finally, the family rose, gathered their children and some belongings, and with hopeless faces, moved away from the cubicle. Lauren approached and sat down. "*Bonjour*, Madame Lafitte, I don't know if you remember me. I was here with a gentleman and we inquired about Tarek Nazari, a young boy of twelve who had been separated from his family."

The woman cocked her head and looked at Lauren's face. "Yes, I remember you. I don't get many Americans here. I remember the two of you."

Lauren shifted her weight forward in the chair, resting her forearms on the desk. "We found a stable home for Tarek with *La Bonne Nouvelle* Church you sent us to. He'd been there only one week when he was taken away to a *foyer* in Lyon. While he was still here, he was getting settled in a home, the most normal life he'd had for months. I'd like to request that he be able to come back." Lauren tried to keep the emotion from her voice, but then she couldn't help herself. "Don't you think a child would be better off in a home than in a *foyer* in a city he doesn't know? He can be reunited with his father either way, can't he?"

Madame Lafitte looked perplexed. Her eyes scrunched behind her glasses. "Nazari, Nazari. That name sounds familiar to me. Something has happened in that case. Let me see." She leaned toward her computer screen and typed something, changed screens several times, typed again. With each minute of delay Lauren's muscles became more taut. Was it good news or bad? Was Tarek's sad story going to have a happy ending?

"Here, I knew it sounded familiar. The boy is returning to Cavaillon because his father has been located."

Lauren's hands flew to her mouth as she gasped, and her eyes filled. "Really? Thank God!" Her eyes raised up involuntarily as tears spilled down her cheeks. She wanted to laugh and cry at the same time. All of her rusty emotional gears must be springing into use at once.

"Yes, it is very good news." A smile that looked genuine spread across Madame Lafitte's face. "His father and uncle have been staying in Avignon. They thought Tarek was there but weren't able to find him, since he was here. When you and your friend came, at least we had a way to contact him, but we only found out late yesterday where the father was."

"Oh, that's wonderful. What's next, Madame Lafitte?"

"We have sent for Tarek to return here to Cavaillon tomorrow. His father would be on his way today, but we didn't have a place for him to stay, so that has been delayed."

"Maybe the lady who helped Tarek has enough room for his father as well. Or she may know someone who does." Lauren didn't know if Madame Bénétreau would be willing to take into her home two grown men in addition to Tarek. Someone at the church would help. She was sure of it.

"Getting Tarek back with his father is a top priority, Madame Lafitte. They have been separated for over three months and Tarek has been living on the streets. This is an emergency, don't you think?"

Madame Lafitte looked up at Lauren, perhaps startled by the urgency in her voice. "Yes, it is. We will send for Mr. Nazari and his brother. You can let me know if someone from *La Bonne Nouvelle* can help."

"I'll call her now." Lauren already had her cell phone in hand. Her fingers shook as she dialed Madame Bénétreau's phone number. Fortunately, the woman answered.

"Madame Bénétreau, Tarek's father has been located." She grinned when she heard the woman's cry of joy on the other end of the line. "We need a place for the three of them to stay. Can the church help?"

"Yes, yes, we will find a way. They can stay here in one of the offices if nothing else. I don't have room for all of them, but someone in the church will, or even someone in the community. What a happy day! Praise God for his oversight in this situation. When is Tarek returning to Cavaillon?"

"He'll be here tomorrow." It was a whirlwind trip to Lyon for Tarek, but at least he was on his way home. Or, on his way back to Cavaillon, which would become home for the Nazari family.

When Lauren hung up, she nodded vigorously to Madame Lafitte. "They have space. They can all be taken into the care of the church, no problem."

"Wonderful." Madame Lafitte smiled again. She must see many tragic cases every day. At least this was a happy story in a sea of sad ones.

As if to confirm Lauren's thoughts, the woman said, "It is not every day that we have such a good ending to an awful situation. Many of these stories are not so happy. So many are rejected and have to leave. Now, of course, it will take Tarek's family time to get settled, but at least they will be together."

Lauren couldn't stifle a grin and a giggle escaped her throat. Calm, serene, steady, bland Lauren. All the descriptions she'd been given over the years. Maybe none of those were really her. She was about to find out. For now, she felt pure joy. Even when she thought of Mark, the pain was subsiding, because she knew she still felt something for him. Something that maybe—probably—would grow and blossom.

ଓ ଓ ଓ

Mark hated the smell of a hospital. Sure, those smells were often clean and floral, maybe pine or fruit-scented from whatever cleaners they used. The act of waiting in a hospital made one aware of smells, sounds, and expressions on faces. There were a few desperate and worried faces in the waiting room. Most others seemed happy, since they awaited a birth.

He and Logan were waiting for a happy reason, but it was still long. For poor Dina, it would be even longer, since she'd been in labor for over ten hours.

Sitting beside Mark was Logan, whose eyes bobbed shut several times in the last hour. He claimed he'd napped a bit during his all-night vigil by Dina's side, after Mark had gone home at Logan's insistence. "No reason for you to lose sleep over my baby."

Mark couldn't argue with that but did stay as long as he felt it would comfort his friend. "How about I bring coffee tomorrow morning? And breakfast?"

Logan had complied with a sleepy smile and the following morning Mark followed through with hot coffee and steaming egg-bacon biscuits.

"Is it normal for labor to go this long?" Mark handed Logan his biscuits, realizing he himself was totally clueless about the birthing process.

Logan's eyelids fluttered again, then opened. "Um—yeah, I think it's not unheard of. Especially for a first baby. A lucky woman has a couple hours of labor and that's it. Other times it can go quite a while. And it seems really painful. Poor Dina. I know my wife and if she's expressing pain, she's feeling a whole lot of it."

Mark nodded with a grimace. For Dina's sake, he hoped the little guy would make his appearance soon.

"Logan Simpson?" A male nurse called from the front of the room.

Despite his sleepy state, Logan shot up like a tin soldier. "He's coming?"

"He's coming. We saw the top of his head," the nurse said with a grin. "Come this way, Mr. Foster."

Logan exchanged a look with Mark, who had stood and held up a hand. "I'll wait here for you if you want me to."

"I'll get you when you're able to come see him. If it gets too long, just feel free to leave, Bro. I appreciate your being here and all."

When Logan followed the nurse and disappeared from view, Mark looked at the magazines on the end table. Too distracted. He had a ton of things to do at home but wanted to support Logan in whatever way he could. Aside from that, he was having loads of trouble getting back into a routine of any kind. What a good way to put that off. A smirk tugged at his mouth.

He glanced down at his phone. It was blinking, indicating a new email. A quick glance revealed a list of ads and client emails. And one from Lauren that must have been sent a few hours ago. He swallowed. Lauren had written to him. What could she want to say? She'd been wrong about her feelings? Would she simply ask how he was doing?

One way to find out and may as well get it over with, though his finger hovered too long over her message. Finally, he jabbed it with one finger and skimmed her words.

He read, "Hi Mark, I hope you had a good flight home and are doing well settling back into your life there. I was so glad to see you. I wanted to give you some news about Tarek. His father was located in Avignon and he and his brother, Tarek's uncle, will be coming day after tomorrow to Cavaillon. Tarek was transferred to Lyon yesterday, but will be returning tomorrow. Thank you for all you did to help with this. I know you'll be happy about it, so I wanted to let you know. Take care, Lauren."

Mark stilled. A lump tightened his throat. *Take care?* He shook his head. He should be overjoyed about Tarek. And he was, he really was. He felt good about the part he'd played in the boy's life. Lauren's message gave good news, wonderful news, really. So, why did he feel a mixture of victorious joy and crippling pain?

Mark took a long breath and looked all around the room, glancing right and left, up and down, distracting himself. Trying to. Lauren's message to him was clear. Nothing had changed. That message could have been from anyone—a neighbor, a casual friend. What a fool he was to keep allowing his emotions to swing east and west as if on a string held in her hands. He had to stop. Logan was right, he couldn't even be friends with her, if he was ever going to heal. That wasn't his way. He'd always tried to stay at least amicable with former girlfriends. But Lauren Abbott was rooted deep in his psyche, in his heart, like a massive, ancient tree whose roots gnarled everywhere, indistinguishable from the earth where they lay. For his future's sake, he had to let her go.

He pushed "reply". Typed, "That's great news, Lauren. I was happy to be able to help in any way I could. Say hello to him for me. Mark."

It hurt to type such bland, casual words that ignored all the history they had. *Let go, Mark. It's time, and you know it.* He pushed "send" just as his eyes began to burn.

℘   ℘   ℘

Lauren leaned back in the straight wooden chair at Madame Bénétreau's kitchen table to glance out the front window. No one yet.

"You've looked out the window ten times, Lauren." Madame Bénétreau chuckled and refilled Lauren's teacup. A cloud of steam scented with cinnamon rose up over the table.

Lauren grinned. "You are just as happy as I am, I know. I just saw him a few days ago, but it seems like so much longer. This is such a big day for him."

"I hope they aren't—" Madame Bénétreau stopped, and she rose, peering down the hall through the front window, covered with a lacy valance. "They may be here now."

Lauren stood up and followed Madame Bénétreau toward the front door and out to the porch just as a car pulled to a stop in front of the house. The rear car door swung open and Tarek slid out. Lauren pulled the gate open as he ran toward her. She leaned down and he thrust himself into her arms. She encircled his small frame with both arms and squeezed him as tears moistened her lashes. He'd never shown her that kind of attachment before. A lump formed in her throat.

Lauren pulled back and said, "I'm so sorry you had to leave, Tarek. I don't know why they did that when you had just gotten settled with Madame Bénétreau. But at least you're back, and tomorrow you'll see your father."

He grinned and it lit up his face. She'd never seen him smile so broadly. He was going to be a handsome young man, with dark eyes and olive skin. "Thank you for bringing me back."

"I didn't do anything, but I told them I thought you should be *here*. That's when they told me they had found your father." She stood up with him and they turned.

His gaze wandered to Madame Bénétreau, who stood behind Lauren. He smiled at her and went to stand by her side, suddenly shy, but clear about where he belonged. The woman placed a hand on his shoulder and said, "Welcome back, Tarek. I'm so glad you've come back." Her eyes were moist with unshed tears, but she was smiling.

The driver of the car had gotten out and pulled Tarek's canvas sack full of his meager belongings from the trunk. He took it to Tarek, nodded toward the women, and said, "I'll leave you all, then."

"*Merci, Monsieur!*" Lauren and Madame Bénétreau called out in unison.

After the car drove away with a scrape of gravel, Tarek turned to Lauren and asked, "When is my father coming?"

"Tomorrow. He's coming tomorrow in the afternoon," Madame Bénétreau told him.

"You will come and meet him?" His dark eyes beseeched Lauren's.

"Don't you want to meet him in private? You haven't seen each other in such a long time."

But Tarek shook his head. "You *must* meet him. I will tell him you are my friends. That you help me." He looked back and forth from Lauren to Madame Bénétreau.

"I'll be here, then. I'll see you tomorrow." Lauren pushed through the metal gate and turned for a final wave. He needed time to get resettled with Madame Bénétreau.

Deep contentment poured into her as she looked back in time to see Tarek and Madame Bénétreau disappear through the front door. Everything would be okay with him. He'd gradually develop a new life, learn French, make some friends, grow up. What a blessing to have had a role in helping him get settled and find his father.

Now she had to think about settling herself. It was time to go back to the States. She knew. She missed Mark and needed to see him, to set some things straight. Where to begin? She'd know when she got there. Maybe he'd written to her after her news about Tarek.

She scanned her mails and texts. There was a text from Jean-Pierre that said, "I'm free tonight. Dinner? Please?" She smiled and typed back, "I'm having dinner with a friend tonight, but we will get together soon." She had to have closure with him and let him know she was leaving France.

Scrolling down, she saw a note from Mark and eagerly clicked on it. She scanned his message and frowned. He sounded cold. Maybe angry. Of course, he had a reason to back away, but that wasn't his style. Maybe he just needed some space. She wished she could talk to him about Tarek, about what she'd learned about herself, about her emotional process. When she got back to Virginia, she'd tell him everything.

Later that evening, she sat across the table from Claire at her favorite bistro. Under a summer sky that was still bright at eight in the evening, a colorful umbrella extended overhead. Laughter from a nearby table wafted up into the night.

Claire scanned the menu. "This looks good. Le plat du jour is rabbit with mustard sauce, and the *formule* has *mousse au chocolat* for dessert. I might get that."

Lauren closed her menu. "Claire, I'll be going back to the States soon. Probably next week."

Claire looked up from her menu, no surprise on her face. "Of course. I knew it would likely be soon, and I understand." She reached out to touch Lauren's arm. "I never thought you were going to stay forever. You have to go back to Mark, don't you?"

Lauren flushed. "I—uh—yes. I think my feelings for him go deeper than I realized, you were right about that. I think I really love him again. Seems weird, doesn't it? Falling in and out of love isn't my usual style, but with Mark it's different. I hope it's not too late. I need to see him and talk. Also, well," she shrugged, "it's just time for me to go."

Claire smiled a gentle smile. It extended friendship that surpassed the short weeks she and Lauren had known each other. "My guess is that you never really stopped loving him. You just had other things to figure out. Lauren, I've enjoyed so much having you work with me. I've loved getting to know you as a friend. I hope we'll stay in touch."

"Yes, of course. I feel the same." Lauren leaned forward and grasped both of Claire's hands in hers. "And Claire, I can't thank you enough for allowing me to work with you. It was a wonderful experience and gave me some direction for my future career."

Claire's eyebrows lifted and a smile stretched at the same time. "Really? In what way? You're interested in catering?"

"Yes, very much." Lauren nodded and took a sip from a goblet of sparkling water. "I came here knowing I still wanted to work with food, but not in a restaurant. I didn't know for sure what I'd enjoy, until you gave me the opportunity. I'm going to explore catering more when I get back home. I'll take my time, though. I have a lot of things to sort out."

"And if that's not what you want to do, you'll find your way. I know you will. You're very talented with both food and décor. You have the knack, the gift. I'm sure you'll find a wonderful way to use it to bring joy to people who gather."

Lauren smiled. "I like the sound of that. People who gather. It's strange, I—I never really had a stable homelife as a child, and I sometimes wonder if my efforts to make food and events for people isn't a desire to create family of some kind. Pseudo family."

Claire listened intently then tilted her head to one side. "There's nothing wrong with that, Lauren. If you have to create a family-type gathering, do it. If you do it for others as part of your career, that means you'll always give *and* receive joy. It'll never get boring, always be bringing happiness to others, even once you have your own family."

Her last words caused a pang deep inside Lauren's soul. Her own family . . . would she ever have one? With Mark? With someone else? She had the bitter impression that Mark had moved on and closed her out of his life, and that realization left a void like a crater. The words she'd said to him before he left had been a mistake. A misguided, fearful mistake.

She returned her mind to Claire's words. They would give her direction. *God* would give her direction through the people he'd brought into her life during this trip. He'd spoken, as she'd asked him to. And now, it was time to go home and put the pieces together, home where she belonged.

ଓ   ଓ   ଓ

Lauren looked at her watch and lifted her eyes to exchange a conspiratorial glance with Madame Bénétreau. She looked down at Tarek, who shifted his weight and paced beside her on the platform. The train was due in two minutes, if it was on time. Most French trains were timely. She silently prayed that this one would be, too.

The sound of an engine chugging and a shrill whistle filled the air before they saw the front of the train appear. It seemed to take forever, but was only two more minutes before the train from Avignon slowed to a halt and the metal doors slid open. People began pouring out of each door, lugging suitcases, gathering children, calling to those waiting on the platform for them.

Lauren wouldn't be able to recognize Tarek's father once he also came through the door, but she watched Tarek's face, vigilant as he stared at the train, eyes combing each passenger that disembarked. Finally, he broke away from Lauren's hand on his shoulder. She watched his dark head bob as he dodged through the crowd. His destination was a tall, thin weary-looking man. As she looked more closely at the man's face, she saw he was already weeping. And so was she.

As the two reached each other and Tarek's skinny form disappeared into his father's embrace, Lauren's tears flowed unhindered. She felt a hand in hers, as Madame Bénétreau squeezed. Lauren squeezed back. She looked up and the woman's face, too, was wet with tears and stretched with a broad smile.

Several minutes later, Tarek and his father made their way back through the crowds to where Lauren and Madame Bénétreau stood. Trailing behind was a man that must be Tarek's uncle. When they reached the women, Tarek's father nodded his head in a small bow and said, "I am Hassan." He gestured to the man beside him, more burly than Hassan but his face clearly showing they were in the same family. "My brother, Salah. We are very grateful to you. My thanks to you are insufficient."

Madame Bénétreau stepped toward them. "We are very honored to help your family, Mr. Nazari. I will take you to a place you all can live for a while until we find you a more permanent home. You will be able to catch up with each other."

It was time for Lauren to leave them, to leave Tarek and Madame Bénétreau. A hello and a goodbye. Madame Bénétreau would take them to the next step in their journey, but she had her own journey to continue.

"I am so happy you are together, finally," she told Mr. Nazari and his brother. She looked down at Tarek, whose face was traced with a measure of joy she'd never seen before. Her heart felt like it would burst open with happiness. "Tarek, I need to say goodbye now." A troubled look flashed across his face. She leaned down to meet him at eye-level. "I have to go back to America, but I'm so glad we had time together. I will stay in touch with you and one day I will come see you again."

Tarek nodded as tears formed in the corners of his dark eyes. He lunged at her and she drew him into her arms. She held tight, feeling she was holding a fragile doll. All that would change. He was on the way.

When she pulled back, his tears had traced a path down his cheeks. She was nearly sobbing as well, but felt full, so full and complete.

"Thank you, Lauren. Thank you very much." His quiet child's voice held more strength and conviction than it had the first day they'd met.

"Thank *you*, Tarek. You helped me too." Lauren grinned when Tarek looked confused by her statement. "It was wonderful to meet you and I will pray for you every day. And I'll write to you, I promise."

He nodded. "Me too." Maybe he would or wouldn't, but at least Madame Bénétreau would keep her in the loop.

She said good-bye to Mr. Nazari and his brother and left Tarek and Madame Bénétreau with a final tight hug. It would only get better now for the Nazari family.

And she knew the same was true for her.

Chapter Nineteen

Lauren breathed deeply and closed her eyes. The slightly acrid scent of lavender filled her nostrils. When she opened them again, before her rolled out rows of lavender, fluffs of deep and variegated purples as far toward the horizon as her eyes could see. In the distance stood a stone abbey, a centuries-old sturdy contrast to the delicate floral fields surrounding it.

She turned to Jean-Pierre who sat beside her on the hillside. "Thanks for bringing me here to the lavender fields. That was the one thing I hadn't gotten a chance to do during my visit."

Jean-Pierre gave a slight bow of his head. "At your service, Mademoiselle. It was your final request before leaving me and leaving your beloved France."

She gave him a feigned frowned and swatted his shoulder playfully. "I'm not leaving *you*, exactly. I just need to go home."

He was looking at her carefully as she spoke, his eyes brimming with sadness. "I'm sorry you are leaving, Lauren. You'll miss the melon festival in July." His lips curved into a small, solemn smile. "And I'm sorry about what happened in the restaurant. I've told you this before, but I wanted to make sure you knew. I am a compassionate man, but I do have a temper. I was very moved by the dinner for the refugees, the presentation, especially. I'd never really thought so much about it before."

Lauren nodded, touched by his statement. "It's such an awful situation. But it ended in a nice way for Tarek. Not perfect, since he still lost his mother, his brother, and his homeland. But he has his father back." A smile spread across her lips as she remembered their reunion. "It was so sweet . . .the father cried and couldn't let go of Tarek." As she spoke a few tears escaped and rolled down her cheeks.

Jean-Pierre reached up and whisked away her tears with two fingers. "You're different now, Lauren. You changed since arriving here. When you came to my brother's house a few days after your arrival, I was afraid you had no emotions at all." He grinned, but then was solemn. "No, not so much that. I felt that you were trapped inside of your body and there was so much you wanted to say, but didn't dare. You don't seem this way as much as before."

Relief and joy washed over her. So, there was a tangible change even evident to others, not just deep inside her own awareness. "I'm so glad. I think I'm starting to heal from things that happened in my past, which I told you about the first time we picnicked together. I still have some things to work out."

"Like Mark?"

She smiled. "Yes, but not only him. Career-wise, and personally, too."

"I think Mark won and I lost." His jaw squared and his lips pressed together as he averted his gaze out to the violet fields.

Lauren pulled her knees up and encircled them with her arms. "I'm not back with Mark at this point. I sent him away, more or less. It's possible he won't take me back, even if I decide for sure that's what I want."

Even as she spoke, something inside her was growing and extending buds and branches in Mark's direction, yet uncertainty hovered there as well. Her longing to see him filled her waking thoughts with increasing frequency. She missed him, craved being with him in a way that was new, insistent.

"The fishmonger." Jean-Pierre threw one hand into the air. "You chose the fishmonger over a successful man like me."

She knew he was joking, but a shadow of hurt seemed to linger in his tone. She leaned toward him and snagged his eyes with hers. "Jean-Pierre, you are a very nice man, an attractive and successful man. But that doesn't mean we are meant to be together. I don't feel that you and I are meant for one another."

He nodded with resignation and a sigh. "Yes, I suppose you are right. It was worth a try, though, wasn't it?"

She grinned. "Yes, it certainly was. I had a wonderful time. I didn't so much enjoy working in your kitchen, but everything else was lovely."

They laughed. He reached out and took her hand, curling his fingers around hers. He pressed his lips into them. Then, leaning forward, he placed a chaste kiss on her forehead. She circled his back with one of her arms and squeezed him around his waist.

"I'll miss you, Lauren. What will you do when you get back? For your job, I mean?"

She stretched her legs back out and her eyes swept across the fields. Her eyes just couldn't get enough of the varied hues of purple. "When I left your restaurant, I had the chance to work for a little while with a woman I'd met in Isle-sur-la-Sorgue who has a catering business. I found that I enjoyed catering, so I'm going to check into that and see if I still like it. I'm not in a hurry, though. I want to be able to try different things."

"A good idea. I know you'll succeed."

"And you found your sous-chef?"

"I'm on my second sous-chef now since you left. She seems to be working out better than the first one."

"And the Michelin star?" She cocked her head. "That was a big goal. Did you get it?"

He smiled. "I will find out soon. And after that I'll try for a second one."

"Please let me know. I'm not sure the stars will really make you happy beyond temporarily." She paused. Tilted her head to look into his face. "I hope you'll visit the church when you have a chance. I'm sorry we didn't get to go together, but you met some of the members at the dinner."

"Yes, I will try."

"And we'll stay in touch." As Lauren spoke, she knew that, though they might stay in touch for a little while, it would likely taper off as life took over for each of them. Especially if she went back to Mark. Claire was another story. She'd surely stay in touch with Claire.

Lauren leaned against Jean-Pierre's shoulder, saddened by the ending of the trip and her goodbye to him, but already sensing the burgeoning anticipation in going home. The trip had told her so much. Despite everything, she got what she came for. And much more.

ભ ભ ભ

Logan had a whole new vocabulary . . . for baby language. Mark shook his head. He never thought he'd see that day, but laughed aloud at his friend. "Are you kidding? What was that again? 'Daddy wuvs his widdle pee wee?' You're killing me, Pal."

Logan's laughter joined Mark's. "Yes, see what the little guy has done to me? He's turned my brains to a bowl of grits." He leaned toward the crib and touched the infant's belly. "I just wuuuuv him!"

The bedroom had been freshly painted and adorned with small sheep and cow appliqués and a gently-dancing mobile hung over the crib. The men gazed down at Logan's new offspring, Dustin, whose eyes occasionally opened to observe the giant humans making ridiculous sounds in their throats. "Yes, I can see, and with good reason," Mark told him. "He's amazing. Look at those little, bitty fingers, and even smaller fingernails."

"He's also asleep again, until tonight at about two a.m. So, why don't we go downstairs and join Dina in the kitchen? I'm glad you were able to come tonight, since our last dinner was pre-empted by special programming."

Mark laughed and followed Logan down the stairs. "And what a long program it was."

"You can say that again. Ask Dina. She told me Dustin might end up being an only child but give her some time. She'll forget the ten-hour labor."

"Don't count on it." Dina's voice rang toward them from the kitchen as they reached the bottom step. She emerged, looking pert and much slimmer than the last time Mark had seen her, her straight, dark hair tucked into a cloth headband. "It's good to see you this side of the hospital, Mark."

A timer rang. She slipped on some oven mitts and pulled a pie from the oven. "Any word from Lauren? Or is that a forbidden topic?"

"Forbidden," supplied Logan in a loud voice. "It's over and we shouldn't talk about it."

"No, it's okay, Dina," Mark said. "It didn't work out, but I did hear from her by email yesterday. While we were there, we were able to help this Syrian refugee boy who'd gotten separated from family. Lauren wrote to tell me they'd found his dad. Good news." He flashed a lame smile he didn't feel, though he was beyond happy for Tarek.

"Oh, how wonderful. I am sorry about Lauren, but it sounds like your vacation turned into a ministry." Dina grinned at him, looking more peaceful than she had in at least three months. When she turned back to her pie, he released his tense shoulders. Maybe the subject would move on.

In the email he'd received, Lauren had recounted in moving detail the reunion between Tarek and his dad. Mark wished he could have been there to see the fruits of all they'd done there, as well as the joy on their faces when father and son were finally reunited. Mark had written to Tarek in order to keep his promise to stay in touch. And because he really wanted to. The letter probably hadn't even arrived yet, and the boy was already back with his father.

And in the email Lauren said she was coming back and wanted to talk to him. What about? Probably to explain her behavior and make sure they were still friends and always would be. It would be difficult to turn down her request for continued friendship, but he knew he had to do it. He hadn't responded to her yet, didn't know what to say. Seeing her would undo the meager progress he'd made since deciding he needed to close the door on their past.

"Hey, Mark, there's someone else I want you to meet." Logan pulled up a stool beside him. "Her name's Sonia and she just moved in down the street. Nice gal. She's a blonde, for a change. We invited her to church and she came with us once. You game?"

Mark grimaced. He'd rather take some time to recover, to process. And to catch up on everything that had grown weeds since his departure, including his business.

He sighed. "Sure, why not?"

CR CR CR

It had been a long flight, with head winds adding an extra hour, but a deep sense of tranquility and peace soaked in as the plane inched its way across the Atlantic. Lauren's mind kept combing through all of the events and memories of her trip to France. It was beyond what she could have done by herself and she marveled at her own progress as well as the closure with Tarek and Jean-Pierre. Mark was another story, but soon she'd see him and maybe they could start . . . somewhere. They could start slowly, if he'd give her another chance.

She'd emailed him but hadn't heard back from him yet. Not like Mark. It had been a long email and she thought he'd have replied by now, especially after all she'd told him about Tarek's reunion with his father. She'd also told him she wanted to see him but didn't tell him why. It would be awkward to explain her feelings in electronic print. In person was better. He probably couldn't imagine that she might still love him. At times she questioned herself—was she sure it was real and wouldn't evaporate one day in the future? No guarantees, but she just knew she couldn't let him go yet, couldn't let *them* go.

As she plodded through passport control her thoughts continued in freefall, fully aware of crossing a divide that was not merely geographical. She hauled her suitcase off the conveyer, and she made her way to Union Station to embark on a short train ride to Baltimore. Her sister, Michelle, had seemed dumbfounded when Lauren called her to say she'd like to stop over for the night on her way back home. She wanted to see Michelle, *needed* to see her. They had to talk, and now was the time. That would complete the circle. This part of it, at any rate.

The train slowed as it approached Pennsylvania Station in Baltimore. Through the window Lauren could see Michelle on the platform fiddling with her phone and shifting her weight from one sandaled foot to the other. She'd had her hair cut and it touched her shoulders in auburn waves. Looked nice against her suntanned skin.

Lauren waved through the train window. Michelle's face showed sudden recognition and she waved back, but her face looked tense. They hadn't had an easy relationship. Normal that Michelle didn't seem overjoyed to see her. Or maybe she understood that they were finally going to face each other and talk.

The sisters hugged and Michelle pulled the canvas tote from Lauren's arm. "Here, let me carry this for you. Did you have a great trip to France? I'm sure you have a lot to tell me."

Michelle's rapid chatter thinly disguised her discomfort, but it would serve as a good buffer until they were able to be in private. Lauren was eager to talk about the elephant that had stood between them for years, but it could wait until then. As they settled into the car and drove toward Michelle's house, Lauren shared some highlights of her trip, emphasizing cultural details and a few things about Jean-Pierre, as well as some good food she'd enjoyed.

She didn't mention that Mark had shown up. She could do that later. The knowledge that she still loved Mark was still a private garden that she savored. In turn, Michelle talked about Justin, their house renovations, and her job at the mortgage company. Normal fare for adult sisters. Yet, nothing was normal about their relationship.

She'd been to Michelle and Justin's home once before, right after they'd moved in, but not since. With all of her trips back and forth to France with Bree, she hadn't had time, she'd claimed. Or, she didn't have enough time off. They'd all been excuses that had reached their expiration date.

Lauren put her suitcase and carry-on in the bedroom that Michelle showed her and rinsed her face in the bathroom. Fatigue was already settling in, with the time change and travel by plane and train. But the urgency to talk to her sister, really talk, simmered down inside her. She hoped that Michelle would be open to digging into neglected and agonizing places.

The tantalizing aroma of tomatoes and basil floated up the stairs as Lauren came down and entered the kitchen where Michelle was stirring a pot with a wooden spoon.

"Smells great."

Michelle turned from the stove and said brightly, "I hope you like spaghetti. This sauce has to simmer a little while. Can I get you something to drink?"

"Where's Justin?"

Michelle stilled, an anxious look on her face. She moistened her lips. "When you called me to say you were coming to visit, I knew that we were going to need to talk. So, I sent him out to play cards with his buddies, or pool, or whatever those guys do."

Lauren grinned, relief cascading through her. "My smart sister. Good move." Her smile faded. "Yes, we really need to talk. First, I want to say I'm sorry. I'm sorry I've been so—so prickly with you over the last few years. You've made efforts and I haven't been very responsive." She held out her hands. Michelle reached out and grasped them, tears building in her eyes, shining before spilling out.

"I hope you'll forgive me for that." Lauren squeezed Michelle's hands, her own eyes stinging. And they hadn't even gotten started yet.

"Yes, of course I forgive you." Michelle's voice came out scratchy. She blinked away fresh tears. "I understand, really. I think—well, I think each of us was like a wounded dog that hides in the corner and bites at anyone who wants to reach out. I probably did the same thing to you or Justin at times."

Lauren's desire to break ground on the difficult discussion had diverted her attention from her thirst. "Oh, I'd love a glass of cold water, in answer to your question." Bringing the past out of its locked trunk was likely to make her thirstier. "And yes, I love spaghetti."

Michelle filled a glass from the dispenser on the refrigerator and handed it to Lauren. "We can sit here at the table." Her voice was small, thin.

Here we go.

They sat down. Lauren took a few gulps of cold water. Her insides trembled as if on a precipice. "Where do we even begin, Michelle? Do you—do you think about Mom still? About what she was like or about her death?"

Michelle didn't seem surprised by the question. "I don't think about her much anymore, especially about how she died, since it was so long ago. Every once in a while, though, when one of my friends talks about going shopping with her mother, or helping her elderly mother out, I feel sort of empty. I'm kind of sad for myself."

Lauren nodded. She looked down at the rim of her glass as the burn returned to her eyes. "Me too. We missed an important part of childhood." She swallowed as her eyes lifted back to Michelle's. "And as awful as that was, I regret that we weren't there for each other. We just coped, as you said, each of us in her own corner." Lauren's voice felt ragged, splintered. She cleared her throat. "It was such a shame that we didn't come together instead of splitting apart."

Michelle nodded, tears flowing freely. "I didn't know how." Her eyes seemed to beg for understanding "We were young. How do you cope with your mother taking her own life when you're sixteen? Even while she was in and out of that psyche hospital, I kept wanting to do something, anything, to get rid of my sadness and my fear for her, so I drank and partied it away. It seemed to help at the time. It made me feel more normal, but also it felt like my only option. Then, you know, as we get older, we start seeing things clearer. Years later I felt bad about leaving you alone. You were younger."

Lauren rubbed her palm down the smooth, wet surface of the glass of water. "I was angry at you for years but didn't even know it. At the time I thought you just didn't love Mom enough or care how she was doing. Underneath that, I felt hurt and alone. I felt abandoned by Mom *and* you. It was like you were fine, you just wanted to have fun. Now I know that was just your way of getting through it."

Michelle looked down at the wood grain table. "I felt guilty for leaving you to cope with Mom by yourself and for abandoning Mom when she needed me. Back then I needed a mom for guidance, since Dad was always gone. But she was like a child most of the time. I felt kind of ripped off. Like, why didn't I get to have my mom bake cupcakes for the second-grade class, or come to student conferences? Why didn't I get a mom I didn't have to be ashamed of? I didn't want anyone calling her crazy, so I just never talked about her. Like she was already dead."

An invisible claw gripped Lauren's inside as Michelle spoke. "I know," she said quietly. "I did the same thing."

After a moment of silence, Michelle looked up and locked eyes with Lauren as a wave of understanding, of shared tragedy passed between them. They reached out simultaneously and grasped one another's hands. The pot on the stove hissed and Michelle pulled her hands back and stood. "Forgot about this," she said, and a small smile emerged.

A panel of light beamed into the kitchen from the window near the stove where Michelle stood, striping the tile floor. Outside the window the foliage on the trees hung still beneath a blazing summer sun. Lauren leaned back in her chair and breathed deeply, peacefully.

"You understand now, Lauren." Michelle returned to the table and slid back into her chair. "It must have seemed to you like I was having a good, old time, but I was dying inside. I stopped the pain with guys, drugs, alcohol, parties. Her voice softened. "I didn't mean to desert you." Michelle's face tightened as she fought a fresh wave of tears then blinked as a few escaped down her cheeks.

"I know." Lauren grasped both of Michelle's hands in hers. "I understand and I forgive you. Will you forgive me for being angry and distant with you?"

Michelle nodded mutely and the two sisters stood up. For the first time in nearly two decades, they hugged each other for a long moment, tightly and sincerely, instead of out of obligation. "My big sister," murmured Lauren against Michelle's auburn waves. She pulled back and looked into her sister's face. "It's not too late, is it?"

Michelle shook her head and let out a broken laugh, smiling and crying at the same time. "Not on your life. But we have a lot of catching up to do. Like, *years*. But you can start with the present. I want to hear all the stuff you didn't tell me. Starting with Mark. What's up with him these days?"

Lauren chuckled and waved the air. Maybe talking about Mark with Michelle would help clear her thoughts. Imagine that, talking about a guy with her sister. Hadn't ever happened, but she was ready to start. "Oh, that'll take a while."

Michelle returned to the stove and placed a pot of water on another burner. She turned and leaned against the counter, arms crossed, a mischievous smile on her face. "Well, we've got all night, Little Sister."

Chapter Twenty

The deadbolt made a hollow clank when Lauren turned the key to her apartment. Still, it sounded like music to her. She was home.

After setting down her suitcase in the foyer, she went to each window in the living room and bedroom and swept the curtain panels open, then pulled open each window. Sunlight flooded into the darkened spaces and swirls of dust danced down columns of light. She'd put cleaning near the top of her list.

But first, Bree. Lauren had again neglected communicating with her friend, aside from short emails to give highlights and also to assuage her guilt. Bree was up to speed on Tarek's predicament but not the resolution. She also knew how things had ended with Mark, but nothing that had happened afterward, from Lauren's visit to Dr. Renard up to the present. All that would take hours of girl time, but she was exhausted.

The night before, she and Michelle had stayed up way too late, but Lauren didn't regret her state of fatigue for such a good cause. Once the sisters were satisfied that they'd covered all the neglected corners, they were content to put the past in its place. After that, Lauren was delighted to talk about life subjects. . . Justin's new job, his occasional depression and Michelle's fears about that, her feelings about her current life, her taste in music and clothing.

"I want to get to know the woman you've become," Lauren had told her.

They painted each other's toenails and gave opinions on hairstyles. They were sisters for the first time in decades. Occasionally, memories bled into their conversation, but would no longer be an electric fence between them.

When Michelle took Lauren to the station for her return trip to Benson, Virginia via D.C., she'd cried again. "These are tears of joy, I want you to know." Michelle gave Lauren a long, tight hug. "I don't want to let you go. I feel like I know you for the first time—ever!"

Lauren smiled, her eyes moist. "Me too. Please plan to come visit me soon. I miss you already." Thankfully, they didn't live too far apart.

They walked side by side toward the train then stopped before its open door. Michelle handed Lauren the canvas bag she carried. "I want an update on Mark as soon as you see him. I mean, if you want to."

"Of course. I'm anxious to see what happens. He still hasn't emailed me and it's been about a week."

Passengers circled past them and mounted the steps to the train. Michelle cocked her head. "He still thinks you don't love him and maybe he's trying to put in some distance to protect himself."

Lauren nodded, her lips pressed tight. Exactly what she thought and not what she wanted to be true. If she told him her current state, which was . . . love, frankly. She loved him. She'd probably never really stopped. That would change his response, wouldn't it?

"I'm trying not to run too fast into the future." Yes, it was a relief just to live that day. "One day at a time. I have my whole life I have to rebuild."

"Yes, I guess you do. Well, you've started with rebuilding our relationship as sisters."

Lauren had smiled and ruffled Michelle's hair. "What a great place to start."

Seeing Michelle was a risk she'd decided to take, but it wouldn't be her last one. She was only beginning to risk and trust. And discover the areas of her life where she'd always backed away in fear. No more. She only hoped her next risk would turn out as well as this one.

Now she was back home. She dialed Bree's number.

"I knew you were scheduled back this week." Bree had picked up after one ring. "I guess you need time now to regroup."

"I stopped overnight to see Michelle."

"Oh." Bree's voice dropped. She knew Lauren's difficult history with Michelle. "Did you talk about—things?"

"Yes, and I have my sister again. We talked about everything, cried a lot, and caught up on twenty years."

Bree laughed. "Oh, that's so wonderful! After all these years. You two can begin again. I'm so happy for you, Lauren."

"Yes, it's wonderful. I feel so blessed, I can't describe it."

"Now it's *my* turn for catch-up. I don't need to catch you up on the last twenty years, but two to three weeks should do it."

"Oh, boy. There's a lot to tell. So much."

After making a lunch appointment with Bree, Lauren checked her phone messages. She thought she'd heard it ping with a new message. Maybe Mark. She looked at email and text and frowned. No message. She hoped he was okay. She texted him. "Hi Mark, I'm back in VA now. Did you get my last message? I'm beginning to worry."

Several minutes later she heard a ping. Mark. "I'm glad you made it back safely. Don't worry, I'm fine. I've been catching up on everything and Logan's wife had the baby. Busy time."

Lauren frowned. Okay, busy. But not Mark. It wasn't his way to respond like this to her. She texted, "Tell Logan I said 'congratulations.' Are you available to get together sometime soon?"

Several minutes passed before Mark responded. "I'll let you know. Have to check my schedule. Welcome back."

She fell back on the couch. She'd hurt him again, she could tell in the tone of his text. Exactly why she hadn't wanted to start again, for fear of hurting him. Which she'd done anyway. At least she had a different response now. She loved him. But could she fully trust it?

Fear seized her for a moment. Could she? Would it all disappear once they were a couple again? Her breath came quickly and she gripped the phone against her chest. Had she reached out to Mark too soon?

Or too late?

☙ ☙ ☙

Mark stared unseeing out his home office window. He'd been at his desk all morning contacting clients, researching deadlines, pulling the pieces of his business back together. Despite careful planning before his departure and some work while he was gone, his desk was in disarray. Like his thoughts and emotions. Staring through the filmy sheer curtains at the sun hitting the maple tree outside his window was soothing. A great way to procrastinate.

He didn't like the person he'd already become with Lauren. Likely, she was hurt and perplexed by his response. But smart girl that she was, she could figure out why in about two seconds. Maybe she thought he'd be faithful, available Mark forever. He'd thought so too, at one time. Not anymore. Her request to get together wasn't going to get in the way of his new direction, one that had been forged as he sat on a return flight from France.

If only he had just said no, he wouldn't see her. But saying no to Lauren had always been an impossible feat for him. Especially if she was asking to meet him. He wouldn't be so cruel again with himself as to entertain the idea that she'd changed her mind. He'd made that mistake once, and it had taken him all the way to Provence.

It wasn't too late, really. He could still say he had too much to do. Or he could cave in. Again.

Mark leaned forward and took a look at his calendar. The next day was Friday. He had a blind date that evening with Sonia, Logan's new neighbor, so if he met Lauren for coffee in the morning, he'd have time to pull himself together emotionally. Theoretically. He'd also meet Sonia with more motivation, since he'd know he was truly available, heart included. Could be a good plan. A sort of anesthetic.

Mark texted Lauren back. "How about meeting for coffee tomorrow at 10? There's new place I've discovered called Daily Grounds over near the Birchwood shopping center. Hope that works."

She responded quickly. "Ten a.m. Friday works fine."

And just then, as if on a signal, his stomach clamped like a vise.

ଓ ଓ ଓ

Lauren circled around the parking lot and finally spied the café, Daily Grounds, on one end. She parked in front of the building. Her palms were moist against the steering wheel and her heart pounded. Why was she nervous about seeing Mark? That had never happened. Not even on their first date.

He'd been so aloof in his messages. He hadn't even called. Just texts or emails. Words on an electronic device could convey hurt, distance, even anger. She was sure of that, because she felt a concrete barrier between them that was three feet thick. How would she ever tell him of her feelings so that he believed her? Trusted her?

Minutes ago, he'd texted her to say he'd be on the terrace. At least it wasn't too hot that day. Maybe there'd be fewer people on the terrace. That would be helpful, since this wasn't a simple coffee date between friends.

She pushed through the glass and spied the entrance to the terrace on the opposite side. On a different day she might stop to admire the earthy décor in the coffee shop, the wood beams on the ceiling, the terracotta tile on the floor, overstuffed chairs in one corner. Only one thought bounced around in her head. Mark.

Lauren pushed through the second glass door to the terrace just as he looked up. Their eyes locked but he seemed tense rather than glad to see her. No warmth washed across his face, no smile, just frozen awareness.

Yet a hot surge swirled through her when she saw his face, his dark eyes so intense just now. Despite his cool distance, he looked handsome, relaxed, and it took her mind back to their dinner date in Cavaillon when she'd been so wildly attracted to him.

Mark rose, gave her a brief, stiff hug. Sat back down. "Welcome back."

"Thanks." She settled into a chair across from him.

"Want something?" His mug already sat between them on the table.

She shook her head. "I will. In a bit. I—I need to talk to you first." She felt suddenly awkward. He tensed and she pretended not to notice. "You're back in the swing of American life now, eh?"

He shrugged. "Have to be. I'm glad it was a slower month in the accounting world." Then he waited. Waited for her to say what she had on her mind. The silence felt thick, heavy.

Although she'd thought over and over about how she'd start this conversation, her mind was blank. She could tell him the latest about Tarek first. That could warm her up and stop the shaking in her left foot.

"You got my news about Tarek. They found his father and uncle in Avignon and they both came back to Cavaillon. The men are staying in a room at the church for now until the city can give them a refugee apartment. They have one available, but it needs some renovation before they can move in. Tarek, his dad, and his uncle will live there together. They started French lessons this week."

Mark nodded, a ghost of a smile tugging at his lips. "I'm really glad. Sounds like our little guy is getting settled. Was it hard for you to say goodbye to him?"

Lauren swallowed as a whisper of sadness slipped in. "Yes, it was, but I was happy for him and so glad I didn't have to leave him in limbo."

"That's good news." Then the warmth drained from his face. "Lauren, I—I almost didn't come to meet you today."

She stared at his closed face and a chill stole over her. "You didn't?"

He shook his head, his gaze glued to the tabletop. "I need to move on, Lauren." His voice almost broke. He cleared his throat.

"No." She reached one hand across the table and entwined his fingers in hers. "Don't. Please."

His fingers barely responded but his head lifted up to face hers. He shook his head. His eyes narrowed but he looked weary. "What do you mean?"

"Don't give up on us, Mark." She kept her tone soft. Mark dropped his eyes to the table again but didn't remove his hand. When he didn't respond she said, "I went to see a doctor to find out if I had my mother's crazy gene. He said the same thing that you did, that I was blocked and so afraid of emotions, my heart couldn't distinguish positive from negative ones. I was shutting them all out." Her words came out in a rush, like a fast-running creek tumbling over smooth stones.

She wanted to say everything before he could stop her, doubt her. "During your visit I *did* feel a lot for you. It started gradually and grew from there. The problem wasn't loving you, Mark. The problem was believing it. I didn't trust myself because I didn't know myself anymore. But while you were there, I saw again all the things I love about you."

Lauren saw the rigidly controlled muscles of his face relax and soften, though he still stared down at the table. Lauren reached out with her other hand and gently lifted his chin so he was looking at her. His eyes were moist. He blinked.

"Mark, I love your heart, how solid it is. You give me a sense of strength and security, but you validate my uniqueness too. You're creative and fun, you're balanced and reliable. I love that about you. I need that. I don't want someone who travels the world and wows everyone with his own self-importance, like Finn. I want *you*, Mark."

He opened his mouth to speak and she continued, "I love the heart you have for people, too, how you committed yourself to Tarek. We made such a great team, didn't we?" She was smiling now, no longer tense. "I love how you were faithful to your love for me when lots of guys would have walked away by now. Thank you for giving me time and space." Two tears slipped down her cheeks.

"So, what are you saying, Lauren?" His voice was gentle, but his eyes remained cool, distant, as if he was hesitant to believe her anymore.

"I'm saying I love you, Mark. I always have, but the fear took over . . . for a while."

His face still looked troubled, but his eyes locked with hers. His jaw tightened. He swallowed, still stiff.

"After I saw the doctor, I understood what you'd been saying all along, that I had repressed my emotions. After that, I started deliberately trying to let them out and they *really* came out, like, all over the place." She laughed then. "You wouldn't *believe* all the different emotions. But then God showed me that I can trust him with risks of life *and* emotions. Risks in loving someone. If I don't risk anything, I'll never know joy or pain and I'll only be half alive." Her voice had softened to a whisper. "He showed me that I still love you, Mark."

"You're sure?"

She nodded. "I love you, Mark. I love you."

"And you're willing to take a risk again?" His voice changed now, thickened. The coldness was gone. Something like a small fire flickered in his eyes.

"Yes, I'm eager to take that risk with you, if you're willing to risk *me*." She was never as sure about anything as she was just then. "If you still want me," she added softly.

He turned his head away and she thought he was angry, but light glinted in the corner of his eye as a tear pooled there. Mark turned back to her, a solemn half-smile on his face. Silvery tears slid down his cheeks. He flicked them away with one wrist. "I have to admit, this was the last thing I expected to hear you say today." He swallowed as he stared into her face. "And of course, I still want you. I love you, Lauren. I was afraid I'd never be able to stop loving you." He leaned forward grasping both her hands in his.

Lauren grinned as they stared into each other's eyes like two love-sick teenagers. "I love you, I love you. I can't seem to stop saying it. It's been backed up and stuck for a year." She laughed and he smiled with her then. "Oh, Mark, my love. I want to kiss you now." Her voice was a whisper. "Can I?"

"Here?" He grinned and glanced around the café terrace where four or five people sat with laptops.

"Yes, why not?" Lauren laughed again, feeling it bubbling up through her worn-out prison of safety. "Risking is the new normal for me. Besides, who cares what everyone else thinks? Your friends who know how long I've strung you along will think I'm manipulating you. Or that I'm fickle or nuts. At one time, that's what I thought, too. But if I love you and you love me, what do we care?"

With a crooked smile that said he'd take the challenge, Mark shifted his chair back to give her space, like he used to do. Lauren rose and went to him. She settled onto his lap, slipped one arm around his neck and touched his chin, which he'd already lifted to her.

She lowered her face to his and covered his waiting lips with her own, pouring her delayed love, all her on-hold feelings into that kiss. Oh, he felt so good, his soft lips against hers. She wanted to dive into him. His arms encircled her, tentative at first, then tightening. His strong arms, the steady strength she needed, circled around her like a secure band of love and commitment. His kiss tasted of coffee and a future bright with rich emotions and experiences. It left her breathless.

Their kiss was long enough to draw some stares, but Lauren didn't care. She could tell Mark didn't either. When she pulled back from him, they stared at each other. The emotion was raw in his eyes, his longing, jagged and clear. She buried her head into his neck, fragrant with cologne, and cuddled into the arms that cherished her, forgave her, loved her.

Finally, she slipped off of his lap and back into her own chair. That kiss had only made her hungry for more. More of Mark. Hungry for a future with him.

"I'm planning to find a good counselor and continue for as long as it takes. I have a lot of baggage to go through a little at a time." She'd looked online just that morning and had a few numbers to call. "And I want to see you. A lot. Is that okay?"

Mark laughed aloud. "Is that okay, she says. I think you know the answer to that." He stopped and again indulged in a long, loving stare. "We're getting kind of sappy, but that's okay."

"You deserve sappy. You've been longsuffering and you deserve all the love I can and *will* pour out on you." Lauren giggled. She didn't know how she'd go home that day after their appointment. She just wanted to stay beside him, near him. Mark was everything she needed and wanted.

"I have a question." He reached across the table to link his hands with hers. He pulled them up and pressed his lips into her knuckles. "Is it too early to propose to you? I don't want you to get away again."

Lauren laughed. "Yes, it's too early. But maybe in a month?" They laughed together.

"Just kidding, no rush," he said. "If we're together again, I'm happy enough for now. I *will* propose, though. Consider yourself warned."

Her eyes found his again and she squeezes his hands. "I can't wait." After a happy sigh she said, "You came all the way to France and found me. After that, I found myself. And after that, I just *had* to find you again."

Her heart had known it all along. Her head had finally caught up. Now they'd found each other. And it was so much sweeter the second time around.

Author's Note

If the fictional character of Tarek has touched your heart, consider that there are 15 million real refugees worldwide. These people are like us, except they have lost everything and find themselves with the daunting task of starting from zero in a new land.

Reaching out to refugees is a way to show our love and Christ's love to victims of unfortunate circumstances. These very circumstances, as horrible as they are, lead to openness to the gospel.

Many Christian ministries are working with refugees. If God calls you to be involved in helping them, you can give to an organization that ministers to refugees and/or participate in a short-term mission trip. Here are a few of the many organizations that have an outreach to refugees:

Greater Europe Mission (planting churches in Europe among refugees)

Call of Hope (Primarily Muslim ministry, including refugee ministry in the Middle East.)

Global Frontier Missions (GFM)

World Venture (Syrian Refugee ministry)

TEAM Mission

United World Mission

CRU (formerly Campus Crusade. Their humanitarian arm is an organization called GAiN)   *more books . . .*

I hope you enjoyed reading *A Promise in Provence*. If you did, please consider leaving a review for me. It would help other readers discover my books and be encouraged by their inspiring truths. You can also sign up to receive updates about new books at

www.Kyle-Hunter.com

For more romantic stories that take you places . . .

Prodigals in Provence (Bree's story)

Bree and Lauren own and run Le Bon Voyage, a travel company specializing in tours to charming Provence, France.

Travis is a TV travel critic accustomed to crossing the globe to film documentaries and write books. But he's been in a spiritual desert ever since losing his marriage and ministry five years earlier.

Between film projects, Travis plans to accompany his elderly mother on a tour to Provence, a long-term dream for her. Bree tries unsuccessfully to block him, sure he's coming to spy on the struggling company for an exposé article.

A diverse group of tourists arrives at the rented villa to spend the week and discover the spectacular villages, vineyards, and history of the Luberon mountain region of Provence. Amidst a series of problems and relational tensions, Bree thinks she has all she can handle . . . until she becomes attracted to Travis.

As Bree and Travis are drawn together, will their hidden wounds drive them apart?

One December

Is there any way to recapture what happened under the moon one December?

Nikki has loved Mike for as long as she can remember. Mike has his own past hurts to resolve, having lost both parents when he was fourteen. He's tried to escape the memories by starting a new life on the West Coast.

At Christmas, he comes back to New York for the first time in three years. He and Nikki rekindle the friendship they had as children and share their newfound faith. Under a Christmas moon, romantic sparks fly... but their mutual attraction takes an unexpected detour.

Nikki is devastated, believing the romance is over. She impulsively takes a one-year teaching opportunity in Paris to face her own fears and to get over Mike.

If they think they can run away from each other, they'd better think again.

"*One December* sizzles with romantic tension, taking the reader on a roller-coaster ride from New York to San Francisco, with a delightful detour in Paris. I couldn't put it down!"

– Elizabeth Musser, author of *The Secrets of the Cross* trilogy and *The Swan House.*

Circle Back Around

Hailey and her father haven't always seen eye to eye, especially in running the failing family textile mill. Frustrated, Hailey leaves the mill and her hometown in North Carolina to start a new life near her sister in Colorado. Only months later her father calls to ask a special favor. He needs heart surgery and asks Hailey to run the mill in his place.

Moving back would devastate Hailey's sister, Hope. Yet Hailey would have an opportunity to possibly save the mill, and at a time when her father needs her most. And maybe he'd even approve of her for the first time in her life.

Filled with self-doubt, Hailey returns to North Carolina and struggles to make a difference at the mill, facing more challenges than she bargained for. Her attractive neighbor, Alex, is almost enough to outweigh the difficulties, but she doesn't know that in the shadows lurks someone who wants to destroy both her *and* the mill.

The Second Chance Series

In **The Second Chance Series**, you'll meet Marissa, Julia, Sydney, and Eden, four college friends who, twenty-five years later, renew their friendships as they find themselves empty nesters and single again. You'll love getting to know these women and following each one in her own book.

Marissa Rewritten (A Novella: Book 1)

Author Marissa Thompson has had a writer's block since her husband died almost two years earlier. Her three closest friends are a comfort. Despite this, things are getting urgent as her career hangs by a thread and repairs on her historic home mount up. Prodded by desperation, Marissa heads to Wilmington, North Carolina for a Civil War research trip. She hopes for inspiration, but receives support from a surprising source, a feisty character from her last novel.

Jarrod Lambert has already lost his wife. He's always been close with his only daughter, a college student, but she seems to be slipping further away from him. In an effort to reconnect with her, he makes an impulsive trip to see her in Wilmington.

Through an accident, Marissa and Jarrod meet and discover common ground. Will it be enough to overcome the obstacles standing between them?

Julia Redesigned (Book 2)

Can a stack of letters provide clues to an age-old conflict *and* a doorway to a new family?

For the last three years, Julia De Luca has juggled her successful interior design business with caring for her elderly mother. Following her mother's death, Julia finds old letters from distant relatives in Italy. They remind her of visits she and her mother made when Julia was a child. Could these letters hold the answer to why their trips to Italy ended abruptly when she was ten years old?

These people whose names she's forgotten are the only family Julia has left on earth. How can she reconnect with them after so many years? Would it be crazy to try?

Her compelling desire to locate her distant family leads Julia on an impulsive trip to Florence, Italy. Along with savoring the sights and flavors of Florence, Julia discovers that families can be messy, that it's not too late to fall in love, and that there's more to Julia De Luca than she ever knew.

Read Chapter One of all books on www.Kyle-Hunter.com

Kyle Hunter writes inspirational romance and women's fiction that sometimes take her characters to faraway places. She lived in France for thirteen years. Currently, she lives in North Carolina where she writes fiction, non-fiction (under the pen name K. B. Oliver and the blog Oliversfrance.com), and teaches French to adults.

www.ingramcontent.com/pod-product-compliance
Lightning Source LLC
Chambersburg PA
CBHW071508110726
47908CB00003B/765